# The Bookshop Mysteries
## A MURDER AT THE CHURCH

### S. A. REEVES

Copyright © 2025 S. A. Reeves
Published by Adventures in Writing.

https://www.adventuresinwriting.com/
https://www.sareevesfiction.com/

All rights reserved. No part of this book may be reproduced or used in any manner without the prior written permission of the copyright owner, except for the use of brief quotations in a book review.

Line and copy editing by Scribendi

Manuscript version 1.1
Build date: 10th July 2025

This is a work of fiction. Names, characters, places and incidents either are products of the author's imagination or are used fictitiously. Any resemblance to actual events or locales or persons, living or dead, is entirely coincidental.

Paperback: 978-1-0687209-6-3
Hardback: 978-1-0687209-7-0
Ebook: 978-1-0687209-5-6

*This book is dedicated to our children Amy and Daniel.*

# About the Authors

S. A. Reeves is the pen name of a husband and wife writing duo, who have been married for over twenty years. They are based near the Peak District in Derbyshire (United Kingdom).

They both like to read and watch murder mysteries, and will frequently stand in front of a whiteboard, plotting the perfect murder—for creative fiction purposes, of course.

This book is written and presented in British English.

This means for our readers in the United States, some words may be spelt different, such as favourite/favorite, behaviour/behavior, labour/labor, analyse/analyze.

These are not spelling mistakes or typos, it's just how us quirky Brits do things.

## Awards Won for A Bitter Pill

## Praise for A Bitter Pill

S.A. Reeves' The Bookshop Mysteries: A Bitter Pill delivers an engaging tale of intrigue, friendship, and unexpected twists in the charming town of Belper. At the heart of the story is Gemma, a passionate bookshop owner with a love for mystery novels, whose life takes an unexpected turn when a real-life mystery falls into her lap. Her companion in crime-solving is Mavis, a sharp-witted older woman grieving the recent loss of her husband yet equally drawn to the allure of a good mystery. Together, they make a delightful sleuthing team, eager to crack the case that, unexpectedly, might be more dangerous than they anticipated.

For mystery lovers, A Bitter Pill is a must-read. It's an addictive tale of crime, community, and the kind of unexpected twists that make a mystery unforgettable. I highly recommend this book, not just for the thrill of the mystery but for the compelling story that keeps you on the edge of your seat. Looking forward to more from S.A. Reeves!

**Literary Titan**

Each intriguing twist and surprising discovery is wonderful. The book is hard to put down, and even after completing it, you'll still feel its warm, comforting atmosphere.

The book keeps readers hooked with its realistic setting and well-developed characters. The mystery slowly unfolds in this well-paced story, with clever twists and turns to keep readers engaged. In the midst of the suspense, Gemma and Mavis's relationship is charming, adding humor and fun to the story. Gemma's natural curiosity and determination push the plot forward, while her friendship with Mavis brings humor and warmth.

The author does an excellent job of creating believable characters, developing good plots, and describing distinctive settings. All of these make this series perfect for both growing and enjoying. If you enjoy reading, solving mysteries, and are curious about small-town secrets and scandals, you'll find this suspenseful and captivating story very enjoyable.

**BookNerdection**

S.A. Reeves's first in a planned series of Bookshop Mysteries, A BITTER PILL starts off strong with immense clarity of vision: it's a classic setup in which two well-meaning and clever women busybody their way into solving a murder in a small town in the UK—with a wink toward the protagonists' self-awareness as consumers of murder mysteries.

As cozy and personable as its eponymous bookshop, A BITTER PILL is perfect for readers who know exactly what they want: a BBC-style murder mystery with small-town personalities navigating small-town concerns while drinking plenty of tea and coffee along the way.

Briskly plotted and charming, S.A. Reeves's THE BOOKSHOP MYSTERIES: A BITTER PILL is a delight by and for murder mystery aficionados.

**IndieReader**

A Bitter Pill is a cozy mystery, and S. A. Reeves certainly sets the stage appropriately for the genre. A bookshop in a small town is the perfect setting. Gemma and Mavis are the ideal protagonists, with their interest in reading mysteries and their Jessica Fletcher vibes.

A Bitter Pill is a the type of novel someone might take on vacation or enjoy over a break from work. The characters are a delight, and the topic of murder never feels too heavy, which is fitting for the sub-genre.

Gemma and Mavis's dialogue in particular is reminiscent of listening to a couple of grandmothers chit chat over tea, and the setting in England only adds to the pleasantry. The Bookshop Mysteries series is bound to be another solid addition to the cozy mystery genre.

**Book Review Directory**

A Bitter Pill is a captivating and compassionate story, and while the book is very much steeped in the Bookworm's cozy, bookish energy, this is very much a murder mystery and its authors and protagonists know the importance of the mystery's pull. Each surprising reveal is exciting, each twist thrilling. I appreciated that Gemma has a near-reckless desire to chase the mystery, but she and Mavis do not lose their level-headed approach.

I'd highly recommend you're armed with a sweet baked treat and your favorite hot beverage, because the only thing that will tempt you to put down this book is the descriptions of the Bookworm café's offerings, which may just drive you to visit your nearest bakery.

A Bitter Pill is difficult to put down, and its cozy spirit will linger with you long after you're finished reading it. I feel as though I've found my new favorite bookshop. Only caveat is that I'll have to open A Bitter Pill to visit it again and again.

**Independent Book Review**

# Join the Reading Club

The Bookshop Mysteries is set in a real town, Belper (Derbyshire) in the United Kingdom, and is set in real locations. If you would like to see what these locations look like, then you can join our reading club to receive a free book: The Locations of the Bookshop Mysteries.

By joining the club we will let you know about new releases, special offers, and exclusive behind-the-scenes details about how we write the books.

https://www.sareevesfiction.com/join

# The Bookshop Mysteries

Love the Bookworm Bookshop and Café? You can buy exclusive merchandise with the Bookworm's logo, from mugs, bags, t-shirts, hoodies and more.

Order from http://sareevesfiction.com or scan the QR Code.

*Also by S. A. Reeves*

***In the Bookshop Mysteries series:***

A Bitter Pill
A Murder at the Church
A Legacy of Lies
A Deadly Deceit

# Contents

| | |
|---|---|
| Chapter 1 | 1 |
| Chapter 2 | 6 |
| Chapter 3 | 12 |
| Chapter 4 | 19 |
| Chapter 5 | 26 |
| Chapter 6 | 35 |
| Chapter 7 | 41 |
| Chapter 8 | 49 |
| Chapter 9 | 58 |
| Chapter 10 | 65 |
| Chapter 11 | 73 |
| Chapter 12 | 81 |
| Chapter 13 | 89 |
| Chapter 14 | 96 |
| Chapter 15 | 101 |
| Chapter 16 | 109 |
| Chapter 17 | 116 |
| Chapter 18 | 125 |
| Chapter 19 | 132 |
| Chapter 20 | 139 |
| Chapter 21 | 149 |
| Chapter 22 | 157 |
| Chapter 23 | 163 |
| Chapter 24 | 170 |
| Chapter 25 | 177 |
| Chapter 26 | 182 |
| Chapter 27 | 195 |
| Chapter 28 | 205 |

| | |
|---|---|
| Chapter 29 | 210 |
| Chapter 30 | 217 |
| Chapter 31 | 225 |
| Chapter 32 | 233 |
| Chapter 33 | 240 |
| Chapter 34 | 245 |
| Chapter 35 | 253 |
| Chapter 36 | 258 |
| Chapter 37 | 268 |
| Chapter 38 | 278 |
| Chapter 39 | 286 |
| Chapter 40 | 292 |
| Chapter 41 | 304 |
| Chapter 42 | 313 |
| *Join the Reading Club* | 320 |
| *Also by S. A. Reeves* | 321 |
| *Bookworm Merch* | 323 |

# Chapter One

On a bright summer Saturday in July, the town of Belper buzzed with excitement about its annual craft fair. Inside *The Bookworm Bookshop and Café*, Gemma Curtis moved gracefully among the shelves of new and secondhand books, packing a selection into boxes. The comforting scent of fresh baked cakes from the café at the back of the store mingled with the familiar scent of paper and ink.

"There's some real classics here," Mavis Rawlings said as she wrapped a fragile volume in protective paper. Her silver hair shone under the store's lights. Though advanced in years, Mavis's spirit was as lively as ever.

Gemma chuckled. "I've selected a collection of books for the fair that should appeal to everyone." They worked in sync, filling boxes with an assortment of novels and non-fiction titles destined to delight the patrons at the St Peter's Church fundraiser later that day. As they worked, Gemma glanced towards the entrance, anticipating the arrival of David, her partner and a local police detective who had promised his help moving the boxes in his spacious car. He was also her ex-fiancé; long story.

"David's never been one for punctuality when it's not detective work," Gemma said, her tone holding more fondness than frustration.

"Give the man a break; he's probably been up late solving a complex case," Mavis said, her eyes twinkling behind her wire-rimmed glasses frame, slightly crooked from years of wear, with lenses that caught the light in a gentle glint.

The bell above the door tinkled, interrupting their chat. In walked David, and the sight of him warmed Gemma's heart. He was really trying in his renewed commitment to their relationship but also in his earnest desire to support her literary passions.

"Ready for a workout, Detective Haynes?" Gemma asked, greeting him with a playful smile and gesturing to the stack of boxes awaiting his attention.

"Crime fighting is nothing compared to this," David said, rolling up his sleeves as he surveyed the mountain of heavy boxes. When David attempted to lift one, Gemma raised her eyebrows.

"Come on! Show those books who's boss!" she said, earning a laugh from both David and Mavis.

"Hilarious," David said, puffing as he manoeuvred the box towards the door. "I've been hitting the gym, so my arms are still a little sore."

"Would you like me to help you with that box?" Mavis asked with a chuckle.

"No, no. I can manage," David said, as his cheeks flushed slightly red.

While David loaded the car, Gemma and Mavis turned in unison and made their way towards the back of the shop, beckoned by the aroma of fresh coffee from the café.

"I can't wait to get the final planning go-ahead for the café extension," Gemma said, her voice brimming with anticipation.

Mavis hummed, her eyes taking in the comfortable reading area they'd created. "It's going to be a splendid space for readers," she said, her fingers traced the spine of a leather-bound classic as they passed.

"Your touch has really transformed this place," Gemma said, admiring the plush armchairs and soft reading lights that lined one wall covered in dark green wallpaper. "I just love seeing our regulars sitting here with their noses in a good mystery."

"Or a romance," Mavis added with a twinkle in her eye, "for those who fancy a bit of heart-fluttering alongside their tea and crumpets."

They paused by the counter, where Ellie Simpson was arranging trays laden with delectable cakes and tray bakes. Her long blonde hair was tied neatly into a ponytail, and she wore a Bookworm branded apron. Despite the unmistakable bump of her pregnancy, she worked with an effortless grace that had customers returning for her sweet confections as much as for the books.

"Ellie, these look amazing," Gemma said, eyeing the chocolate-drizzled eclairs and lemon zest cupcakes.

"Thanks, Gemma!" Ellie said with a large smile. "The rented coffee machine's already at St. Peters, and Sienna and Louise will be there to help serve up these treats. I don't think I can manage all day on my feet there."

"Smart move," Mavis said, her maternal instincts never far from the surface. "You take it easy. Those two are more than capable of holding down the fort."

"Definitely," Gemma said, glancing at the wall clock. "We wouldn't want you to overdo it. Just the smell of these cakes is enough to ensure they'll sell like ... Well ... Hotcakes!" They all laughed.

The bell above the shop door rang again as David entered after delivering the first carload of boxes to the church.

"Ah, there's your knight in shining armour ready for the next lot," Mavis said.

David glanced at the remaining stack of boxes and let out a puff of air in exasperation.

"This is the last load, Sir Lancelot," Gemma said.

"I hope you sell them all so I don't have to carry

them back." David bent to hoist a box, his arms tensing as he underestimated its weight. The box wobbled in his grip before he steadied it against his knee.

"Careful. That box contains collectors edition hardbacks" Gemma said, her voice laced with playful sarcasm.

"You put all the hardbacks in one box," David muttered under his breath. With the box now firmly in his grasp, David edged past displays of bestsellers, his path leading him outside to his parked car in Belper's marketplace.

As David loaded the last box and slammed the car boot shut, he wiped his brow, looking pleased with his efforts. From inside the shop, Gemma nodded her approval and gave a thumbs up before turning to speak to Ellie, who was wrapping the trays of cakes with clingfilm ready for transportation.

"Ellie, we'll head off now. If it gets quiet later, don't wait around; lock up and put your feet up, alright?"

"Will do, Gemma," Ellie replied, her hand resting on her rounded belly. "Good luck with the sale!"

"Thanks," Gemma said. She slipped an arm through Mavis's, and together they exited the bookshop to make their way towards St. Peter's Church, just down the road.

"Beautiful day, isn't it?" Mavis observed as they walked across the market square under a perfect, cloudless blue sky.

# Chapter Two

As Gemma and Mavis entered the churchyard, David stood out against the backdrop of his car. He was chatting with a striking young man.

"Gemma, let me introduce you to James. He's the son of the church warden," David said as they approached, motioning towards the young man beside him. "James, this is Gemma Curtis, the owner of The Bookworm on the marketplace."

James, who was wearing chinos pressed to perfection and a pristine crisp shirt, turned to face Gemma as he extended his hand. "Pleased to meet you, Miss Curtis," he said in a soft and well-spoken voice.

"Call me Gemma, please," she replied. "And this is Mavis. We're delighted to meet you."

James extended his hand to Mavis, and she shook it. "Ah yes, Mavis. We've met before," said James.

"Yes, I've known your father for many years," Mavis said with a smile. "He's the head bell ringer now, isn't he, as well as the church warden?"

"He certainly is," said James.

"His bell ringing demonstration later is much anticipated," Gemma said.

James's smile widened, a hint of pride flickering across his features. "He'll be thrilled to hear that."

Gemma glanced towards the church. A young lady with long blonde hair cascading over her shoulders walked towards them with an airy grace that caught everyone's attention. James's face lit up as he introduced her. "Gemma, Mavis, this is my girlfriend, Rhianna."

"Pleased to meet you," Rhianna said, offering a warm smile. She extended a hand, manicured and soft, to Gemma and then to Mavis, who both returned her greeting with equal warmth.

"I love the perfume you're wearing," said Gemma. "May I ask what it is? Is it orange?"

"Thank you. It's orange blossom," Rhianna said. "James bought it for me last Christmas."

"It's lovely," said Gemma. She looked towards the church as patrons, eager for bargains, had turned up early.

"Well, we best get cracking," Gemma said, eyeing

David's car packed with boxes for her stall. "These books won't sell themselves!"

"Let me help with that," James offered without hesitation, as he rolled up his sleeves.

"Thank you. That's very kind of you," Gemma said, already moving towards the vehicle. She lifted a small box filled with a payment machine, business cards and a large stack of Bookworm branded bookmarks. David and James bent over the boot of the car, grappling with a particularly heavy box between them.

"Steady now," David grunted, his stance wide as they navigated the path leading to St Peter's entrance. The box wobbled precariously, eliciting a chuckle from Gemma, who followed with her lighter box.

They deposited the boxes inside the cool stone walls of the church. The books, once nestled on the shelves of the bookshop, now awaited new hands to lovingly turn their pages.

"Thanks again, James," Gemma said, her voice slightly echoing in the entrance area of St Peter's that led into the nave as they began setting up the stall.

"No problem at all," James replied with a genuine smile.

Gemma's fingers danced between the flaps of a cardboard box, prying it open. The scent of old books wafted out as she lifted the first volume to eye level. James, who'd been shifting another box into place beside her stall, paused and peered over her shoulder.

"Ah, Arthur C. Clarke," he said, pointing at the spine of the well-kept paperback. "A visionary writer."

"He certainly was," Gemma responded. She placed the book delicately on top of the cloth-covered table. "I grew up on tales of space exploration and otherworldly adventures. There's something timeless about early science fiction."

"Isaac Asimov was one of my favourites," James said as he handled a hardback anthology. "His ideas on robotics seemed so far-fetched once, but look at us now."

"The robots haven't quite taken over yet, but we're getting there," Gemma said, admiring the artwork gracing the cover of another novel that she directed towards James. "Did you ever read *Have Spacesuit, Will Travel* by Heinlein?"

"Can't say I have," James answered, looking intrigued with a furrowed brow. "Do you recommend it?"

"I do, it's pure escapism. I imagined myself hopping from planet to planet when I first read this," Gemma said with a nostalgic smile, placing the book centre.

"Never too late for an adventure, Gemma," Mavis chimed in as she eavesdropped on the discussion.

Their conversation was interrupted by the entry of Reverend Simon, whose presence commanded a hush among the early arrivals. He cleared his throat, standing beneath the stained glass that cast kaleidoscopic patterns over the stone floor.

"Friends of Belper," he began, his voice echoing through the sacred space. "Once again, we gather in fellowship at our annual craft fair." As everyone listened intently, he continued, "I now declare the Belper Craft and Summer Fair at St Peter's officially open!"

Gentle applause rippled through the congregation, and James discreetly checked his watch.

"It's been a pleasure helping you set up, Gemma, Mavis," he said, offering a polite nod. "I should see if Dad needs a hand. Enjoy the fair, and I may see you both later." James walked off with Rhianna by his side.

"Such a charming couple," Gemma said to Mavis, as James and Rhianna merged with the crowd.

"They are," Mavis agreed, her gaze following the young pair before returning to the bustle of activity around them. Gemma watched with a contented smile as the local townsfolk filed into the church. The scent of antique wood mingled with the faint aroma of beeswax from the well-polished pews, creating a tranquil and expectant ambience as a man approached their table.

"Ooh, is that a first edition?" he asked, picking up a carefully displayed book.

Gemma nodded and leaned forward. "It is. A 1961 edition of *Catch-22* by Joseph Heller, hardly touched." The man's fingers caressed the spine, and his eyes traced the title.

The buzz of conversation swelled as more locals congregated around Gemma's stall, drawn by the curated collection of literary gems.

"Your stall is always a highlight, Gemma," another familiar patron said as his hands clasped a stack of second-hand novels.

"Thank you, Harold," Gemma said. "Secondhand books ... They're like old friends waiting to be revisited."

Heads nodded in agreement as books were plucked from boxes, pages were gently fanned, and the occasional gasp escaped at finding a long-sought-after title.

"Look at this turnout," Mavis whispered to Gemma. "You've really outdone yourself this year with this selection of books."

"Couldn't have done it without your help," Gemma responded, her gratitude genuine.

As laughter and chatter filled the church, a sense of fulfilment blossomed within Gemma. Each book that exchanged hands was a story set to live in a new home, a treasure passed from one guardian to another. And amidst the joyful commerce of the fair, there was no doubt that today was shaping up to be truly special.

# Chapter Three

A flurry of whispered gasps and the shuffle of feet tore Gemma's attention away from the lady thumbing through a stack of mystery novels. At the church entrance, a dishevelled figure swayed precariously, his steps erratic as he bumped into tables with clumsy abandon. Muffled grumblings and whispers rose from the crowd as the man mumbled incoherently and slurred his words.

"Really now," Mavis said, casting an irritated look at the people grumbling. "This is a house of God. We ought to show some compassion rather than those scowls."

David abandoned his post at the bookstall with a concerned frown creasing his forehead. He approached the man, his voice gentle yet firm. "Are you alright, sir?"

But the reply was lost in a garbled mess, the words tumbling out like puzzle pieces refusing to fit together.

With a steadying hand on the man's back, David coaxed him towards the exit, avoiding the judgmental stares that followed. Gemma caught Mavis's eye, a silent exchange of shared sympathy for the stranger's plight passed between them.

"Sienna, could you watch the stall for a moment?" Gemma asked.

"Of course," Sienna replied.

"Sienna, my dear, could you hand over a cup of tea and a Belgium bun?" Mavis asked. "I think that poor man could use some sobering up."

"Certainly," said Sienna, as she prepared the tea and put the bun in a paper bag.

Gemma's eyes softened with concern as she and Mavis stepped into the courtyard with David and the dishevelled figure. The man sat on the floor with hunched shoulders. "John?" Mavis asked as she crouched beside the man. "John Hargreaves?"

The man lifted his head, squinting his bloodshot eyes. With the gentle prodding of memory, a glimmer of recognition seemed to cross his weathered features.

"Seen him around Belper many times," Mavis said to Gemma. "He's popped by the café before. He was always polite and grateful, just ... down on his luck."

"Yes, I think I have seen him around the marketplace

before too," said Gemma, nodding as she watched Mavis offer the tea and Belgium bun.

"Here you go," Mavis said. John's hand trembled as he reached out, his fingers grazing the cup before securing it with a shaky grip. He brought the cup to his lips, a drop spilling over and darkening the fabric of his worn jacket.

"Thank you," he managed, the words slurred and distant, like an echo from a well.

David folded his arms, concern etched lines across his forehead. "He smells of alcohol," he observed. "Must've had a fair bit if he's in this state."

"Let's give him a moment," Gemma said. "Perhaps the tea will help clear his head." After another few minutes, she said, "I best get back in, as Sienna and Louise are trying to cover both stalls, and it's busy."

"It's okay. You go back, and I'll stay here," said David.

Gemma nodded and walked back into the church, taking her place behind the table covered in books. A lady approached the stall and began scanning the table.

"Can I interest you in anything in particular?" Gemma asked.

"I'm after something fun and lighthearted," said the lady.

"Ah, how about *Bridget Jones's Diary*," Gemma asked with a smile, plucking a vibrant cover from the display. "If you're in the mood for wit tangled with romance, this will wrap you up cosy as a quilt."

The customer beamed at Gemma's recommendation. "Just what I need for the weekend," she replied, her voice rich with anticipation.

"Helen Fielding has a knack for crafting characters you wish were your friends," Gemma continued, her knowledge of genres shining through. She placed the book in a brown paper bag and exchanged it for a crisp five-pound bank note.

"Enjoy," Gemma said, as the customer departed with her new romantic comedy tucked under her arm.

"Busy morning?" James's polite voice cut through the crowd's chatter as he approached the stall, his presence as neat and unassuming as his pressed shirt.

"It is, yes. Lots of eager bookworms here today," Gemma replied, as Mavis rejoined her at the stall.

A man dressed just as smartly as James had joined him. "Gemma, let me introduce you to my dad, Norman, church warden and head bell ringer."

"Pleased to meet you, Norman," said Gemma, as she extended a hand to greet him.

"The pleasure is all mine," said Norman, who nodded a greeting at Mavis.

"I'm looking forward to the bell demonstration," said Gemma.

Norman, an imposing figure who commanded respect, nodded with a warm grin. "It will be a fine demonstration, Gemma. In fact, I'm just about to unlock the bell chamber." His voice resonated with the timbre of the bells he so adored.

"Campanology is quite fascinating," Mavis piped in, demonstrating her worldly knowledge with a nervous flourish. "It requires such precision and harmony." Gemma smiled.

"Quite right," Norman said, before another lady approached. "Ah, Cynthia, come meet Gemma and Mavis from The Bookworm Bookshop." He paused as Cynthia stepped forward. "Everyone, this is Cynthia Norton. She is a volunteer here at St Peter's."

Cynthia Norton's presence was striking, her colourful attire standing out against the atmosphere of the church. Her hair was dyed light pink, and she wore bright red lipstick. Her eyes held a flicker of recognition as she greeted Gemma.

"Ah yes, we've met," Gemma offered.

"Yes, I run the news agents and off licence at the marketplace," Cynthia said. "You've bought biscuits from my shop many times."

"I like your lipstick," said Mavis. "It's nice and bright."

"Thank you. I usually wear pink, but thought I would try something more customary for the craft fair," Cynthia said.

"Cynthia helps here at the church during the week and is a bell ringer in training," said Norman with a smile. "Speaking of which, we had best get on, Cynthia, and get prepared," Norman excused himself with a courteous nod. "The bells wait for no one." He nodded his head towards Mavis and then Gemma and then walked off with Cynthia and James towards the bell tower.

"Good luck!" Mavis called after him.

As Norman's footsteps receded, Gemma faced Mavis.

"How long have you known Norman?" Gemma asked with a smile.

"I've known Norman through the church for many years. My Fred, God rest his soul, was friends with Norman at the bowls club," Mavis said.

"Well, he seems lovely," said Gemma.

Gemma's gaze returned to the stall, ready to guide another patron through the maze of genres and titles. Her eyes twinkled behind her glasses as she recommended another witty romantic comedy, a book called *Chalet Girl*, to an eager teenage girl. "You'll adore the banter in this one," she enthused, her knowledge of the genre as vast as the selection before her. The girl clutched the book to her chest, beaming with anticipation of the cosy evenings ahead.

Suddenly, the jovial hum of the church was shattered by a piercing scream that descended from the belfry. Every head in the church turned, and every voice hushed. The scream echoed through the rafters.

Gemma faced the girl who had just bought the

book. "Please excuse me," Gemma said before dashing towards the sound. Mavis, with surprising agility for her age, was close at her heels, her face etched with concern.

They ascended a narrow spiral staircase, their breaths coming in quick gasps as they climbed higher. The scent of old wood and centuries of whispered prayers clung to the air, growing colder as they approached the belfry.

At the threshold of the chamber, a scene that would forever imprint itself in their minds met them. Cynthia Norton, her face masked with ghostly shock, wailed in Norman's arms. His face was a mask of disbelief, and his powerful hands, which once commanded the bells, were now offering comfort.

On the floor lay a young man, his life story cut short, blood seeped from a gash upon his brow and a cruel wound to his stomach.

Gemma's heart thundered in her chest, and she knelt beside the body. Her hands searched for a pulse in the cold flesh of his neck. There was nothing. "He's gone," she uttered, her voice steady despite the tremor in her soul. "Mavis, get David."

With a nod, Mavis hurried away, her smart attire blurring into the shadows as she hastened to bring help. Gemma remained by the young man, her mind raced with questions.

# Chapter Four

Gemma watched as Norman escorted a wailing and trembling Cynthia down the narrow staircase after suggesting they leave to avoid contaminating the crime scene. Cynthia's sobs echoed off the stone walls of the belfry. The sound seemed to linger and swell in the confined space, much louder than Gemma thought necessary for genuine grief. Gemma arched an eyebrow; something about Cynthia's dramatic display niggled at her, but she shelved the suspicion for later contemplation.

"Take care of her, Norman," Gemma called after them. Her voice was calm, considering that she had just touched a dead body.

"Right then," she muttered under her breath, as if talking to herself made the setting less creepy. Gemma retrieved her phone from her back pocket. "Let's get some snaps of the crime scene. You never know; they may come in handy."

Gemma opened the camera app and began to document the scene, being careful not to disrupt anything; each photograph was a silent witness. She took a picture of the body's awkward sprawl on the floor and the surrounding area. There was a broken blood-stained vodka bottle that lay discarded next to the body. She wondered if the victim had drunk its contents first, as she squared up the bottle in her camera app.

Her gaze fell upon dried, muddy footprints in the dust on the dirty floor. She snapped several close-ups, noting the different treads. One set was heavier; boots, perhaps? And then there it was, an incongruous splash of colour amidst the gloom: a bright pink tube of lipstick in the middle of the room, just a few metres from the body. It seemed a strange thing to find on the floor. Cynthia's maybe? Although it wasn't near where she was standing with Norman.

"Out of place, aren't we?" Gemma's tone was light, almost conversational, as if the lipstick could spill its secrets. She crouched for a better angle as the electronic shutter beeped on her phone. *Mavis will find these photographs interesting*, she thought to herself, although part of her felt awkward photographing a dead body. *That isn't normal, is it? Perhaps I've been reading too many mysteries.*

Satisfied with her impromptu photography session,

Gemma slipped the phone into her back pocket and stepped back from the scene, giving one last glance at the body.

"Poor thing," she whispered.

Heavy footsteps echoed up the stairwell to the bell chamber as David arrived. Mavis was at his side, her face taut with worry.

"Did anyone disturb or touch anything?" David asked. His voice remained steady with a hint of professional detachment.

"Only the murderer," Gemma replied, her hands smoothing the fabric of her jeans. "I had Norman take Cynthia out to avoid any further ... contamination."

David nodded, his eyes scanning the scene before he stooped beside the body and confirmed what they already knew. He withdrew his phone and dialled the station. "This is DI Haynes. I need a crime scene investigator and a pathologist. We have a potential murder." He paused while listening to someone on the other end of the call. "St Peter's church in Belper ... Young man. Looks to be in his early twenties. No confirmed identity as yet ... Thank you." He hung up the phone.

"Thank you for your quick thinking, Gemma," David said, tucking his phone away as he stood. His gaze lingered on her for just a moment longer than necessary. "Would you and Mavis mind heading downstairs? I need to secure the area."

Gemma felt Mavis's arm link with hers, and they

descended the narrow steps. The murmurs from below grew louder, swelling into a cacophony of curiosity and concern as they re-entered the nave.

"Is it true, Gemma? What's happened?" The crowd pressed in, faces drawn and pale.

Gemma's announcement cut through the whispers like a knife. "Someone has been found dead upstairs." Gemma couldn't bring herself to say the word "murdered." She ignored the flutter in her chest and the way her pulse raced; now was not the time to show fear.

A collective gasp rippled through the building. James and Rhianna shouldered their way to the forefront, their expressions a mixture of shock and intrigue.

"Who is it?" James asked, his voice steady despite the gravity of the situation.

"We're not sure," Gemma admitted, her brow furrowed. "But he's young. Early twenties, I think." Mavis squeezed Gemma's arm reassuringly, grounding her as she faced the barrage of questions. "The police are on their way."

The reverend cleared his throat, capturing the attention of the restless crowd. "Ladies and gentlemen," he began, his voice carrying the weight of authority and concern, "in light of the current circumstances, it would be prudent for us all to vacate the premises. The remainder of today's event is, regrettably, cancelled."

Chatter filled the church, along with murmurs of agreement that fluttered through the gathering like leaves in a breeze as stallholders nodded and exchanged looks of understanding.

"Please, return tomorrow when the police have concluded their investigation to collect your belongings and stock," the reverend added, ushering everyone with a gentle wave towards the exit. The faint sound of police sirens wailed in the distance.

Gemma watched as everyone filed out of the church, their faces full of concern and shock. Mavis, ever the comforting presence, stood beside her, offering silent support with a reassuring pat on the back.

In the gardens of St. Peter's, the scent of fresh cut grass mixed with the soft floral notes drifting from the nearby rose bushes. As Gemma and Mavis lingered near the roofed gateway to the church, a fleet of cars arrived in a symphony of flashing lights. Uniformed police officers spilled out onto the path in front of the church entrance, their movements brisk and purposeful. Among them, Gemma spotted a familiar face; Dr Susan Thomas, a crime scene pathologist and one of David's colleagues.

"Afternoon, Reverend," Dr Thomas said in greeting. Her professional demeanour was softened by the nod she gave to Gemma. With a briefcase in hand and a no-nonsense stride, she followed the reverend, who was already leading the way back to the church.

Together, Gemma and Mavis stepped aside, making room for the procession of law enforcement.

Mavis leaned closer, lowering her voice to a conspiratorial whisper. "Did you find anything interesting up there?"

Gemma glanced at the cluster of police cars parked by the church's entrance. Her mind replayed the chaotic scene she had committed to memory. "There was a broken vodka bottle," she said, her eyes narrowing as she pictured the jagged shards. "It might have been the murder weapon. It was covered in blood, and the victim looked to have taken a nasty blow to the head before being stabbed with the broken bottle."

Mavis gasped. "Really? That's quite gruesome." She arched a brow, the lines on her forehead deepening with intrigue.

"And boot prints," Gemma continued, her voice barely above a murmur. "Muddy boot prints all over the dust. It rained cats and dogs last night, didn't it?"

"Curiouser and curiouser," said Mavis, the corners of her mouth twitching upwards.

"Then there was this bright pink lipstick," Gemma added, her tone thoughtful. "Just lying there a few metres from the body."

"Ah," Mavis said. "The plot thickens. A clue, do you think?"

"Maybe," Gemma replied, the hint of a smile playing on her lips. "I may have taken some photos of the crime scene." Mavis smiled. "They may come in handy," Gemma said, quickly justifying her actions.

"Do you think we'll need them?" Mavis's eyes gleamed with a mix of excitement and concern.

"Well, we'll have to see what David and his team come up with," Gemma said as her gaze drifted over the concerned faces mingling in the gardens. Gemma and Mavis looked at each other and gave a knowing nod. The cogs of curiosity were already beginning to turn.

## Chapter Five

Back in the bookshop the next day, Gemma fluffed a cushion on a reading nook's seat before unlocking the front door with a soft click, signalling the start of another day within Belper's marketplace.

"Seems eerily quiet today, doesn't it?" Mavis asked, emerging from behind a shelf stacked with the latest fad dieting books. They always sold well before the summer, as people like to shed those extra few pounds before their holidays. Mavis peered at Gemma with a look of concern in her eyes.

"Understandably so," Gemma said, straightening a stack of hardcovers. "After yesterday's grim discovery at the fair ... Well, it's shaken everyone up."

"Have you heard anything back from David?" Mavis asked, her voice low, almost hesitant.

"Only that he was working through the night. He must be exhausted," Gemma said with a sigh.

The jingle of the door announced new customers; a couple seeking refuge from the sudden downpour of summer rain. Gemma greeted them with her trademark bubbly warmth and guided them towards the latest bestsellers. They left with satisfied smiles and a paper bag rustling with fresh adventures.

More patrons drifted in and out, a gentle stream of book lovers and caffeine seekers. Gossip had spread quickly through the town, and Gemma had many people ask her about what had happened. She couldn't blame them; Belper was such a peaceful town, so a brutal murder in a church of all places was not what the townsfolk were used to. Gemma navigated that morning's sales with ease; the new point-of-sale system beeped contentedly as she scanned each purchase.

"Isn't this just a dream?" Gemma enthused, tapping the sleek screen. "No more battles with the cash drawer. It used to require a good whack and a prayer just to give up the change."

Mavis chuckled. "I'm usually all fingers and thumbs with these gadgets, but even I have to admit, this one's quite the charmer."

Gemma glanced up, catching Mavis's eye over a tower of cosy mystery novels. "How's your garden coming along? The competition's just around the corner, isn't it?"

Mavis beamed at the mention of her beloved pastime. "Oh, I'm certainly entered into the competition. The best garden and the prize marrow categories this year." She patted her hair into place. "I've got my work cut out for me, though. Mrs Colchester's roses have been the talk of the town, and she's won thrice already."

"Your garden is a slice of Eden if I ever saw one," Gemma said. "If anyone can give Mrs Colchester a run for her money, it's you."

"Thank you." Mavis's cheeks flushed a delicate pink. "My friend Barry's coming around later to lend a hand. I'm giving him advice on roses, and he's an expert at growing large marrows."

The bell above the door jingled as David entered. Weariness was etched onto his face. "Man, that was a busy night last night," he said with a sigh while approaching the counter.

"Everything alright, David?" Gemma's brow furrowed in concern.

"Could do with a strong coffee. It was a long night. Hardly slept," he replied, his voice gravelly with fatigue.

"Come on. Let's head to the back. Ellie will sort you out a strong coffee," Gemma said, motioning towards the café.

They settled into the comfy chairs, and Ellie approached. "Hello, David, what can I get for you?"

"A double-shot espresso, please," David said, as he smiled at Ellie while rubbing his temples.

"Going for the hard stuff, I see," Gemma teased, eliciting a half-smile from him. "I'll have a latte, please."

"Earl Grey, for me, please," said Mavis.

"Your rocket fuel coffee is on the way," Ellie chirped before turning away to work her magic with the espresso machine. Ellie shortly returned with a tray and set the drinks on their table.

"Here you go, David. Hope this perks you up," she said.

"Thanks, Ellie," they all said in unison, before Ellie retreated to the counter, her attention reclaimed by the steady stream of customers waiting for coffee and cake.

David picked up the small espresso cup and downed his double shot in one gulp before letting out a large sigh. He looked up at Gemma and Mavis as he took on a more stern demeanour. "We made an arrest last night for the murder," he announced.

Gemma's heart skipped at the news; she wasn't expecting an arrest so quickly. Mavis let out a soft gasp, her delicate features folding into a frown. "Who was it?" Mavis asked, her question hanging in the air.

"Wait," Gemma interjected, touching her friend's arm. "First, who was the victim?"

"The victim was a local man called George Peters," David said, the syllables tasting bitter on his tongue. "He was only twenty-three but already had quite the criminal record; shoplifting, minor drug possession, antisocial behaviour."

Mavis pursed her lips, the gears in her mind turning like the precise mechanisms of her cherished grandfather clock. "So it's possible he had enemies then," she surmised, her tone a mix of curiosity and concern.

"Yes, George was the sort of person to collect enemies," David said, nodding.

"Still, nobody deserves murder. No matter how undesirable their behaviour," Gemma said as she leaned forward. She narrowed her eyes in concentration as she processed David's words. "And who have you arrested?" Her voice was steady.

David hesitated, his gaze shifted to the empty cup before him. "John Hargreaves," he said, his voice a shade grimmer than before. "The homeless man who caused that commotion at the church."

Mavis's teacup clinked against the saucer with a slight tremor from her hand. "John?" she asked, shaking her head in disbelief. "But he's such a kind soul, always polite and mild-mannered."

"Kind or not, the evidence is quite compelling," David replied, meeting Gemma's inquisitive stare. "The vodka bottle found at the scene is covered in his fingerprints. Traces of vodka and ketamine inside it matched what was in his system; a blood test confirmed that. And the muddy prints ... they match his boots perfectly. Not to mention blood stains and spatters on his clothes."

Gemma sat back, the information hitting her like a gust of icy wind. "That does sound damning," she said, frowning. "But how did he even get into the church? Surely it's locked at night? Were there any signs of a break-in?"

"Indeed, it usually is locked, and no, there were no signs of a forced entry," David said, scratching his chin. "However, we found a newly cut set of keys in John's belongings hidden beside the church where he'd been bedding down." A silence fell over the trio, broken only by the distant murmur of conversation and the gentle clinking of cups from the café.

"New keys ..." Gemma said. Her mind raced as she tried to piece the puzzle together. It didn't sit right with her. The thought of John Hargreaves with his weathered face and gentle demeanour, being capable of such violence, surely not.

Mavis rested her cup with a decisive click. "This doesn't add up," she declared, her silver hair catching the light as she gave her head a firm shake. "John may have his troubles, but this ..." she said, leaving the sentence unfinished yet laden with doubt.

David sighed. His broad shoulders slumped and fatigue showed in his eyes. "I understand it's hard to digest," he said, his tone apologetic. "But the facts are the facts. Until proven otherwise, all signs point to John Hargreaves." Gemma's fingers drummed the tabletop.

"Still," Mavis persisted, her brows knitting together in consternation, "it all seems too convenient, doesn't it? All that evidence laid out like a breadcrumb trail straight to poor John." She glanced towards David, her eyes sharp behind her glasses.

David ran a hand through his hair, his gaze weary. "He was under the influence of ketamine," he reminded them, though his voice lacked conviction. "Not exactly in a state to think about covering tracks."

"But, even so," Gemma said, her own scepticism mirroring Mavis's, "to have those keys ... It suggests a level of planning that doesn't align with someone in such a stupor." She shook her head. "Something about this just doesn't feel right."

"Has he said anything in his defence?" Mavis enquired, her tone softening with concern.

"Not yet," David replied. "We've had to wait for the alcohol and ketamine to clear his system; they're a nasty mix. So far, he's not contesting anything."

Mavis reached for her tea, her hand trembling. "Poor soul," she murmured, taking a sip. "Whether or not he's guilty, it's a sad state of affairs."

David glanced at his wristwatch. "Right. I've got to get back to the station. I thought you would want to know what's happening," he said, pushing his chair back with a soft scrape against the wooden floor.

"Of course, David," Gemma said with understanding, rising to her feet as well. She leaned in and gave him a grateful peck on the cheek. "Thank you for keeping us updated. I appreciate it."

He smiled. "It's quite a shock, I know," he admitted, "but the evidence we have against him ... it's pretty damning."

Mavis, who had been listening intently, nodded. "No, it doesn't look good," she said, her voice laced with a mixture of disbelief and concern. "Hard to believe it, though."

With a last nod, David turned and made his way towards the door. His figure was silhouetted against the bright entrance before he slipped out into the bustle of the marketplace.

When the door closed, Gemma said, "This just doesn't sit right with me." Her voice was low and troubled.

Mavis met her gaze. "I agree," she said. "It couldn't hurt for us to take a closer look, could it? After all, if the police already have their man, it's not like we'd be interfering."

"You're right," Gemma replied, a spark igniting in her eyes as she contemplated their next move.

"Pop around to mine this evening?" asked Mavis. "We can set up the dining room again; turn it into our little investigation headquarters like last time." Gemma chuckled, the twinkle returning to her eyes as she envisioned the scene. "I'll have the kettle on and the notepads ready. Are the Bookworm detectives back in business?"

Gemma smiled, her spirits buoyed by the prospect of delving into another mystery with her trusted companion. "I believe we are. I look forward to it, Mavis," she said.

## Chapter Six

Gemma eased her VW Beetle to the curb, the engine's gentle purr falling silent as she switched off the ignition. She exited the car with a folder tucked under her arm and approached the quaint stone facade of Mavis's house. When she rapped on the door, Mavis answered with her usual grace. Her silver was hair glinting and her spectacles were perched on her nose, framing warm eyes that welcomed Gemma inside.

"Come through," Mavis said, leading Gemma past the hallway lined with framed photographs of smiling faces. They stepped into the garden and were greeted by the heady scent of blooming roses.

A man sat in a cushioned chair on the patio, his attention fixed on the vibrant flowerbeds before him. At the sound of their arrival, he looked up, revealing a face etched with lines of kindness.

"Gemma, this is Barry Spencer," Mavis said, her hand sweeping towards the man who rose to his feet. "Barry, meet Gemma Curtis. We work together at The Bookworm Bookshop."

"Hello, Gemma. A pleasure to meet you." Barry tipped his cloth cap with the genteel manner of a bygone era.

"Barry and I have been helping each other with our gardens for the competition," Mavis continued. "We're both vying for the coveted best garden title this year and, of course, for the marrow-growing contest." She gestured towards the lush vegetable patch where robust marrows lay. "Barry here is quite the expert," she said. "His jumbo marrows took the second place prize last year, and he has come first before too."

"Merely a fortunate harvest," Barry said. "Though I must say, Mavis's marrows are shaping up splendidly. Nice and plump and firm." He nodded approvingly towards the burgeoning crop.

Gemma's eyebrow arched and a ripple of amusement crossed her features at the unintended innuendo. "Seems like you've got everything well in hand here," Gemma said with a smile. "And it's always good to have friends with green fingers when there's a competition afoot. But if you don't mind me asking, aren't you both competing for the same prizes?"

"We are, but I've won the marrow-growing prize multiple times. For me, it's the taking part that's important and not the prize. It's been nice working with Mavis," Barry said, his affable smile putting Gemma at ease. "I think it's Mavis's turn to shine this year."

Mavis clapped her hands together, delighted. "Oh, Barry, you're too kind. Wouldn't that be nice? But now, come, let's have some tea. Are you okay with Earl Grey, Gemma?"

"Yes, that would be very nice, thank you," said Gemma. She was a coffee drinker usually, but tea on a nice summer's evening was quite refreshing.

They settled around the patio table, her folder momentarily forgotten, as Gemma enjoyed the evening sun. She leaned forward, resting her elbows on the weathered garden table as Mavis poured the steaming tea into floral-patterned cups.

"There's been some trouble in the competition this year," Mavis began, her voice dropping to a conspiratorial whisper. "Someone is going around sabotaging the gardens. Can you imagine? Just last week, the Tomlinsons woke up to their dahlias absolutely decimated."

"Good heavens," Gemma murmured. "That's very unsporting; it's downright malicious. Do they know who did it?"

"No, and it's got us all on edge. They haven't touched Mrs Colchester's prized petunias yet, though. She's won three years running now," Mavis said, her eyebrows knitted together in worry. "It's put quite the damper on things, I must say."

"You have a locked gate though, right?" asked Gemma.

"I do, yes, but there's nothing stopping anyone jumping over it or over the back fence from the alleyway."

"Perhaps there's a way to keep your garden safe," Gemma suggested, her mind already racing through potential solutions. "Jack might have some ideas. He's quite tech-savvy. You remember Jack, the young man who helped set up our new point-of-sale system at the bookshop?"

Mavis perked up, the cloud of concern lifting at the prospect of help. "Oh, yes, he's a clever one. Do you think he would know what to do?"

"Let's find out." Gemma fished her phone from her pocket, her fingers deftly composing a message. She hit send, and within moments, the device buzzed with a reply.

"Jack says he's got something in mind and can come by after work tomorrow," Gemma read aloud. "That should put your mind at ease."

"Marvellous!" Mavis exclaimed. They sat admiring Mavis's roses and drinking their tea when Barry changed the subject from gardening to something more sinister.

"Such a tragedy about that young man at the church," Barry said, breaking the silence. He adjusted his cap. His fingers lingered on the brim out of respect. "He was a troubled lad, I'm afraid. Had quite the reputation for stirring up trouble." His tone carried an undercurrent of regret, as though speaking ill of the deceased left a bitter taste.

"How do you mean he was troubled, Barry?" Mavis asked.

Barry leaned back in his chair with a contemplative look. "He had it in for that homeless chap. Bullying him, he was. Although I was surprised to hear they'd charged him for murder. He was such a mild-mannered man." He glanced at Gemma and Mavis, searching their faces for a sign of shared understanding.

"How do you know this, if you don't mind me asking?" asked Gemma.

"I volunteer at a food hub at the Baptist church. John would regularly pop in for something to eat and drink. I used to enjoy our chats together, but he did mention that he was having trouble with a local man tormenting him. He eventually told me who it was. I said he should inform the police, but John said the police wouldn't want to deal with a homeless man. I guess he must have just snapped in the end."

"Such a sad situation all around," Gemma said, the empathy in her voice as soothing as the tea they sipped.

Barry glanced at his watch and then stood, stretching his legs with a soft groan of contentment. "Well, ladies, it's been absolutely lovely, but I should get home. I need to water my garden now the sun is setting."

"Thank you for the delightful company, Barry," Gemma said warmly, watching as he gathered his things.

"The pleasure is all mine," Barry replied. "And thank you, Mavis, for the tea and the roses' advice. I'll see myself out."

As he ambled towards the gate, Gemma turned to Mavis with a playful glint in her eye. "Barry seems nice," she teased with a wink.

Mavis let out a chuckle. "Oh, he's a good friend from the gardening club, and a widower too, bless him. But that's all there is to it," she clarified, brushing off any insinuation with a wave of her hand.

"Of course," Gemma said, taking the hint to drop it. "Shall we head inside? I've got some notes for us to look at."

"Yes, of course," Mavis said, rising to her feet with sprightly energy. "I've set up in the dining room already and turned it back into our investigation room."

Together, the two women made their way into the house, leaving the serenity of the garden behind. As they crossed the threshold, Gemma felt the thrill of a new chapter unfolding. She was eager to unravel the tangled threads of the murder that had shaken their peaceful town to its core.

## Chapter Seven

They entered the dining room, and Gemma eased into the plush comfort of one of Mavis's floral dining room chairs. A white sheet of paper that would serve as their makeshift investigation board was stuck to the wall, ready to assist in their detective work.

Mavis emerged from the kitchen with another pot of Earl Grey and a china plate of freshly baked coconut macaroons. Gemma smiled in anticipation. She took a macaroon and let its crumbly texture dissolve in her mouth. "Mavis, these are lovely," she said, the rich taste of coconut sending a ripple of comfort all the way to her toes.

"It's one of my favourite recipes," Mavis replied, settling next to Gemma. They both turned to the blank canvas before them on the wall. It was a clean slate, ready to be filled with the murky details of a crime and a potential miscarriage of justice.

"Right then," Mavis said. "Let's start at the beginning."

Gemma nodded, her mind already sifting through the facts. "George Peters, our victim," she began, her voice steady despite the gravity of the topic. "He was a young lad. In his early twenties." Her glasses caught a glint of light as she recounted the grim discovery. "Found him in the bell chamber of the church. Head wound ... and a nasty stab in the abdomen." She paused, her brow furrowed in thought. "He must have died there the previous evening or night. Sometime between when the chamber was cleaned the previous day and when it was unlocked the morning of the craft fair. No clue why he was there at that time, of all places."

They sat momentarily in silence. George Peters had been no saint from the sounds of it. But who would find themselves driven to take such violent actions? And why within the hallowed quiet of the church's bell chamber? Gemma felt a renewed surge of determination. She liked solving puzzles, and this would be a particularly tricky one.

Mavis used a marker to add a note in her neat cursive on the white paper. "Body discovered by Norman Howard and Cynthia Norton," she dictated to herself.

"They unlocked the room, ready for the bell demonstration, and discovered the body already there," Mavis continued as she scribbled. Her marker squeaked a full stop at the end of the sentence.

Gemma leaned back in her chair and considered the facts Mavis had laid out before them. They seemed straightforward enough, but she knew appearances could deceive.

"John Hargreaves," Gemma mused aloud. "The prime suspect." She stood to add her own contribution to their makeshift investigation board. "Boot prints matching his were all over the scene. And then there were the fingerprints on the bottle that was used killed to George; the same bottle laced with vodka and ketamine." She paused, her heart heavy with the implications. "They found a set of keys on him too ... Keys for the church and the bell chamber."

"Looks damning indeed," Mavis agreed, a furrow creasing her brow.

"Yes, it doesn't look good at all, does it?" Gemma said. She capped her marker and placed it on the dining room table, giving Mavis an expectant look.

"Odd, though, isn't it?" Gemma pondered, her fingers tapping rhythmically against the tabletop. "According to David, John hasn't said a word to clear his name. Not one alibi or plea of innocence."

"Could be he's still reeling from the drugs and

alcohol in his system," Mavis offered, her tone betraying a hint of scepticism. "That ketamine is quite a powerful drug, isn't it? I saw something about it on the tele once."

"True," Gemma said, nodding thoughtfully. "He might not have grasped the gravity of his situation yet." They sat in contemplative silence for a moment.

"Regardless," Gemma said, breaking the quiet. "We'll find the truth. We owe it to George ... and to John, if he's innocent." Gemma fanned out the contents of her folder across Mavis's dining table. "I printed some photos I took when I was alone in the belfry with the body." She selected a particular print from the table. "Sorry in advance, Mavis," Gemma said, her voice carrying a tinge of apology as she affixed the photo onto the paper taped to the wall. "This one's a bit ... stark."

Mavis waved off the concern with a flutter of her hand, peering over the rim of her spectacles. "Oh, pish-posh. I've seen my share of the macabre in my day. Let's have a look then."

The photograph, though less vivid than reality, still showed the grim finality of George Peters' earthly departure. He lay crumpled on the floor, his eyes closed as if in peaceful slumber, oblivious to the violence that had claimed him.

"Goodness," Mavis whispered, but her gaze remained unflinching.

"Here's another," Gemma continued, picking up a second photograph. The photo was of a bright pink lipstick tube nestled amongst the dust and shadows of the bell chamber. She placed it next to the first photo, on the wall, with a piece of Blu Tack. "I can't shake the feeling that it feels important."

"Could Cynthia have dropped it there?" Mavis asked, leaning in closer, her curiosity piqued.

"Maybe it's her usual colour. I've seen her wear it at her shop on the marketplace," Gemma replied. "But why would she have a colour with her that she wasn't wearing that day?"

"Ah," Mavis said, her lips pursing in thought. "It could be nothing, or it could be something. Something we need an answer to."

Gemma stepped back, arms crossed, as they both studied the growing collage of clues. "Let's keep digging, Mavis. There's more here. I'm sure of it," she said. Gemma leaned closer to the pictures on the wall, studying them. "Barry said George was no angel," she murmured. "He'd been giving John a hard time for months. But is it enough to justify desperate measures?"

"Everyone has a breaking point," Mavis said, settling into her chair with a thoughtful tilt of her head. "But John? He's always been so nice and polite, even when times were tough. I can't picture him orchestrating such a violent act."

"Yes, it does sound out of character from what you've told me," Gemma conceded. "And with vodka and ketamine in his system, it feels like it would take more than luck to pull off an attack like that. He could hardly walk when he staggered into the church."

"Aren't you friends with the pharmacist at the supermarket? Could she shed some light on it?" Mavis suggested.

"Yeah, that's a good idea. Jen will know more about the effects of that drug and what he'd be capable of if he ingested it," Gemma said. "I'll pop in tomorrow and see if she can meet for a coffee on her break."

"Good plan," Mavis said with a smile, although concern clouded her eyes. "Something that also doesn't sit right, though, is how did John get hold of this drug? Is it easy to get? I don't really know much about it, to be honest."

Gemma shook her head. "I don't know. I guess anything like that is easy to get from the seedy underbelly of society; not that I thought this town had an underbelly."

"Indeed. I hope we're not barking up the wrong tree with John. Such a nice man. Very well spoken and gentle. Not one to harm a fly, let alone … Well, it just seems out of character."

"I know what you mean." Gemma stood, stretching her back, feeling the day's investigations weigh upon her shoulders. "We'll figure this out, Mavis. And we'll make sure that we uncover the real culprit."

Mavis's lips twitched into a smile. "I have every faith

in our abilities. After all, if we can't trust our instincts, what can we trust?"

"You're right there." Gemma's response was determined. With Mavis at her side, the truth couldn't remain hidden for long.

Gemma returned to her chair and tapped the pen against her chin. "So," she began, "let's look at our next steps." She glanced at Mavis, who was perched on the edge of her seat with an air of keen anticipation. "First things first. I will speak to Jen to find out about the effects of the drugs John had taken. We should then speak to the reverend to see if there's any CCTV footage. I noticed there were cameras outside the church. It could give us a clearer picture of who had access to the bell chamber."

"Right you are," Mavis chimed in, smoothing the crease of her cardigan sleeve. "And let's not forget that lovely James and his girlfriend, Rhianna. They are a similar age, from the looks of it. They might know more about the victim from high school, possibly?"

"Good point," Gemma said, nodding. She was already ticking off the tasks ahead.

"What about David?" Mavis ventured with a hint of mischief twinkling in her eyes. "You mentioned seeing David tomorrow night. Will he divulge anything?"

Gemma smiled. "Oh, it's just a matter of asking the right questions, but I don't want to let on that we are investigating. He might tell us not to, and where's the fun in that?" The two women chuckled.

Gemma rose from her chair, gathered her notes and tucked them into her folder, her eyes bright with the thrill of the chase. "I best be off. It's been a long day."

"Just about ready for the land of nod myself," said Mavis as she tried to stifle a yawn.

## Chapter Eight

The next day, Gemma arranged a whimsical display of new romantic comedy arrivals when the bell announced the entry of a customer, a heavyset man wearing jeans and a T-shirt. Gemma glanced up and offered a welcoming smile. "Good morning," she said, but the customer barely acknowledged the greeting, marching straight to the counter, where Mavis stood polishing her spectacles with a handkerchief. Gemma walked back to the counter to join Mavis.

"I'm looking for *The Labyrinthine Compendium of Phantasmagorical Oddities*," the customer demanded, his voice laced with expectancy. Gemma exchanged a bemused look with Mavis, whose eyebrows arched in surprise.

"Oh, I can't say that one rings a bell," Gemma

admitted, tapping keys on the computer behind the counter. "Let me just have a look in our system." Gemma's fingers danced over the keyboard as she searched for the book.

"Here we are," Gemma said, her tone still cheerful despite the frosty atmosphere. "It appears to be quite a niche title, but I can order it in for you. It should only take a couple of days."

"Unbelievable," the man huffed, his impatience boiling over. "What kind of bookshop doesn't stock a simple book?"

"Ah, well," Gemma said, while attempting to embody the patience of a saint, "with millions of new books released every year, it's challenging for any shop to have them all on hand, but I can get it for you." Gemma paused before speaking and then took a deep breath. "Would you like me to place an order for the book?" Gemma smiled, even though the customer's disdain hung in the air between them.

The customer responded with a derisive snort. "No, I'll just order it online. They can have it delivered to me by tomorrow," he declared, as if the mere thought of waiting over twenty-four hours, and walking back to the shop, was an affront to his very existence. With that, he spun on his heel and marched out of the shop, the bell above the door jingling angrily in his wake.

Gemma let out a sigh, her forced smile faltering as

she turned to Mavis. "Can you believe the nerve? Some people seem to take pleasure in being difficult."

Mavis, who had been observing the exchange, shook her head. "It's as if they're trying to prove a point about the convenience of online shopping. As if we don't already know." Her voice was tinged with the wisdom of her years, but not without a note of bewilderment.

"True," Gemma said, chuckling in an attempt to brush off the unpleasant encounter. "At least most of our customers still appreciate the charm of a physical book bought in person."

"Oh, speaking of which, how is your little experiment with stocking those e-readers going?" Mavis enquired, peering over her glasses with genuine curiosity.

"About as well as a chocolate teapot," Gemma admitted with a grin. "I've sold a few, but there's just not much appetite for them here. People come to the Bookworm for the tactile joy of flipping through pages, not screens."

"Nothing quite matches the smell of an actual book," Mavis said. "Especially a nice musty, secondhand one."

Gemma nodded, her annoyance from earlier fading as she glanced at her watch. "Mavis, I need to dash. Could you hold the fort?" she said.

"Of course," Mavis replied. "You're meeting that pharmacy friend of yours, aren't you?"

"Yes, that's right," Gemma said with an assertive nod. "I'm hoping Jen can shed some light on the cocktail of drugs."

"Such a dreadful business," Mavis said with a sigh, the corners of her mouth turning down in concern. "I hope you get the answers you need."

"I'm sure I will." Gemma offered a supportive smile before slipping through the door.

The walk was brisk, and Gemma moved with purpose, her mind churning with questions only Jen could answer. Fifteen minutes later, she arrived at the supermarket, its automatic doors sweeping open to welcome her into a world of fluorescent lights and busy shoppers.

The pharmacy counter stood to her right. A short but orderly queue of patrons waited patiently for their turn. Gemma hovered near the counter, her gaze searching for Jen's familiar face.

"Ah, Gemma!" Jen called out, spotting her friend from behind the shelves. "My lunch break starts soon. I'll meet you in the café."

"Take your time," Gemma responded, her voice carrying a note of gratitude across the distance. She watched Jen disappear back into the organised chaos of her workspace before heading towards the café.

After ordering two lattes, Gemma found a quiet corner table at the back of the store and settled to wait. Before long, Jen, in a crisp white lab coat, entered with her flame-red hair cascading over her shoulders. Gemma looked up, and a smile bloomed across her face.

"Jen, over here!" she called out, waving her over.

"Sorry I'm late. Queue from hell," Jen said in apology, slipping off her jacket and draping it over the back of the chair before sitting opposite Gemma. "So how are things with you and David? I heard you were back together?" she asked, her voice bubbling with genuine interest as she reached for her steaming latte.

Gemma's cheeks coloured slightly at the mention of David's name. "We're ... taking it slow, trying to figure things out again," she said. "But it's good. Thanks for asking."

"I'm pleased for you, Gemma," Jen said, her eyes crinkling with a smile as she took a careful sip of the latte.

"Thank you," Gemma said. She chuckled, feeling the warmth of camaraderie between them. The conversation shifted seamlessly as Jen leaned forward, lowering her voice as if to share a secret. "I heard about that murder at the church. Terrible business. It's not something you'd expect in Belper."

Gemma nodded, her humour fading. "It's shocking. Makes you think we're living in some gritty Channel 4 drama rather than a sleepy town."

Jen let out a soft laugh, shaking her head in disbelief. "I heard they arrested a man who had been sleeping rough near the church. Is that right?"

"Yes, that's right," Gemma replied, her tone measured, betraying nothing of her personal quest for answers. "But there's talk around town ... whispers that something doesn't add up."

"Really?" Jen's eyebrows lifted in curiosity. "What have you heard?"

"Nothing concrete," Gemma hedged, careful not to come across as too involved. "Just bits and pieces here and there. You know how people talk."

"Of course," Jen agreed, nodding. "Rumours fly fast in a town like this."

"David mentioned something odd," Gemma began, being careful not to make it look like she was investigating a murder. Her gaze was fixed on the gentle swirl of milk in her coffee. "Something about the murder weapon." She paused, considering how to phrase her next words. "It was a vodka bottle, but there's more to it. It had traces of both vodka and ketamine."

Jen raised an eyebrow as she processed this information, her pharmaceutical expertise already piecing together the implications. "Ketamine?"

"Yes," Gemma continued, her voice dropping slightly despite the bustling café around them. "And when they arrested that man, they found the same substances in his system. But here's what puzzles me; if he was under the influence like that, could he have unlocked the church with the keys the police found on him? And then commit such an act?"

Jen leaned back in her chair, the fiery strands of her hair catching the light from the window as she shook her head. "Mixing alcohol and ketamine is incredibly dangerous," she said. "Too much ketamine, and it's lethal. Even without hitting that threshold, when combined with alcohol, it would sedate someone significantly. Coordination, planning, precise movements; all would be significantly impaired, in fact, nearly impossible. That's not even considering the impact of the vodka alone, depending on how much he consumed."

Gemma's brow creased in thought, her investigative instincts kicking in despite her attempts at nonchalance. The pieces didn't fit. She pondered Jen's words.

"Hardly the state you'd expect for someone capable of murder," Gemma mused out loud, almost to herself. Jen nodded in agreement, her professional opinion solidifying Gemma's growing suspicions.

"Whoever did this ..." Jen said, her tone underscored with a professional certainty that resonated with Gemma's intuition. "If they were on a cocktail like that, the likelihood of them being able to carry it out diminishes dramatically."

The puzzle pieces hovered in the air between them, a picture incomplete and increasingly complex. With every new shred of information, the web of mystery only seemed to grow denser.

"I just can't see how he'd be capable of anything, let alone murder," Jen said, her voice tinged with frustration. "If you were planning something ... illicit," she said, her eyebrows knitting together in thought, "you wouldn't choose ketamine. Amphetamines would be more up your alley as they're stimulants. They sharpen you up; not slow you down."

"Is ketamine hard to come by?" asked Gemma. Her question was casual, almost indifferent.

"On the streets, they call it Special-K," Jen said with a shrug, as if discussing the weather rather than the illicit world of drug dealing. "It's around, though not as common as some other drugs. You could get it if you knew the right people. Not something I endorse as a medical professional, obviously."

"Yes, of course," Gemma said, nodding slowly. Her mind was already churning with possibilities, scenarios where the true perpetrator was still at large. Gemma thought it best to steer the subject towards something else. "Speaking of getting things ... Are you and your husband all set for your holiday this year?"

A smile broke across Jen's face, her features softening as she embraced the welcome change of topic. "Majorca for ten days," she exclaimed, her eyes gleaming with the prospect of sunshine and escape. "I'm counting down the days."

"That sounds lovely. I bet your kids will love that," Gemma replied, her smile mirroring her friend's enthusiasm. "I haven't even thought about holidays yet. I quite fancy a long weekend by the coast."

With their empty cups signifying the end of their break, Jen rose from her seat as she prepared to dive back into the methodical world of prescriptions and dosages.

"Thanks for the coffee, Gemma," Jen said warmly. "It's been lovely to catch up, and good luck with ... everything."

"Thanks, Jen. Enjoy Majorca," Gemma said, watching as her friend disappeared back into the bustle of the supermarket.

## Chapter Nine

When Gemma arrived back at the store, she spotted Mavis perched behind the counter with Geoff Dunsworth, Belper's own brick-and-mortar maestro.

"Good afternoon, Geoff!" Gemma said with her signature bubbly enthusiasm. "To what do I owe the pleasure?" she asked, although she knew why he was there. A wave of excitement washed over her.

"Ah, Gemma," Geoff replied, his rough builder's hands smoothing over his work-worn jeans before shaking Gemma's hand. "Just the person we've been waiting for."

Gemma settled next to Mavis. "I come bearing good tidings," Geoff said, his voice rich with anticipation. "The Council has given the thumbs up. Your plans for the café extension are approved. We can break ground whenever you're ready."

A surge of elation coursed through Gemma, brightening her face into a wide grin. Ever since Mavis had invested in the bookshop, it had been their dream to expand the café into a larger haven for book lovers and event goers.

"Really?" Gemma clapped her hands together, unable to contain her glee. "This is fantastic! We'll be able to host more author signings, poetry readings ... Oh, and the clubs that use us will adore having more space!"

"Well, there's nothing standing in your way now," Geoff said as he unfurled a set of detailed plans across the counter top. The crisp paper crackled under his hands as he smoothed out the edges, revealing the future of Gemma's beloved bookshop in sketched lines and architectural symbols.

"Here we are," Geoff announced, pointing to the layout with an air of pride. "We'll get the foundations going without a hitch. Once we've got the shell up, we can shape your extra space without so much as a pebble out of place inside the shop."

Gemma leaned forward, and Mavis edged closer too.

"Without breaking through the main wall first?" Gemma clarified, her brows raised in pleasant surprise.

"That's right," Geoff said with a nod. "That way,

you can keep serving your customers without too much interruption, apart from some noise."

"Brilliant!" Mavis exclaimed, clapping her delicate hands softly. "Less fuss, more cake."

As they shared nods of approval, Geoff retrieved another document from his leather satchel, this one laden with figures and dates. He laid it next to the plans, and Gemma's gaze shifted from the dream to the due diligence required to make it a reality.

"Right, here's the payment schedule," Geoff began, tapping the top sheet. "Sixty-three thousand pounds all in, with twenty thousand needed upfront to cover initial costs."

The numbers were substantial but not unexpected. Gemma and Mavis exchanged a glance and both nodded. It was a leap of faith they were ready to take together.

"Consider it done," Gemma said with resolve, her voice steady. "I'll arrange the transfer for the deposit."

"Excellent." Geoff stood, extending his hand to each of them. His handshake was firm, and his strength took Gemma by surprise, but the deal was done.

"Thank you, Geoff. We appreciate everything," Gemma said with a smile, her grip matching his in confidence.

"Anytime, ladies. I'll see myself out," Geoff replied, tipping an imaginary hat before departing into the marketplace.

As the door's bell signalled his exit, Gemma turned to Mavis, her heart swelling with anticipation. "Can you believe it, Mavis? Our little bookshop is about to enter a new era."

"It is indeed very exciting," Mavis responded, her smile soft yet triumphant.

Gemma and Mavis spent the rest of the day greeting customers and making sales. The evolution of their bookstore was within their grasp, and it was exciting. All afternoon, Gemma looked up from the counter towards the café and imagined the new and larger space filled with patrons and the various clubs and societies that now used the space. Hosting events was becoming a large part of the bookshop's business, and it was exciting. As the working day drew to a close, Gemma turned to Ellie with a warm smile, watching as the young woman gathered her things, a hand resting gently on her baby bump. "Goodnight, Ellie. Take care of yourself and the little one," Gemma said.

"Will do, Gemma. See you tomorrow!" Ellie responded, her steps unhurried.

"I wish Ellie would take it a little easier," said Gemma.

"She'll be fine. I think she likes the distraction from the pregnancy, and she told me that keeping moving helps with her back," Mavis said as her eyes brightened with the prospect of their next errand. "Shall we pop over to see the reverend?"

"Yes, let's go," Gemma said.

Mavis chuckled, adjusting her spectacles with an air of resolve. "Lead the way."

"I'll drive us there, and then I can drop you home afterward. Jack said he'd meet us at your house," said Gemma.

"That would be lovely," said Mavis.

After locking the bookshop for the night, they strolled through the marketplace to the coppice car park, where Gemma's VW Beetle awaited. Their journey was brief, but the silence begged to be filled with the day's discoveries.

"I spoke to Jen earlier today," Gemma began, her grip on the steering wheel relaxed yet controlled. "She gave me quite the insight into ketamine and alcohol. It's all rather troubling."

Her interest piqued, Mavis tilted her head. "Oh?"

"Turns out, ketamine is an anaesthetic; it would have made John quite docile." Gemma's brow furrowed as she considered the implications. "But when mixed with alcohol, it's incredibly dangerous. Could be fatal if the dose is too high."

"Goodness," Mavis murmured, her face etched with concern. "Are we thinking that someone tampered with that vodka bottle? They knew what they were doing?"

"I think it's possible." Gemma's tone was grave, the weight of the situation settling between them like a shadow. "It's not just reckless; it's calculated. And that means we could be dealing with someone who had intent to harm John as well as murder George."

Gemma reversed the car into a spot alongside the grounds of the church's aged stone facade. She killed the engine and turned to Mavis.

"From what Jen told me," Gemma said, her fingers drumming on the steering wheel, "and considering how that mix would sedate rather than stimulate, it seems unlikely John could have managed all ... that." She gestured towards the church where the tragedy had unfolded. "Unlocking doors, drawing George into the belfry, committing murder, locking everything up again and escaping while under the influence of a drug like that, let alone alcohol; no, it doesn't add up."

Mavis leaned back, her expression pensive. "This just reinforces my thought that John wouldn't perform such a devious act. I just don't think he'd have it in him. Murder, that is."

"True. Based on the effects Jen described," Gemma said, shaking her head, "Remember how he was the next day? He was barely able to string two words together. How would he have been in a fit state to carry out a murder? No, my gut tells me John's been framed."

Mavis nodded, absorbing the gravity of Gemma's deductions. "But by whom? That's the million-pound question," said Mavis. They both knew the implications were serious. If John was innocent, then the real perpetrator was still at large; a chilling thought.

"Let's talk to the reverend," Gemma said, with newfound resolve. "Although, let's not make out that we are investigating. Let's keep it ... casual." Mavis smiled, and with that, they stepped out of the car, the church door beckoning them forward and the mystery calling them ever deeper into its enigmatic embrace.

## Chapter Ten

Gemma and Mavis stepped through the large welcoming doors of St. Peter's Church. The scent of polished wood and incense enveloped them, reminding Gemma of Sunday services as a child. Gemma's gaze fell upon the stout door in the corner, guarding the narrow stairs to the belfry. She noticed the brass padlock glinting in the light; shut and locked. With a frown creasing her brow, she approached for a closer inspection.

"Locked," she confirmed, running a finger along the cold metal. "Looks like it's always kept this way."

"Makes sense. Those stairs are very steep," Mavis said, peering at the lock through her glasses. Gemma nodded.

They moved on, their footsteps echoing as they traversed the foyer and entered the main nave. Ahead, the altar loomed, an anchor of faith in the sea of pews. Near it stood Reverend Simon, his head bowed in what seemed like quiet contemplation, prayer ... or maybe catching a quick nap.

"Reverend Simon," Gemma called out cautiously, not wishing to startle the man.

At the sound of his name, the reverend lifted his head with a jolt. He waved a hand and made his way towards them, the tails of his cassock sweeping over the ground.

"Ah, Gemma, Mavis! What a delight to see you both," the reverend said in greeting. "Your presence is always a blessing." He clasped his hands together. "Let's sit?" He gestured towards the front row of pews.

The pew creaked as Gemma and Mavis settled beside the reverend. A shaft of sunlight streamed through the stained glass windows, casting kaleidoscopic colours across the nave.

"How have you been coping, Reverend, after ... well, after everything?" Mavis's voice was soft, but carried a motherly concern.

The reverend, a portly man in his mid-sixties, sighed with his hands clasped in his lap. "It has been quite the ordeal, Mavis. A terrible shock, indeed. To think that such a crime could occur in God's house ..." His words trailed off as he shook his head, disbelief etched into the lines of his face.

Gemma leaned forward. "It is shocking," she said,

her voice steady yet warm. "But you handled it with such grace, Reverend."

"And I must thank you, Gemma," he said, turning towards her with a grateful smile. "Your quick action that day, keeping the crime scene undisturbed. It was most astute. And you too, Mavis, fetching Detective Haynes ..."

A blush crept onto Gemma's cheeks at the praise. "No problem at all, Reverend. I suppose being David's partner may have taught me a thing or two about detective work." Her attempt at humour was light, but the gravity of the situation still hung in the air.

She shifted in her seat, her investigative instincts bubbling to the surface. "Did the police share anything with you about their findings?" Gemma asked, locking eyes with the reverend.

He hesitated before answering. "They've been rather tight-lipped, I'm afraid. Crime scene officers came here to look for clues, but once they concluded their investigation, they took poor George's body to the coroner's office." The reverence in his tone spoke volumes about the sanctity he felt had been violated.

"And nothing else? No other leads or information?" Gemma pressed.

"Well ..." Reverend Simon paused, his eyes clouded with concern. "They informed me they took poor old John into custody. I must say it came as a complete shock. I always thought he was such a good-natured and kind soul. I thought I knew him well."

Mavis nodded, her lips pursed. "John always seemed so gentle," she added, echoing the reverend's sentiment.

Gemma leaned back into the pew, her mind raced with the details of the case. She glanced at Mavis and saw her own worry reflected in her friend's eyes. "I noticed some CCTV cameras outside," said Gemma, as she glanced to the back of the church. "Did the cameras catch anything ... peculiar that evening?"

With a sigh and a troubled expression, the reverend said, "I'm afraid someone recently vandalised our security system." He gestured towards a door at the back of the church. "The camera covering that door and those covering the main entrance and driveway were tampered with."

"Vandalised?" Gemma asked, her thoughts already racing ahead.

"Yes. Someone knew where to cut; a large section of cable removed, just like that," he said, snapping his fingers. "Made it quite impossible to repair swiftly."

"Didn't the cameras catch whoever cut them?" asked Gemma.

"I'm afraid not. They seemed to know how to approach the camera without being seen," he answered.

Mavis pursed her lips again. "So they took advantage of the camera's blind spots?"

"Seems so," the reverend admitted. "There's a blind

spot by the side fence. Whoever did this must have known about it. I hadn't considered it until now ..."

"What about inside the church? Any cameras there that might've caught something?" Gemma asked, trying to mask her eagerness.

"Ah, no," he replied, with a sad shake of his head. "The church is a sacred area. There have never been cameras inside. It's where people come for time alone with their thoughts and God."

"Then the person responsible would have to know their way around, not just the church but the camera angles too," Gemma mused out loud, more to herself than to them.

"Norman's been working on getting everything repaired. It's quite costly, but we can't leave the church vulnerable. There's an appointment set for next week to fix them up," Reverend Simon said, his voice tinged with hopelessness over the invasion of their peaceful sanctum.

Gemma brushed her fingers against the grain of the aged oak pew as she feigned curiosity. "Reverend Simon, do you think John broke in to commit this dreadful act?" She tilted her head, watching his reaction while already knowing about the keys found on John.

"Break in? Oh, no. No signs of forced entry anywhere," the reverend said. "He must have had a set of keys, somehow."

"Stolen, perhaps?" Mavis chimed in with a mix of concern and intrigue.

"Norman and Cynthia each have a key, as they help me run the church. I have a set too." He stood and gestured for them to follow him into the small office tucked away beside the nave. "Plus, there's a spare in the key safe; still accounted for." The reverend spun some tumblers on the small combination lockbox screwed to the wall. With a click, the small metal box swung open, revealing the untouched spare keys.

"Ah, so you three each have your set of keys, and these are the spare. That means someone made a copy of the keys?" Mavis asked, her voice steady but her eyes wide with the implications.

"Quite possibly. In fact, that seems highly likely." Reverend Simon said with a sigh, closing the safe with a sense of finality.

Gemma's mind was alight with questions, but she pocketed them for later, pressing on to another line of enquiry. "Reverend, did you know the victim well?" Her question was casual but pointed, her gaze locked with his.

"George? Only by reputation and the trouble he caused John." The reverend's expression softened at the mention of the homeless man who had sought refuge at the church. "I never met young George personally, but it was clear he enjoyed making life difficult for others. A troubled soul."

"I wonder if Norman's boy, James, knew him. They were around the same age, I think," said Gemma.

"James?" The reverend paused, pondering. "He might have, yes. They both attended Belper School around the same time, I believe. A good lad, that James. Always willing to lend a hand with his dad here."

"Could be worth asking," Gemma suggested, planning her next steps.

Mavis's voice, soft but insistent, pulled Gemma back from her thoughts. "Reverend, do you have any information about the funeral arrangements?" She watched as the vicar's kind eyes clouded with uncertainty.

"Ah, I'm afraid not," Reverend Simon replied, his hands clasped together as if in silent prayer. "The family is still in a state of shock, and they've kept to themselves since ... well, since the incident."

"Please let us know if anything comes up," Gemma offered with sincere warmth. "The community will want to pay their respects." She stood, and Mavis and Reverend Simon followed her lead.

"Of course," he said, a grateful smile gracing his lips. "I'll be sure to pass on any information."

As they edged towards the doors, Gemma reached out a hand to touch the reverend's arm. "And if you need someone to talk to, Reverend, our bookshop is more than just books and coffee. You can come and see us anytime."

"Thank you, Gemma. It's usually the other way

around, isn't it? People coming to me." The twinkle in his eye was brief but genuine.

"Everyone needs a listening ear sometimes," Mavis said, as they stepped out into the daylight, descended the stone steps and said their goodbyes to the reverend.

"That was interesting," Mavis said, buttoning up her cardigan.

"It was indeed. Much to think about," Gemma said, leading the way to her car. As they settled into the seats, Gemma turned the key in the ignition. "Jack should be at your place by now with some contraptions to ward off the garden saboteur."

# Chapter Eleven

Gemma's car pulled up outside Mavis's house on Sandbed Lane. She looked over at the young man perched atop the front garden wall. Jack, with his cropped brown hair and lean silhouette, was the spitting image of youthful nonchalance. His ripped blue jeans and black heavy metal T-shirt spoke of a rebellious streak, but the warmth in his wave as Gemma and Mavis approached was nothing short of familial.

"Evening, Jack. How's your mum?" Gemma asked as she stepped out of the car.

"Gemma, Mavis," Jack said, as he hopped off the wall. His bicycle, its paintwork chipped and handlebars slightly askew, leaned against a lamppost. "Mum's doing well. Thanks for asking," Jack replied. "She sends her regards."

"Come on through. You can bring your bike and put it in the garden," Mavis beckoned. "I made a carrot cake." Jack lifted his bike and carried it into Mavis's house, careful not to knock anything in the hallway.

Mavis led them through to her garden; an idyllic setting and a small slice of paradise that was alive with the buzzing of bees and the sweet scent of her, hopefully, award-winning flowers.

"Tea?" Mavis asked.

Jack nodded. "Yes, please."

"Tea would be lovely," Gemma said, taking a seat at the garden table adorned with a lace tablecloth.

Mavis returned from the kitchen, balancing a tray with a steaming teapot and a cake. "Here we are." She poured three cups of tea.

"Looks delicious," Gemma complimented, accepting a cup. The carrot cake, moist and rich with spices, sat temptingly on the plate before her. "Nothing beats your baking, Mavis. I best not have too much, though. Going for dinner with David soon," Gemma quipped, fork already diving into the cake.

"Flattery will get you everywhere," Mavis responded, with a twinkle in her eye.

Once they had finished their refreshments, Jack delved into his backpack and emerged with several sleek, green camouflaged devices. He set them on the table, their lenses blinking like vigilant eyes. "I've got just the thing to protect your garden, Mavis," he said with a grin.

Mavis peered curiously at the equipment, asking, "What are these contraptions, Jack?"

"Trap cameras," he explained, as he arranged them methodically. "They're equipped with AI — that's artificial intelligence — which means they can tell if they are looking at a person or an animal. If it's just the wind playing tricks, they won't bother recording."

"A ... I ...?" Mavis's brow furrowed in concentration. "Sounds very high tech."

Jack chuckled. "It is, but simply put, the camera's brain learns what to look for. It'll ignore a rustling branch but catch a fox, or more importantly, the garden vandals. It can even set off an alarm when it detects something."

"Goodness," Mavis murmured, impressed despite not grasping all the details. "Well, as long as it means I don't have to spend my nights glued to the window with binoculars."

"These cameras will be your eyes and ears," Jack affirmed. "The noise from the alarm will be enough to scare anyone or anything away."

Mavis turned to him, concern etching her features. "And how much do I owe you for these clever gadgets?"

"Oh, nothing," Jack said, waving away the thought. "Consider it a friendly loan until after the garden competition."

"Such a kind boy," Mavis said, her voice rich with gratitude. She watched as Jack strode across the lawn, placing two cameras strategically; one aimed at the flowerbeds and another towards the marrows.

Once the cameras had been placed to not be accidentally set off by Mavis when sitting on the patio, Jack dusted off his hands and slung his backpack over one shoulder. "They're all set up and working. If anything happens, give me a ring. I'll pop over with my laptop to check the footage on the memory cards. I've set the alarm to only sound after 8pm, and stop at 8am, so you can tend to the flowers without making a right racket."

"Thank you," Mavis said, as Jack lifted his bike from its resting spot on the lawn. "I appreciate it."

"Anytime, Mavis," he called back, flashing a grin before walking his bike to the side of the house to leave by the gate.

"Such a good lad," Mavis said, turning to Gemma with a fond smile. "His mother must be proud." Gemma smiled and nodded back. They collected the empty teacups and deposited them in the kitchen before heading into the dining room; their makeshift investigation space.

"I'll need to shoot off soon and get ready for my meal with David," Gemma said. "But it would be a good idea to make some notes on what we discovered today." Gemma picked up a pen from the dining room table and took off the lid.

Mavis settled herself onto a chair, her keen eyes

reflecting concern. "This murder. It's been niggling at me."

"I agree," said Gemma. "It feels too orchestrated, and certainly not the work of some transient soul with no connections or resources."

"My thoughts exactly," Mavis exclaimed. "And then there's the matter with the church's CCTV. It's all a bit too convenient, isn't it?"

"Too convenient by half," Gemma said, scribbling on the large sheet of paper fixed to the wall. "Someone knew where to go through that fence and how to incapacitate the camera without leaving an easy fix. That requires knowledge and planning. If John had planned it and tampered with the camera, why would he ensure he was so intoxicated before carrying out such a plan? A little dutch courage, sure, but a bottle of vodka laced with Ketamine?"

"Norman, he's been a church warden for years now." Mavis leaned forward. "He's always so particular with church matters. I've grown to know him well over the years. For the cameras to be out of action this long ... Well, let's just say, Norman is meticulous about things being right."

Gemma nodded, tapping the pen against her lips. "The reverend did say that the repairs are booked in. It could just be how long it took to get an engineer's appointment."

"Yes, that's probably it," Mavis said. "I should go and have a chat with him, casual like. See what he says about the situation?"

"Absolutely," Gemma assured her, adding another line to her growing list of enquiries on the large sheet of paper.

Gemma sat on a dining room chair, her hand fidgeting with the pen. She glanced at Mavis, a thoughtful furrow deepening her brow. "And then there are the church keys."

"Ah, yes," Mavis said, as if she'd just remembered something important. "If all other keys are accounted for, someone must have had a new set cut for the church. It's the only way."

"Right," Gemma agreed, her mind whirring. "Norman and Cynthia both have a set, and then there's Reverend Simon." Gemma raised a finger. "Oh, and the spare in the key safe." As she spoke, Gemma stood and jotted down points in neat bullet form on the wall, each tap of the pen punctuating their significance. "But have we verified that Norman and Cynthia still have theirs? The police have the set used that night, but what if ..."

"Exactly, dear," Mavis interjected, tapping the side of her nose with a knowing look. "Reverend Simon said they've got them, but is that definite, or are we just assuming? We could do with finding out if Cynthia and Norman still have their keys."

"Definitely," Gemma echoed, her scrawl growing

more determined on the paper. Mavis leaned in closer, lowering her voice as if the walls could whisper secrets. "We should also have a word with Cynthia. See how she's coping. Maybe bring up that pink lipstick found at the scene. Could be nothing, but ..."

"Her trademark shade," Gemma concluded. "We'll tread lightly, though. No need to unsettle her more than necessary."

"Of course." Mavis nodded. "And where does your intuition point to? If you had to guess ..."

Gemma paused. "I wouldn't call it suspicion," she hedged. "But Norman and Cynthia seem to have loose ends in need of tying." She met Mavis's gaze.

"Unanswered questions tend to linger like the last leaves of autumn, don't they?" Mavis mused.

"Indeed, they do," Gemma replied, standing to stretch her legs. Gemma glanced at the ornate clock perched on the mantle. "I really should go," she said, as she stood.

Mavis looked up at Gemma. "Yes, enjoy your date with David."

"Thanks," Gemma replied, a warm flush creeping into her cheeks. "We're trying that new bistro on King Street. Supposed to have a lovely ambience."

"Ah, I've heard good things about that place," Mavis enthused. "Their lemon tart is supposed to be divine. You must try it."

"I'll make sure I do. David is more of an apple pie and custard kinda guy," Gemma said with a smile.

"Enjoy yourself. You can tell me all about it tomorrow," Mavis said, as Gemma headed towards the door.

## Chapter Twelve

The cheerful honk of a car horn broke the quiet of the evening. Gemma stood from her sofa and peered out the lounge window. She saw David's expectant gaze from his car idling at the curb. She smiled and waved. Baxter, her loyal chocolate Labrador, wagged his tail, mistaking the signal for an imminent walk.

"Sorry, boy," Gemma said with a chuckle, scratching behind his ears. "I only just let you out. Tomorrow, I promise a really long walk." She could almost swear Baxter understood as he gave a resigned huff and padded away.

She grabbed her handbag and made sure to lock the house behind her. Sliding into the passenger seat of David's car, she leaned over and planted a kiss on his cheek. His response was a warm smile, as crinkles formed around his eyes. For tonight's date, Gemma had chosen a summer dress that fluttered with every movement, while David had opted for a crisp pair of trousers paired with a smart shirt. The engine hummed as they set off towards town.

"How was your day?" David asked, glancing her way with genuine interest.

"Ah, the usual chaos," Gemma replied, rolling her eyes fondly as she recounted the tale of the customer whose temper had been raised by the absence of *The Labyrinthine Compendium of Phantasmagorical Oddities* on the shelves of the Bookworm. "He couldn't fathom why such an essential book wasn't in stock."

"Impossible to cater to every obscure literary request, though, isn't it?" David asked, his tone both understanding and pragmatic.

"Yep, but I don't think he got the memo," Gemma said. She hesitated for a moment before sharing the piece of news that had brightened her afternoon. "But there's good news too. The planning permission for the café extension finally came through!"

"That's amazing news." David beamed. "You've worked so hard for this."

"Thanks. Mavis and I are really excited by it. Geoff starts work on the construction soon." The drive into town was short, and after parking the car around the corner, they entered the bistro. David held the door open for Gemma, ushering her into its cosy confines.

The soft burble of conversation, accompanied by the clinking of cutlery and glasses, set the backdrop for an evening of culinary delight. Rustic wooden beams adorned with fairy lights crisscrossed the ceiling, casting a golden glow over the small, linen-draped tables that huddled together like old friends sharing secrets.

"Ah, this is lovely," Gemma said, taking in the quaint charm of potted herbs on windowsills and the delicate aroma of rosemary and thyme danced through the air.

The host led them to a corner table, where a flickering candle added an intimate touch to the setting. As they settled into their chairs, a young waiter with an earnest smile presented them with menus bound in worn leather.

"Would you care for something to drink while you decide?" he asked, his pen poised above a small notepad; none of that ordering on an iPad here.

Gemma glanced at the wine list, her eyes lighting up at the sight of a familiar favourite. "I'll have a large glass of the New Zealand, Marlborough region, Sauvignon Blanc, please."

"And for you, sir?" the waiter asked, turning to David.

"Just a pint of coke, no ice, please," David replied, giving Gemma a wink. "You get more coke if you skip the ice."

She rolled her eyes and smiled. "Some things never

change," she teased, the playful banter between them as comforting as the soft jazz notes that floated from a hidden speaker.

Their drinks soon arrived, the white wine reflected the candle's flame like a captured star, while David's coke, sans ice, promised a satisfying quench. They sipped and perused the menu.

"Seared scallops sound nice," Gemma said, tapping the description of the starter with her finger. "What about you?"

"Chicken *goujons* for me," David declared with mock sophistication, pronouncing *goujons* with an exaggerated French accent that had Gemma chuckling.

"Chicken nuggets by any other name," she quipped, but the sparkle in her eyes betrayed her amusement.

"Ah, but these are gourmet. Give anything a French name and it immediately becomes refined and a little posh," David said with a smile. "They come with a tomato compote; very fancy."

"Tomato ketchup, you mean?" Gemma joked.

"Oh, I hope so," said David.

"Main course?" Gemma queried, perusing the hearty options. "Lamb cutlets with *dauphinoise* potatoes," she decided with a nod, already imagining the savoury flavours.

"Right, then. I'm going for the mighty burger. Extra bacon, onion rings." David's eyes gleamed with anticipation. "It's a special occasion, after all."

"Should I call ahead for an ambulance? Looks like you might need help rolling out of here afterward," Gemma joked, her laughter mingling with the cosy ambiance around them.

"Wouldn't be the worst idea," David said, chuckling and patting his stomach with feigned concern. "But what a way to go!" With their orders placed, they leaned back in their chairs.

Gemma broke the comfortable silence between them, her eyes alight with gossip. "Did I tell you about the garden competition Mavis has thrown herself into? Her friend Barry is showing her the ropes on how to grow prize marrows. You should see them. They're enormous!"

David chuckled, his laugh rich and hearty. "Large firm marrows, eh?"

Gemma couldn't help but release a burst of laughter, shaking her head at David's easy humour. "It's all fun until someone plays dirty, though. Someone's been sneaking around, vandalising some of the competitors' gardens."

"Really? That's quite sinister for a gardening contest," David said, raising an eyebrow in mock alarm.

"Jack's set up some cameras in Mavis's garden to catch the vandal. Hopefully, we'll have the mystery solved soon if they attempt it in Mavis's garden." Her tone held a hint of pride at their proactive approach.

"Smart move, but make sure Mavis puts up signs

she's recording. It could help if she needs the footage for evidence," David advised, taking a sip from his drink.

Gemma's brow furrowed. "Why would you need a sign?"

"Even criminals have rights," he said with a shrug.

"Seems silly, but I'll let Mavis know," Gemma conceded with a playful eye roll.

As their starters arrived — a pair of artfully arranged scallops for Gemma and golden-brown chicken goujons for David — Gemma's thoughts drifted towards the grimmer topic that had been weighing on her mind.

"Has that man you arrested, John, said anything new?" she asked, picking up her fork and probing a seared scallop.

David shook his head, his expression turning sombre. "No, not really. He claims he can't remember a thing from that night. Now he won't speak at all, even though he's been charged."

"That makes no sense. Why wouldn't he protest his innocence?" Gemma's voice was tinged with confusion and concern.

"It is strange," David agreed, glancing at her before continuing, "but he's refusing to say anything."

"Refusing?" Gemma echoed in disbelief, the scallop forgotten on her fork. "But that's just ... it's not right."

"I agree," David said with a nod. "But until he talks, we're at a standstill to get his side of the story."

Gemma sighed. She took a bite of a scallop, the delicate flavours momentarily distracting her from the puzzle of John's silence.

When they had finished their starters, the waiter whisked away the empty plates. Moments later, he returned with a flourish, setting down a plate of succulent lamb cutlets in front of Gemma and a towering burger for David.

"Wow, that's a sight to behold," David declared, eyes wide as he regarded the extra bacon and onion rings crowning his meal.

Gemma chuckled, admiring her own dish before seizing the moment to delve deeper into the case. "So, any further evidence come to light?" she asked, slicing into the tender meat. She wasn't sure if she should probe like this, but she needed to know.

"Actually, yes," David replied, his mouth full of an ambitious bite. "We found a pair of gloves near where John slept. No fingerprints on any door handles or such, but we found them on the bottle of vodka and the keys."

"And they're definitely his gloves?" asked Gemma.

"Yes, we have already tested them for DNA," said David.

"Odd, isn't it?" Gemma mused, savouring a forkful of lamb. "To be meticulous with door handles but careless with the murder weapon and have prints all over it?"

"Very," David agreed, wiping his lips with a napkin. "But considering he was intoxicated at the time, I doubt he was thinking straight about covering his tracks."

"True," Gemma conceded, though something still gnawed at her.

Their main courses eventually surrendered to their appetites, and the waiter reappeared for dessert orders. Gemma opted for the lemon tart that Mavis had recommended, while David chose the apple crumble with crème anglaise. It didn't take long for their desserts to arrive.

"Yours looks nice," Gemma said, eyeing the crumble with a hint of dessert envy.

"Apple crumble's my favourite. Can't beat it," David said with a grin, digging into the warm, sweet layers. Gemma smiled, taking a delicate bite of her own dessert. Once they had finished, David settled the bill. They rose from their table, the cosy ambiance of the bistro giving way to the warm night air outside, and David drove them back to Gemma's house.

"Thanks for dinner, David," she said, stepping out onto the pavement.

"Anytime. I really enjoyed it," he replied in a soft voice.

Gemma closed the car door and turned back towards him. "Would you like to come in for a coffee?" she said. David's smile widened, and he nodded, shutting off the car's lights.

"I'd love to," he said.

# Chapter Thirteen

It was a fine, sunny morning, and Gemma bounced around the bookshop in a delightful mood. She surveyed the store with a sense of contentment. Even with everything that had gone on recently in town, she felt on top of the world. Nothing could bring her down off this cloud.

"How was last night?" Mavis enquired, as she flitted between the bookcases, dusting off the world literature section.

Gemma smiled. "It was wonderful, Mavis. The food and ambience in the restaurant were just perfect. We chatted for half the night. It felt like those early days all over again," she said, her voice harbouring a hopeful note.

"That sounds lovely. It's nice to see you two getting on so well," said Mavis.

"David told me a little more about the murder case too. He let me in on some rather intriguing information."

Mavis's eyes twinkled with curiosity as she clasped her hands together. "Oh, do tell! But perhaps save the juiciest bits for later? How about popping over to mine after work? We can dissect every detail."

"Yes, we best discuss it later. Prying eyes and all that. Tea at your place sounds perfect," Gemma said, nodding. "I'll bring Baxter along. A bit of fresh air and a stroll would do us good."

"Delightful!" Mavis beamed.

Together, they turned their attention to the children's book section, where a colourful rug lay rolled up in the corner. With a swift tug, Gemma unrolled the rug across the floor. Mavis positioned a plump chair front and centre, ready to captivate some young minds.

"The little ones are going to love it, lost in stories while their parents get a nice break in the café," Mavis mused, smoothing out the creases in the rug.

"It was a brilliant idea, Mavis," Gemma said, admiring their handiwork. The thought warmed Gemma as she glanced around the bookshop. The bell above the door signalled the arrival of a parade of young children, along with their parents.

"Right this way," Gemma beckoned, guiding the procession towards the patterned rug. She ushered the children to their spots, their chatter bubbling like a brook as they settled down. Gemma turned to the adults, who looked on with grateful smiles at the thought of offloading their kids for an hour.

Gemma gestured towards the café. "Parents, you are all welcome to relax in the café if you wish," Gemma said.

"Thank you," murmured a mother. "Could murder for a cuppa. Not stopped this morning. Been up since six with this one."

"I can imagine. Sounds tiring," Gemma replied. As the parents retreated, the clamour from the rug crescendoed until Mavis took her throne. The chatter died down as each child gazed up at Mavis.

"Ready for a tale or two?" Mavis asked, her voice carrying the gentle lilt of a lullaby.

Gemma leaned closer to a mother nursing a cup of tea. "Watch this," she whispered. "Mavis is like the pied piper."

The mum chuckled, watching in awe as her usually restless son sat transfixed by Mavis's melodic tones. "She's quite something," the mum agreed, taking a sip of her tea.

Mavis's voice, rich with warmth and whimsy, danced across the room as she unfolded the tale of *The Very Hungry Caterpillar* to her audience. The children perched on the rug were fixated on every turn of the page. Gemma watched from a distance, and she even found herself enchanted by Mavis's rendition. Who would have thought a caterpillar eating lunch would be so thrilling?

With the last page turned and the caterpillar's transformation complete, Mavis closed the book with a gentle clap. "Now, my dears. Do any of you have questions about our hungry little friend?" Mavis asked.

A forest of small hands shot up into the air, eager for Mavis's attention. She pointed to a girl with pigtails who asked with earnest curiosity, "Can caterpillars really eat all those foods?"

Mavis chuckled. "Well, while strawberries and chocolate cake might tempt them, I think most caterpillars stick to munching on leaves. But isn't it fun to imagine what else they could nibble on?"

Nods of agreement rippled through the group, but another hand remained determinedly raised. A little boy with scuffed shoes and a furrowed brow declared, "I need a wee."

His mother, previously lost in the moment's tranquillity in the café, rushed over, her hands fluttering in an apologetic dance as she led her son away. Laughter bubbled among the parents.

As Mavis continued with another story, Gemma made her way to the café counter where she could hear snippets of conversation from the mums and some dads who were sitting around a couple of tables that had been pushed together.

"Did you hear about that George Peters?" one mum

murmured, her tone hushed yet laden with an edge of disapproval. "I heard he was no good, always causing trouble."

"Seems harsh to speak ill of the dead," another countered, her eyes darting around as if expecting a reprimand.

"Maybe," the first conceded, stirring her tea with more force than necessary, "but being dead doesn't make him a saint, does it?" Gemma made herself look busy behind the café counter when another snippet of conversation caught her ear.

"Of course, you know Cynthia from the off-license," said one mother, lowering her voice to a conspiratorial whisper. "Poor woman was being intimidated by him too."

"Who? George Peters?" asked another mother.

"Yes. He was quite a piece of work, apparently."

Gemma stepped from around the counter and edged closer to the group, feigning casualness while her heart thumped with either excitement or trepidation. She couldn't tell which. She joined the conversation.

"Sorry, I couldn't help overhear," she began. "Intimidation? How would you know about that?" Gemma asked, her tone laced with concern as she abandoned her pretence of indifference. The mum glanced around before leaning in.

"Cynthia confided in me once. I know her from my

yoga group. She said George was threatening her for free smokes and booze. Can you imagine?"

"Th ... that's dreadful," Gemma said, as her mind raced. "She must've been terrified."

"Scared out of her wits, she was," the mum confirmed, nodding gravely. Cynthia's tear-streaked face at the crime scene had painted a picture of shock and sorrow, but now, with this new information, it took on a different shade. Having George out of the picture could make Cynthia's life much easier, as horrible as it sounded. She made a mental note to dissect this potential motive with Mavis later.

Time slipped by unnoticed as the children's laughter bubbled through the bookshop. Mavis, with her charming knack for storytelling, held court among the little ones. When she closed the last storybook, releasing the spellbound audience from her gentle grasp, the room erupted in applause from tiny hands.

"Bravo, Mavis!" Gemma cheered, her eyes sparkling with delight at the sight of such joy.

"Wasn't it just wonderful?" Mavis said, beaming, her cheeks flushed with the success of their endeavour. Gemma and Mavis surveyed the space they had transformed into a storytelling corner.

"Quite the triumph, I'd say," Gemma said, locking eyes with Mavis. "The café was abuzz, and the books have worked their magic once again."

"Indeed," Mavis agreed, her spectacles catching the

light as she nodded sagely. "We shall have to make this a regular affair." Gemma nodded.

"We should certainly make it a trial for a month and see how it goes," said Gemma. "And look," Gemma pointed towards the children's book shelves. "Some of the parents are buying copies of *The Very Hungry Caterpillar*. As the families began to leave, Gemma called out, "You're all welcome back next week. We are running story time at the same time."

One of the mothers turned around. "Oh, we'll be here. It was lovely."

## Chapter Fourteen

Later that evening, Baxter, a paragon of canine obedience, sat at Gemma's feet, lapping up water from a bowl Mavis had placed for him. Gemma looked at Mavis and sighed contentedly. "Mavis, that children's book reading was such a hit."

"Absolute pleasure," Mavis said, beaming from her cushioned garden chair. "The little ones were so engaged!"

"The parents were over the moon to have a break," Gemma said with a chuckle. "But oh, the things you overhear. There's a bit of chatter about Cynthia that's been swirling around."

"Ooh, do tell," Mavis said, but before Gemma could start, there was a knock on the back gate. "Come in!" Mavis called out, unfazed. Barry walked through the gate, his usually cheerful demeanour clouded like a summer sky before a storm. Concern etched into Mavis's face as she rose. "Barry, you look as though you've lost a pound and found a penny. Sit down. I'll pour you a cup of tea," she said, her voice laced with warmth.

"Thank you, Mavis."

Mavis shuffled to the kitchen. She returned with another cup and poured him a tea with a splash of milk.

Barry's hands shook as he accepted the steaming cup from her. "It's my roses, Mavis. Someone's butchered them; snipped right through the stems."

"Good heavens!" Mavis exclaimed, her hand flying to her chest.

"Who would do such a thing? That's just cruel!" Gemma said. Baxter sensed the shift in energy and nuzzled closer to Gemma's leg.

"There's just no need for such senseless vandalism," Barry said, as he frowned. "I'm so upset, angry too. I've spent weeks nurturing those roses."

Gemma watched as Barry's hands tightened around his cup.

"Seems I'm not the only one," Barry said, his voice low and strained. "A few other competition entrants have suffered the same fate."

"What about your marrows?" Mavis asked, her voice full of concern. "Have they been damaged?"

"They left those untouched, thank goodness." Barry

sipped his tea, his eyes distant. "You need to be extra vigilant, Mavis."

Mavis nodded and said, "Our friend Jack has put some cameras around the garden. We're keeping a watchful eye out, aren't we, Gemma?"

"Absolutely," Gemma replied, as she offered a supportive smile. "But what about your garden, Barry? Any chance your neighbours caught something on camera?"

Barry shook his head, a look of resignation passing over his face. "No cameras. Neither me nor my neighbours. We're blind to it, I'm afraid. It must have happened in the dead of night. I just wanted to come over and warn you, Mavis."

"That's very kind of you, Barry," said Mavis.

"Least I could do," he said.

"How many others have had their gardens vandalised?" she enquired, the concern clear in her voice.

"Four, including myself," Barry said, his hands clenched into fists on his lap. "All contenders for the same category."

"That feels like a correlation of sorts," Gemma said, her analytical mind sorting through the details.

"It does, indeed," he confirmed with a heavy sigh. "No one else's produce or ornamentals have been targeted; just the flowers. Just those who might win. Not that I'm saying I may have won, but the other gardens targeted were all winning material."

"Don't put yourself down, Barry. Your garden is lovely," said Mavis. "So, this is happening to people with a good chance of winning a prize in the flower garden category," said Mavis. It wasn't a question but a conclusion spoken aloud.

"Seems to be the case," Barry grumbled.

"What about Mrs Colchester's blooms?" Mavis asked. "She's won several times before."

"Ah, yes. Her garden is spectacular," Barry said, nodding. "Thankfully, her garden remains untouched; for now. She's as alarmed as the rest of us, perhaps more so considering her past victories."

"Terrible business. It just won't do," Mavis said, shaking her head.

Barry rose from his seat, the lines of worry etched across his forehead. "Afraid I must dash. Need to see about salvaging what's left of my roses; or find something suitable to replace them before judging next week."

"Of course, Barry," Gemma said, rising as well. Her heart went out to him; the competition was the talk of the town in the gardening fraternity.

"Thank you for the tea, Mavis," Barry said, as he tipped an imaginary hat in Mavis's direction. "And sorry to bring such gloomy news on such a fine day."

"Think nothing of it," Mavis assured him. "We're here for each other; come rain or shine."

With a nod and a weak smile, Barry exited through

the gate, leaving Mavis and Gemma alone with their thoughts and the last of the evening sun filtering through the leaves, casting dappled shadows on the lawn.

"Such a shame," Gemma muttered. "Such mindless vandalism."

"It is shocking. What's Belper coming to? A murder at the church, and now this," Mavis said, her gaze lingering on the closed gate.

"I know it's not great," Gemma said, "but the camera's should help deter anyone looking to cause trouble." Gemma helped collect the cups and place them on the tray.

Mavis chuckled. "Our very own electronic guard dog."

"Not as cuddly as the real thing, though," Gemma said, as she rubbed Baxter's head. "Shall we go for a walk? Baxter's champing at the bit."

"Yes, let's," said Mavis.

Baxter, sensing the impending adventure, perked up and wagged his tail with anticipation. Within moments, they were ready, and they left Mavis's house and ventured towards the fields. Baxter trotted ahead, his leash slack in Gemma's gentle grip, while Mavis walked beside her friend, their footsteps in sync.

## Chapter Fifteen

It was a pleasant evening as Gemma and Mavis strolled through the fields at the top of Belper. Baxter darted through the grass, chased butterflies and spun around to catch his own wagging tail. The simple things in life.

"Look at him go," Mavis said. "I wish I could bottle up some of that vitality."

Gemma smiled. "He seems to have an endless supply, doesn't he? Makes me tired watching him." They continued to walk through the fields. It was still warm but not too hot as the sun started its descent. It was just right; a perfect evening.

"I can't believe someone targeted Barry's garden. It's not right," said Mavis.

"Does it worry you?" Gemma asked. "For your own garden, I mean?"

Mavis let out a sigh. "There's nothing I can do except hope that Jack's cameras and alarms are enough of a deterrent. If they're brazen enough to go after Barry, then ..." she trailed off, leaving the unsaid hanging between them.

"Yet you seem so calm about it all," Gemma said, as she admired her friend's composure.

"Life has taught me there are far bigger storms to weather than worrying about my blooms winning prizes," Mavis said, as she looked out across the fields. "Barry's garden had a real chance of winning the best garden prize this year, though. Marrows may be his passion, but he has taken to growing roses very nicely."

Gemma chuckled. "You're very gracious, Mavis. Not everyone would take it in stride like you do."

Mavis gave a wistful smile and patted Gemma on the arm. "Graciousness has its place. And besides, we've got more pressing mysteries to unravel, haven't we?" Mavis switched topics with the ease of a seasoned conversationalist. "What's the latest you've heard about the murder?"

Gemma glanced at her friend, noting the glint of intrigue in Mavis's eyes. "David mentioned a glove found in John's belongings," she said, her voice dropping to a conspiratorial whisper as Baxter darted through the grass, oblivious to their discussion.

"To stop fingerprints on the door handles," Mavis said, tapping a finger against her lips.

"Yes, but here's the sticking point," Gemma continued. "The vodka bottle — the supposed murder weapon — had John's prints all over it."

Mavis stopped walking, her expression contemplative. "So, either he was careless after consuming the vodka, or ..." She paused, inviting Gemma to consider the alternative.

"Or it's a setup," Gemma concluded, the pieces of the puzzle aligning in her mind. "If John drank from the bottle, then his prints would be all over it. If he passed out, someone could have taken the bottle and then ensured his prints were on the keys, leaving him passed out, none the wiser."

"Yes, my money is on poor John being framed," said Mavis. "It's far too easy to pin the crime on him if he's not in charge of his faculties."

Gemma nodded, feeling a sense of alignment with Mavis's intuition. "It seems like an easy way to cast blame on a vulnerable target," she agreed, her thoughts already racing ahead to what this revelation meant for their investigation.

As they continued their walk, somewhere in the distance, a church bell chimed the hour. Baxter's barks echoed through Squirrel Woods, a small copse of trees between some fields. Gemma and Mavis ambled along. The buttercups spread on the ground in a sea of vibrant yellow, and they watched a butterfly flit from one flower to another. Gemma hoped Baxter didn't see the butterfly and try to chase it.

"Did David mention if John has pleaded his innocence?" Mavis asked, turning her attention back to Gemma.

"He only mentioned that John said he couldn't remember a thing," Gemma said as she looked at Mavis. "Since then, not a word more. It's as if he's sworn himself to silence."

"Curious," Mavis mused, her brows twitching in thought. "A man wrongfully accused would surely fight tooth and nail to clear his name. Do you think the cocktail he was on has caused amnesia?"

"It could be. The amount he consumed could affect his memory," Gemma said, but there was a note of scepticism in her voice. She knew David would have pressed for any fragment of memory, any sliver of an alibi. But nothing so far had come to light. They stepped out of the copse, and the woods gave way to open fields where the distant sound of machinery hummed as farmers tended to their crops.

"Earlier today, at the book reading," Gemma began, her words finding a rhythm with their steps, "I overheard one of the parents share something rather intriguing," Gemma said.

"Interesting. Do go on," said Mavis, who seemed quite excited at the idea of a lead in the case.

"She claimed Cynthia had been intimidated by George." Gemma glanced at Mavis, watching for a reaction.

"Intimidation?" Mavis exclaimed, her interest piqued. "Well, that adds a sordid layer to our little mystery."

"Doesn't it just," Gemma said, as she stopped walking and looked at Mavis. "Apparently, he wanted free cigarettes and alcohol from the shop," Gemma continued, recounting the tale with a hint of disbelief. "But it's the why that has me hooked. What could George possibly hold over Cynthia? What's he intimidating her with?"

"That's the question," Mavis said, her mind already turning over the puzzle pieces. "It gives Cynthia a motive; stronger than most. We must unearth what this intimidation was about."

"Could just be idle gossip, though? You know what people are like for tittle-tattle," said Gemma.

Mavis considered the question. "I have often found that where there is gossip, there's at least a hint of truth," Mavis said.

Gemma nodded. "Well, we can easily find out from Cynthia herself." Gemma gazed out across the field they were crossing. "Do you think," she mused aloud, "that Cynthia's reaction was genuine? When she found George's body, I mean. Anyone would be shocked to the core upon finding a body like that, but if that body had been causing you so much torment, well, one might be relieved."

Mavis stopped and turned her attention to Gemma.

The insinuation in Gemma's question was startling. "It's hard to tell," she replied with a thoughtful frown. "Her sobbing seemed a bit ... extreme. Theatrical, even."

"If it had been me finding the body, I think I would be more in stunned shock," Gemma said. "You are right, though, Mavis. Theatrical is a good word for it." Gemma paused. "And then there's the matter of her lipstick; the one found at the crime scene. It's unmistakably hers; that garish pink is hard to miss."

"Quite so, but we already discussed that it could have easily been dropped while she was tidying up the belfry with Norman the day before," Mavis said, her fingers plucking at a loose thread on the cuff of her cardigan. "I feel our next step is to uncover more about this intimidation business. If it's true, it certainly paints a motive."

Gemma nodded. "You're right. Tomorrow, I'll stop by the corner shop. I know Cynthia, not well, but enough to strike up a conversation. Maybe she'll let something slip about what's been going on. Even if she doesn't say anything, hopefully, I can pick up on her body language."

"Good idea," Mavis said, nodding. "I think I'll have a chat with Norman. He's part of the model railway club that meets at the old Strutt School Community Centre. They're gathering tomorrow, and I've known him long enough that he might just open up to me.

There's a baking group that meets there, too. I can use that as my cover."

"Cover? Spoken like a true spy, Mavis," Gemma said, as she let out a small chuckle, imagining Mavis with a disguise, sneaking around behind pillars.

"You always need a cover story. I've read enough spy thrillers to know how it works," said Mavis. "What's your cover story for seeing Cynthia?"

Gemma considered the question. "Oh that's easy. I'm a hungry customer buying biscuits," she said.

"Perfect. She'll never suspect a thing." Mavis let out a laugh. Even though it was a grave situation with the murder, Gemma sensed that Mavis was actually quite enjoying the thrill of the case.

"It will be interesting to get Norman's insight, though. He seemed a lot calmer than Cynthia that day," Gemma said, as they approached the edge of the field.

"Norman has always been a calm man. In all the years I've known him through the church, I've never seen him worked up about anything. Even when the church roof developed a nasty leak a few years ago," Mavis said.

Baxter, even though he'd been running around non-stop, showed no signs of tiring and scampered ahead, giving chase to a particularly nimble squirrel.

"Look at him go," Gemma called out, her eyes following the exuberant dog. "Where does he get his energy? I'm tired just watching him."

Mavis smiled as she fished out a treat from her handbag and called Baxter. Upon spotting the reward, he bounded towards her with a joyous bark.

As they finished their walk and arrived back at Mavis's house, Gemma unlocked her car.

"Do you want to pop in for a cuppa?" Mavis suggested, but Gemma glanced at her watch and shook her head.

"Better not tonight, Mavis. I've got to work through the shop's accounts and keep them up to date. Besides, Baxter here looks like he could still do with a rinse after all that rolling around."

"Of course." Mavis's voice held a thread of disappointment that Gemma noticed.

"We should have a meeting tomorrow night, though, if you are free?" asked Gemma, knowing full well that Mavis would love to meet. "Discuss what we found out from Cynthia and Norman."

"Yes, that sounds like a lovely idea. I look forward to it." Mavis gave a quick pat on Baxter's head. "You two take care now."

"Always do," Gemma said, as she opened the car door and Baxter leapt onto the backseat. He settled down quickly, the sign of a well-exercised pooch.

# Chapter Sixteen

The next day, Gemma stood amidst the familiar embrace of the Bookworm. The espresso machine spluttered and hissed, bathing the store with the rich aroma of freshly brewed coffee. The morning rush, if you could call it that, had dwindled to a steady stream of customers. Gemma glanced at Mavis, who was sorting a line of Miss Marple novels into the correct order.

"Looks like it's quietened down," Gemma said. "I'll pop over and have a word with Cynthia now." Her voice had dropped to a conspiratorial hush.

"Alright," Mavis called after her. "Good luck with operation biscuit."

"Have you been in the spy novels again?" Gemma asked with a smile.

"I may have picked up some old Le Carré, for reference, of course," Mavis said. "Tinker Tailor Shopkeeper Pensioner." This made Gemma laugh out loud, and with a wave, she stepped out of the shop and walked to the opposite end of the marketplace, where Cynthia's shop stood. Gemma pushed through the corner shop's door and headed straight for the biscuit shelf to pick up a packet of custard creams.

Approaching the counter, Gemma found herself second in line. Ahead of her, a flustered gentleman with a loaf of bread tucked under his arm listened as Cynthia talked at him. The man's eyes darted around, looking for an escape without seeming rude.

"... and then I told him, 'That's not how you do inventory these days,'" Cynthia said, oblivious to her captive audience's discomfort.

"Ah, yes, very interesting, Cynthia," the man murmured, edging backward ever so slightly. The opportunity finally arose when Cynthia took a breath and the gentleman seized it. "I must be going. My wife will wonder where I've got to," he said, with forced cheerfulness.

"Of course, don't let me keep you," Cynthia replied, but her tone suggested she would happily continue the conversation.

As the man scurried away, Gemma couldn't help but smile. She always thought Cynthia could talk the hind legs off a donkey. Gemma placed the custard creams on the counter. "How are you holding up, Cynthia?" Gemma asked, looking Cynthia in the eyes.

Cynthia clasped her hands together and let out a dramatic sigh. "Oh, Gemma, it's been awful," she exclaimed, her voice quivering theatrically. "To think that I stumbled upon that poor young man's body ... It's been like living in a nightmare!" Her eyes searched Gemma's face for sympathy.

Gemma nodded, her mind ticking over this display. *She's laying it on thick*, she thought. "By the way," Gemma said, watching Cynthia's reaction, "did you ever get your lipstick back? I saw it on the floor of the bell chamber. Looked like it was yours."

Cynthia blinked, her expression one of genuine surprise. "My lipstick? I don't know what you're ... Oh!" Her hand fluttered to her chest. "You must mean the pink one."

"Yes, that's right," Gemma said. "I saw it on the floor while I was standing guard there. Did you drop it when you found George?"

"Must have," Cynthia replied, a touch too quickly, colour rising in her cheeks. "In all the confusion ..."

"Only I remember you were wearing red that day, not pink," Gemma continued, her tone casual.

"I wear many colours. Where are you going with this, Gemma?" Cynthia's voice rose in pitch. *Quite defensive*, Gemma thought to herself. A customer at the back of the shop turned his head, drawn to the commotion.

"Oh, nowhere," Gemma said, as she raised her palms in a gesture of peace. "Just curious. You mentioned once how you almost always wear pink."

"Mostly, yes, but I like a change every now and again," Cynthia said in a tone that implied changing the subject.

"Of course. I'm just saying, I quite like the pink," Gemma said. She could feel the tension radiating in the air. Still, it was a strangely defensive outburst to something so seemingly innocent.

"Right, well, I should get these back," Gemma said, motioning to the biscuits as she handed over the exact change. "Thank you, Cynthia," Gemma added, before turning to leave. Her mind raced with questions. She paused and turned to face Cynthia again. "Cynthia, if you don't mind me asking ... did you know George?"

Cynthia busied herself with straightening a stack of newspapers on the counter, avoiding Gemma's gaze. "Well, I knew of him, but didn't know him as such."

"Hmm." The sound escaped Gemma's lips before she could stop it, and she immediately regretted it.

"What is that supposed to mean, exactly?" Cynthia's eyes met hers. Gemma felt the piercing stab of Cynthia's gaze. Thank God, they weren't laser beams.

"Only that I've heard whispers around town," Gemma said, her words deliberate, careful not to push too hard. "People talking about how George might have been trying to extort you."

The colour drained from Cynthia's face, leaving her looking even more washed out against the dreary backdrop of her shop. "Where did you hear such nonsense?"

"Bits and pieces here and there," Gemma replied. "You know how these small towns are. Gossip and all that."

"Look, Gemma," Cynthia said, her voice cracking like thin ice underfoot, "you solved that Dominic Westley murder, and we're all very impressed. I've had a traumatic experience, and I think you should mind your own business." *Traumatic due to finding a body or traumatic due to being intimidated*, Gemma thought.

Gemma leaned in as she locked eyes with Cynthia. "Traumatic because George was extorting you? I wouldn't blame you. That sounds horrible," she said. Gemma's heart pounded. She probably could have handled this better.

"Mind your own business, Gemma! That's the last time I'm going to say it!" Cynthia's voice was sharp, and her hands clenched into fists on the counter. "Can you please leave now."

Before Gemma could respond, the bell above the door jingled and James sauntered in, smiling. Gemma felt a sense of relief at the friendly face. Cynthia straightened her back and smiled as if nothing had happened.

Oblivious to Cynthia's previous outburst, James

headed towards the magazine rack and picked up a glossy classic car magazine. With the magazine in hand, he headed to the counter, where Gemma and Cynthia stood.

"Hello, Gemma, Cynthia," James said in greeting.

"James," Gemma said, trying to sound cheerful. "How's Rhianna?"

"She's doing well, thank you," he said. "I'm meeting her later this afternoon." He looked at Gemma and then Cynthia. "What are you two discussing? You both went awfully quiet when I came in. Is everything okay?" he asked, an eyebrow arched in polite enquiry.

"Nothing in particular," Gemma said, as she offered a reassuring smile. James laid the magazine on the counter, pulled his wallet from his pocket and paid. Cynthia remained silent as she handed him his change.

"Take care, both of you," James said, as he pocketed his change. He rolled the magazine and placed it under his arm before exiting the shop.

Gemma let out a silent breath; one she hadn't realised she'd been holding. The shop felt colder now. Cynthia remained silent and stared at Gemma, who thought it best to leave.

"Blimey, that was awkward," Gemma whispered to herself as she walked back to the Bookworm. The encounter had left her mind spinning and not in the way she'd hoped for when she set out that morning.

Once she arrived back at the Bookworm, she

composed herself and walked in. She paused for a brief second to appreciate the comforting aroma of coffee and cinnamon.

Mavis stood behind the counter, engrossed in a novel. "How did it go?" she asked, looking up from her book.

"Interesting. I think," Gemma mused. "Pretty bad, actually. That didn't go how I expected it too. "Gemma approached and leaned on the counter. "Let's just say Cynthia's reactions were ... revealing," Gemma continued, keeping her tone conspiratorial. "But we'll unravel that tangled web later, away from prying ears."

Mavis glanced around the shop, ensuring no curious browsers were within earshot, before looking down at her watch. It was a delicate piece, a gift from her late husband, that always kept impeccable time. "Goodness. Look at the hour," she said with a flutter of her hands. "I must dash off to the Strutt Centre. Norman will be there with the model railway club."

## Chapter Seventeen

Mavis entered through the heavy door of the old Strutt School, an imposing Edwardian building that opened in 1909 and was now a bustling hub for the town's hobbyists and social butterflies. Mavis knew the building well, as she used to attend school there as a child. But now it was used for various clubs, societies and local council youth clubs.

Mavis paused in the entranceway and scanned the notice board that was peppered with announcements and schedules before locating the room number for the model railway society. As she ascended the stairs, each step resonated with memories of youthful laughter that once echoed through the halls. At the top of the stairs, she walked down the corridor and into a room that was a hive of activity. Tables were adorned with meticulous model landscapes with rail tracks and locomotives. The club's members were huddled in earnest discussion over their handiwork.

Mavis spotted Norman by a table, where he was explaining the delicate art of painting model trees to an attentive listener. Noticing Mavis, Norman waved, and he excused himself from the conversation with a friendly nod.

"Ah, Mavis!" he said, as she approached.

"Hello, Norman," Mavis said. "I must say your elm trees look positively lifelike." Mavis crouched a little lower to inspect the model landscape before her.

"Thank you," he said, with a chuckle as he brushed off the compliment with a modest wave. "It's all in the brushwork."

"Well, I'm quite certain there's more talent to it than technique alone," she replied, her tone light but sincere.

"So, what brings you to the model railway club, Mavis? Thinking of beginning your own collection? I warn you, it's addictive," said Norman as he gestured to the models on the table before him.

"No, no," Mavis said with a chuckle. "I'm here for the baking club down the corridor. I was just walking by and saw you. Thought I would pop in and say hello." Mavis wasn't comfortable fibbing, but she thought it was necessary to maintain her cover. She was sure Miss Marple would also stoop to such measures for a case.

"Well, it's great to see you," Norman said.

"How have you been holding up, Norman? I've not

seen you since ... Well, you know," Mavis said, her voice lined with concern.

. "Ah, well ..." He shifted uncomfortably, clasping his hands together. "Truth be told, I've been better. The whole affair shook me up something rotten. Haven't set foot in the belfry since it happened."

"Understandable," Mavis said, nodding sympathetically. "Such things take time to settle. You're doing remarkably well, considering."

"Thank you, Mavis," he said, offering a smile. "That means a lot."

"It's quite the ordeal to process," Mavis said, her eyes soft with empathy as she regarded Norman. "And poor Cynthia; she was particularly distressed that day. How is she holding up?"

Norman fidgeted with a tiny paintbrush. "Oh, Cynthia ... yes, she was very upset," he said, his voice trailing off before he added with an anxious chuckle, "Though I wouldn't be surprised if she saw it as an opportunity to cosy up for some comfort."

Mavis tilted her head, her curiosity piqued. "Whatever do you mean by that, Norman?" Her gentle tone encouraged him to confide in her.

He exhaled a heavy sigh, and his shoulders slumped. "Well, in the strictest confidence?" he asked.

"Of course."

"It's just that Cynthia has ... she's taken a liking to me over the years. Likes us to be alone together." He glanced away, his eyes focusing on a distant point in the room. "At the last bell practice the day before the fair, she went so far as to try to kiss me."

The revelation struck Mavis like the clang of the church bell itself. "Goodness, Norman! And your feelings? Surely you don't ..."

"No, no," he interrupted, shaking his head. "Not at all. I'm devoted to my wife, as you well know."

"Of course," Mavis said with a sympathetic smile. She reached out, gave his hand a reassuring pat, and leaned in. "It must be quite flattering, though, in a way, that Cynthia harbours affection for you," she said, her voice lowering to a whisper.

Norman's face twisted into a grimace. "Flattering?" He looked around to ensure no one was eavesdropping on their conversation. "It's a nuisance, Mavis. I've been happily married for over four decades. I'm not in the market for a fling, but Cynthia ... Well, she's persistent." His voice quivered ever so slightly. "I'm terrified Margaret will find out."

"We've known each other for many years, Norman. Your secret's safe with me," Mavis assured him. "By the way, do you know if she got her lipstick back? It was near poor George's body."

"Her lipstick?" Norman blinked, confusion knitting his brows together.

"Yes," Mavis said, as though discussing the weather.

"A bright pink lipstick was found on the floor when they discovered the body."

"Well, she did try it on at the bell practice the day before. She may have dropped it then." Norman rubbed the back of his neck, his discomfort apparent. "I don't recall Cynthia wearing pink the day of the fair. If memory serves, it was a darker shade. A red, perhaps." He cleared his throat, adding, "Not that I make a habit of noticing such things."

"Of course not," Mavis said. "Understandable," she said, nodding thoughtfully.

"Why the interest in lipstick, Mavis? It seems an odd thing to fixate on under the circumstances."

Mavis shuffled closer, and her voice dipped, punctuated only by the occasional whistle of a model train. "Oh, it's no big deal. I was just wondering if she got it back. Those fancy cosmetics cost a fortune these days."

"Ah, I see," he said. "That's very thoughtful of you."

"Did either you or Cynthia know George well?"

"George?" Norman asked. "I'd heard of him, yes. I didn't know him personally, though. My James has told me that George was the school troublemaker." He glanced around before leaning in. He lowered his voice until it was barely audible above the ambient sounds of the community centre. "But Cynthia ... she had more dealings with him than most."

Mavis feigned surprise, her eyes widening just enough to sell the act. "Oh? What sort of dealings?"

"Intimidation and extortion. Well, so she said," Norman whispered. "He'd apparently been extorting her for free cigarettes and booze from her shop. Vile business."

"Goodness. That's dreadful! But what could he have had over her to demand such things?" Mavis enquired, her heart rate ticking up a notch with every question.

Norman shook his head, a shadow crossing his face. "She wouldn't tell me. Not the specifics. Only that she was terribly upset about it. Cynthia confided in me, but I couldn't get her to go into detail."

Mavis shook her head in sympathy. "Poor Cynthia must have been terrified out of her wits."

Norman nodded. "She was scared, Mavis. Shaking like a leaf on a windy day," he said. "But then, very strangely, she stopped talking about it. As if she'd never mentioned it at all." He fiddled with a tiny painted figure, placing it beside the model train tracks. "I told her to go to the police, but she snapped at me something fierce. I didn't dare bring it up again. Don't really know why she mentioned it in the first place if she was only going to stop saying it."

"Don't blame you," Mavis replied, noticing his nervous movements.

"Knowing this about Cynthia's relationship with George, did you think her reaction to finding George was ... well, a bit much?" Mavis ventured, watching Norman.

He paused, a model tree held midair between his fingers. "Well, her reaction was somewhat flamboyant now that you mention it, but that's Cynthia through and through. Everything she does is a little overdramatic." Norman let out a laugh. "She doesn't seem to do subtle." Norman hesitated, the lines on his face deepening with thought.

"I hate to say this under the lord's watchful eye, but if George was intimidating her, then him being gone solves a problem for her, doesn't it?" Mavis asked. She let the implication hang in the air for a moment, her heart ticking up a beat as she watched the realisation dawn in Norman's eyes. "Of course, I'm not saying ..." Mavis began, but Norman cut her off with a sharp look.

"Let's not wander into wild speculation, Mavis. Cynthia may be many things, but a murderer? No, I don't think so." Norman shook his head.

"Oh, Norman, I never meant to imply that Cynthia could be involved in something so dreadful," she said. "It's just that the whole situation feels so peculiar, doesn't it?"

Norman relaxed slightly. "Yes, it feels strange," he admitted, almost to himself. "But Cynthia? No, I don't think she would harm a fly."

"Anyway," Mavis said, "the police seem to have already arrested the culprit. That chap who was rough sleeping. John, I think his name is?" Although she didn't believe John could be responsible, now wasn't the time to let that detail be known. "From what I heard, he was drunk. His fingerprints on the murder weapon. Very shocking. They even found a set of keys with him."

"Yes, yes. I heard an arrest had been made. He had been sleeping rough on the church grounds. I had asked him to move on once, but the reverend took pity on him and turned a blind eye to him sleeping outside the church," said Norman. He then seemed to double-take as he processed what Mavis had said. "You said he had a set of keys?"

"Yes, well, so I heard. I don't know for sure," Mavis said.

"I don't know how he would get those. Cynthia and I both have a set ..." Norman put his hand in his trouser pocket, pulled out a set of keys and shook them before putting them back. "The reverend has a set, and there's a few spares in the office."

"John had one of the spares? It doesn't seem likely." said Mavis.

"I'm not sure. I'd have to bring that up with Reverend Simon."

Mavis nodded. "Perhaps he snuck into the church and stole a set. Shocking," she said. "It's a shame the church's cameras were on the blink and couldn't record him entering the church for the keys, or to commit the murder," Mavis said. Norman looked at her in surprise.

"How do you know about the broken cameras?" he asked.

"Oh, Reverend Simon mentioned it when I bumped into him the other day. He said vandals had broken the outside cameras," Mavis said.

"That's right. I have an engineer booked to come and fix them. These vandals are real pests. Stuff like this costs the church a fortune," Norman said.

"I can imagine. It's just not fair, is it? John must have broken the cameras," Mavis said. Of course, she didn't actually believe that, but she couldn't let on her true thoughts. Not while deep undercover.

"That would make sense," said Norman. "It's so calculated and devious that it's rather chilling." Norman returned his attention to the model trains. He brushed his fingers against the textured landscape. "I best get back to the model railway meeting, Mavis. There's a chap here who knows a thing or two about painting techniques for slate roofs, and I've got this model barn that's giving me grief."

"Of course, Norman. And thank you for your time," Mavis replied, with genuine warmth in her smile. "It was lovely to catch up with you." She hesitated a moment before adding, "And send my regards to your family. Your son James is such a lovely boy. He's quite the gentleman; a credit to you and your wife."

"Thank you, Mavis. That means a lot," Norman responded, his chest puffing out with pride. "James is a good lad."

## Chapter Eighteen

Later that evening, in Mavis's dining room, Gemma fidgeted with the coffee mug in her hands, tracing her finger around the rim. Mavis, perceptive as always, leaned forward with a concerned tilt of her head. "You're awfully quiet tonight. Is everything alright?" Her voice was warm.

Gemma smiled. "I'm fine, Mavis," she said, setting her mug on the table. "I was just thinking about my meeting with Cynthia. It didn't go as well as I'd have liked."

"Oh, I'm sure it's not as bad as you think." Mavis placed her hand on Gemma's arm as a touch of reassurance. "Tell me. What happened?"

"Well," Gemma began, "it all started off pleasantly enough. Cynthia was her usual self, being the centre of attention but polite. But then ..." She hesitated.

"Go on," Mavis said.

"I asked Cynthia if she had got her lipstick back. It was innocent enough. I thought I would start soft with my line of questioning," Gemma said, recalling the shift in the atmosphere.

"And then?"

"Cynthia's demeanour changed. She became quite defensive, almost ... hostile." Gemma's words hung between them. "To be honest, I think I went in too quickly asking questions. I wasn't very subtle."

"Defensive?" Mavis asked. "That doesn't sound like a simple case of misplaced makeup. You may have touched a nerve without realising it." Gemma nodded. "It sounds like an over-reaction. All Cynthia had to say was, 'Oh yeah, I dropped it. Thanks.'"

Gemma bit her lip. "I don't see why she would get so defensive about it, though," she said carefully. "Unless ... unless Cynthia dropped it the day before."

Mavis leaned forward. "I have another theory," she said.

"What is it?" Gemma said, leaning in, her curiosity piqued.

"Norman mentioned Cynthia has taken quite a shine to him," Mavis divulged, her voice dropping to a whisper. "Always trying to find an excuse to be close to him, if you know what I mean?"

"Really?" Gemma's eyes widened in shock.

"Although, Norman told me that in the strictest of confidence," Mavis said.

"I understand," Gemma said, as she placed a hand on Mavis's arm.

"The day before the murder, while they were rehearsing and then tidying up the bell chamber for the fair, Cynthia tried to kiss Norman," Mavis continued.

"Did he, you know …?" Gemma's question trailed off, but Mavis understood.

"Return her affections?" Mavis asked. "Oh, heavens no!" Mavis chuckled. "If anything, Norman was quite irritated by it. He is, after all, happily married."

"Of course," Gemma said, as she looked towards the window. "It's an interesting detail, though. Cynthia never mentioned that. Not that she would, I guess." Gemma twisted the silver chain around her neck and looked at Mavis, who was sipping her tea as if they were discussing nothing more consequential than the weather. "Cynthia's reaction to finding the body; the tears, wailing and clinging on to Norman. She was all over him, like ivy on an old brick wall," Gemma said.

Mavis set her cup on the table. "Well, to be fair," she began, her voice steady but not without empathy, "she had just seen a dead body. It's only natural she'd grab a hold of someone nearby."

"True," Gemma conceded. "But didn't her crying strike you as a little overdramatic?"

"Perhaps," Mavis agreed, nodding slowly. "People do have different ways of coping with shock, though."

"Did you have time to ask Norman about the lipstick?" Gemma's enquiry was casual.

"I did," Mavis confirmed. "Norman wasn't certain. He reckons she wasn't wearing her usual pink the day they rehearsed and tidied up ahead of the craft fair. So it would be rather odd if she dropped it there, but he couldn't be certain of it."

"Odd indeed," Gemma said. Her mind whirled, trying to piece together the fragments of information. "Are we focusing too much on the lipstick, I wonder?" Gemma voiced the nagging doubt aloud, watching a moth flutter against the window, drawn to the artificial glow. "Could it be a red herring?"

"It's possible," Mavis said, her voice tinged with uncertainty. "But we shouldn't discard that detail entirely. Even the smallest clue can unravel the whole mystery."

"You're right, as always, Mavis," Gemma said, feeling the weight of each potential lead. "We'll move on from it for now, but keep it in the back of our minds. I asked Cynthia if she knew George. Her whole demeanour shifted at that point. At first, Cynthia played down knowing George, just in passing, really. But when I pressed about the intimidation ... Oh, she bristled like a startled cat and accused me of interfering."

"That was rather strong of her," Mavis said in a

surprised tone. "Norman did mention the intimidation. Cynthia had confided in him, though he said she clammed up about it after a while. It's peculiar. One minute, it was her biggest problem and source of worry. Next minute, it was forgotten and not mentioned again."

"Yes, very peculiar," Gemma said. "If Norman and Cynthia are such good friends, why would she stop confiding in him? There's something else there, hidden away. More to George's hold over her than we're seeing."

"Perhaps," Mavis said. "Yet her attempts to snuggle up to Norman seemed to irk him to no end."

"True," Gemma said, as she stared up at the case board on the wall. "But if she's holding back from Norman, then she's burying secrets deep. Secrets that could unravel everything."

"Or implicate her further," Mavis added. "Her actions are making her seem like she has a lot to hide."

"Good point," Gemma said. "We need to know what those secrets are, though how we'll coax them out into the light, I don't know," she said, as she shrugged.

"Let's not rush ourselves," Mavis said, her voice as soothing as the chamomile blend she favoured on restless nights. "Sometimes the answers find us when we least expect it. She is a person of interest, so let's see how she reacts or if she says anything over the coming days. If there is any guilt from involvement, she'll be over-thinking your conversation with her. She may give up some details by mistake."

"Hopefully before anything else happens," Gemma said, as she stood to stretch her legs. "For now, we let the questions simmer."

"Like a good stew," Mavis said with a smile. "All the flavours come together in their own time."

Gemma smiled and took comfort in Mavis's unerring optimism. Mavis's pen danced across the paper with a squeak as she jotted down every detail, her handwriting a series of loops and whirls.

"What should we do next?" Mavis asked, as she tapped the pen against her chin.

Gemma sighed. "Honestly, I'm not sure," she said, collecting her thoughts. "I hate to jump to conclusions, but Cynthia certainly seems to be involved in some way."

Mavis arched her brows, and a look of mild shock crossed her face. "Do you think Cynthia committed the murder?"

Gemma chewed on her bottom lip. "It's hard to believe she would commit such a brutal act," she confessed, her voice tinged with doubt. "But I can't shake the feeling that she's more involved. The intimidation gives her a powerful motive, but on its own, is that enough? Or is there more going on? That's what we need to establish."

"Cynthia could be in cahoots with someone else,"

Mavis said, leaning against the polished wood of the dining table.

Gemma shrugged. "It's a possibility, but we need proof beyond gut feeling."

"We need to dig into Cynthia's story," Mavis said. "Does she have an alibi? She had the means; she had keys and access to the church. We could argue she had opportunity too, if we can't find an alibi."

Gemma nodded. "How to get the alibi, that's the question." The thought hung between them, weighty and unanswered.

Mavis pursed her lips. "I'm not sure. Perhaps we should sleep on the idea. Fresh eyes in the morning and all that." There was wisdom in Mavis's words.

With a heavy sigh, Gemma conceded, "You are right. We can't solve this now." Together, they tidied up the dining room and capped the pens. The remnants of their investigative endeavour disappeared into drawers and folders.

"Goodnight, Mavis," Gemma said.

"Goodnight," Mavis replied, escorting Gemma to the door. "And don't fret. We'll crack this. Let your mind rest, and the solution will present itself. It always does."

## Chapter Nineteen

The next morning, Gemma leaned against the marble countertop of her sleek kitchen, which looked like something out of an Ikea catalogue. She cradled a steaming mug of coffee in her hands. On the TV, the BBC news presenter discussed the latest social media trend sweeping the nation; a dance kids were filming on their phones that looked part Hokey Cokey and part spasm, she wasn't sure. Gemma's attention was only half there; she was already mentally organising the day ahead at the Bookworm.

The sudden trill of her phone cut through the hum of the television. Gemma placed her coffee mug on the counter and glanced at the phone screen. Worry pinched at Gemma; calls from Mavis this early were unusual.

"Good morning, Mavis. Is everything okay?" Gemma asked, her voice laced with concern.

"Morning. It's those camera alarms Jack installed; they went off last night! They were very loud. Woke me up with a terrible fright." Mavis's voice fluttered with agitation over the line.

Gemma straightened, her body taut with shock. "Are you alright? Was it an intruder?"

"I'm fine. Yes, it was intruders. It was around three in the morning when the blasted things started wailing. I threw open my bedroom window and hollered, and would you believe it; a bunch of kids scattered from my garden like pigeons!" Mavis said, her usual calm demeanour replaced with fluster.

"Kids? At that hour? You should have called me right then, Mavis!"

"Oh, Gemma, I couldn't wake you," Mavis said, her tone apologetic yet firm.

"I insist. Next time, call me day or night. I'm going to ring Jack now to see if he can swing by your place and collect the video from the cameras."

"Thank you. I appreciate it," Mavis replied, her voice steadying with the comfort of Gemma's decisive action.

"Stay put, Mavis. I'll be in touch soon," Gemma said, before ending the call. Her fingers flew over her phone's screen, the message to Jack concise and urgent: "Need u at Mavis's ASAP. Intruders last night. Can u make it before work?" The response was almost immediate; a buzz that made her heart jump. "On it. Need a lift, though. I need to take the memory cards from the cameras."

"Be there in 5," she typed back, urgency propelling her movements as she downed the last of her coffee. She grabbed her bag, slinging it over her shoulder, and left the house, the door clicking shut behind her.

Gemma strode to her car with haste. The engine sprang to life, and soon she was weaving through the streets of Belper. Jack waited outside his house. He slid into the passenger seat. "Thanks, Gemma. What's happened then?"

"Trouble at Mavis's house. She had intruders in her garden in the early hours," she replied, keeping her eyes on the road. "Let's not keep her waiting."

They soon arrived at Mavis's house, and she greeted them at the door. Gemma wrapped her in a gentle embrace.

"Are you alright?" Gemma asked, her voice warm with concern.

"Those rascals gave me quite the turn, but I'm fine," Mavis said, as she ushered them into the kitchen. "Couldn't see much in the dark, but the alarm scared them off."

Jack rubbed his chin. "Good thing we set up those cameras. They probably didn't even know they were being filmed."

"I put up a small sign saying there were cameras, but

I doubt they could read them at that time of night," said Mavis.

Jack excused himself and went into the garden, leaving Gemma and Mavis in the kitchen.

"Tea, Gemma?" Mavis offered, reaching for her floral teapot as if normalcy could be restored with the simple act of brewing tea.

"Let me do it, Mavis, while you go through the camera footage with Jack," said Gemma.

"No, that just isn't proper. You are my guests."

Gemma smiled; typical Mavis. The perfect host, even during trying times. Gemma decided to relent. "Thank you, Mavis. Tea would be lovely," Gemma said, taking a seat at the kitchen table.

Jack returned from the garden and placed the memory cards on the kitchen table. Mavis had been fussing over a tray of scones, but she paused to watch him pull a laptop from his bag. He flipped open the lid with a flourish, like a magician about to conjure up an illusion.

"Ready for the grand reveal?" Jack teased, his voice carrying an exaggerated suspense.

Mavis nodded, clasping her hands together. "Let's see what we've got then," she said. Gemma leaned forward and peered at the screen. She watched Jack insert one memory card after another, files cascading onto the computer's desktop like pieces of a puzzle waiting to be assembled.

"Here goes," Jack announced, double-clicking on the first video file. The footage was grainy, but the image of the rosebushes bathed in the weak moonlight was unmistakable. A pair of shadowy figures clambered over the fence with the clumsy urgency of youth, heading straight for the roses.

The sudden blare of the alarm sliced through the silence of the kitchen, making Gemma jump despite knowing it was coming. On the screen, the startled children whipped their heads towards the camera, their eyes wide and faces illuminated.

Mavis inhaled, her shock audible. "Oh, my ..."

"Recognise them?" Gemma asked, her voice low and serious.

"Yes," Mavis replied, a tremor in her voice. "Those are Mrs Colchester's grandkids."

"Looks like she's playing dirty," Gemma said, a hint of disappointment threading through her words. "Sabotaging the competition's gardens so she can take home the prize." She shook her head. "That's not the spirit of the town's garden contest."

"Never would have thought she'd stoop this low," Mavis muttered, the betrayal etched into the creases of her face. "And using her grandkids, no less."

"Quite despicable, really," Gemma agreed, her lips pursing in disapproval. They sat in silence, absorbing the implications of what they'd just witnessed.

Jack's fingers glided over the laptop's keyboard, his

focus unbroken as he located and clicked on the second file. The screen flickered to life with another view of Mavis's garden, the lens taking in a wider swathe of greenery where the moonlight played hide and seek with shadows. And there they were, two figures with youthful gaits, visible against the backdrop of tended perennials.

"See that?" Gemma said, pointing to the screen, her voice a mix of dismay and concern. "One's got secateurs in their hands."

Mavis leaned forward, squinting at the screen. "Barely fourteen, I'd reckon," she murmured, and her face tightened with worry.

Gemma sighed. "It's a slippery path, alright. From vandalising gardens for grandma to who knows what tomorrow? Armed robbery?" Bitterness laced Gemma's voice. "Could you send these to my phone, Jack?" she asked, turning to their impromptu tech support, who was already nodding.

"Of course," Jack replied, his movements efficient as he sent the files to Gemma through WhatsApp.

Gemma chewed on her lip, contemplation clouding her brow. "What do you want to do about this, Mavis?"

The older woman folded her arms as she stared at the frozen image of the children caught mid-mischief. "I'll need to think on it ... and discuss it with Barry," she said with a decisive nod. "Best not to overreact just yet."

"Agreed," Gemma said.

After Jack closed his laptop with care, slipping it into his bag with a soft thud, he stepped outside into the garden to replace the memory cards in the cameras. In mere moments, he returned, hands free of tech, eyes confirming the task done.

"I left the cameras going, just in case our visitors decide to do an encore," he said.

"Can't see them risking it again after the scare they got," Gemma said, "but you never know with kids today."

Jack glanced at his watch. "I need to dash to the sorting office, or I'll be late for my shift," he said, urgency creeping into his voice.

"Let me drop you off. I'm heading to the shop anyway," Gemma offered.

"I'll come along," Mavis declared, her eagerness to be part of the unfolding story clear in her bright eyes.

## Chapter Twenty

Later that morning, Gemma navigated the aisles of the Bookworm, weaving between customers like a dancer in a crowded ballroom.

"Excuse me," a voice called out, just as Gemma was about to restock a shelf. She turned to find a lady peering eagerly at her from under a mop of unruly hair. "Do you have Frank Herbert's *Dune*?"

"Right this way," Gemma replied with a pleasant smile, guiding her towards the science fiction section. She reached for a deluxe hardcover edition and handed it over. "One of my favourite science fiction epics," she confessed, her eyes lighting up behind her frames. "The layers of imagination in Herbert's world are far more vivid than any movie adaptation could capture."

"Couldn't agree more," the customer mused, running her fingers over the embossed cover. "Films just don't compare. They strip away the magic of your imagination."

Their exchange bubbled into a short but spirited debate about the merits of literature versus cinema. A shared understanding that a book's power lies within its ability to conjure unique worlds within the mind's eye.

"Shall we?" Gemma motioned towards the counter after their friendly discussion wound down.

"Of course," the woman said with a chuckle, following her lead.

At the counter, Gemma scanned the book as the customer produced a bank card. When the transaction was completed, the customer took the bagged book. "I have a date with a sandworm," she quipped.

"Enjoy your journey to Arrakis," Gemma said.

As the door closed behind the departing customer, Mavis leaned against the counter. "Never been one for those space stories myself," she admitted.

"Ah, but they're such fantastic voyages of the mind," Gemma said, her enthusiasm undimmed. "Like *Project Hail Mary* — it's my current favourite. Same fellow who wrote *The Martian*, Andy Weir."

"Interesting," Mavis said, although Gemma wasn't sure Mavis was sold on the idea. "I think I'll stick to adventures set on *terra firma*. Give me a good romance or a murder mystery any day."

"Can't argue with that," Gemma said. The bell above the door jingled again, signalling another arrival.

Gemma glanced up to see Barry striding into the shop. Concern etched his face as he found Mavis, who was tidying the counter.

"Thank you for getting in touch, Mavis," he said, his voice earnest as he approached. "I came as soon as I could."

"Barry, let's talk over a cuppa in the café, shall we?" Mavis suggested, gesturing towards the back of the shop.

"Good idea," Gemma agreed, leading them through the bookshelves towards the café. They settled at a round table. "What would you all like?" asked Gemma.

"Breakfast tea, please, with a splash of milk," said Barry, as he got comfortable in his chair.

"Earl Grey for me, please," said Mavis.

Gemma caught Ellie's attention. "Ellie, could we have some drinks, please? Earl Grey for Mavis, breakfast tea and a splash of milk for Barry, and I'll have a skinny latte."

Ellie nodded in acknowledgement, busying herself with their orders. "Coming right up!" she said. Soon enough, Ellie brought over their drinks, placing them on the table with a kind smile. "Anything else you need, just holler," she said, before returning to the counter.

"Thanks, Ellie," Gemma said.

"Right then," Mavis began, accepting her steaming teacup from Gemma. "I had some unwanted visitors in my garden last night; scared me half to death they did."

"Oh, that doesn't sound very good. Are you okay,

Mavis?" Barry replied, his brow furrowing as he took a sip of his tea.

"Yes, yes. I'm fine," said Mavis. "Jack's cameras worked wonders, though," Mavis continued. "Caught the whole thing, and the alarm sent them scurrying off like rats from a sinking ship."

"Did you see who it was, Mavis?" Barry asked, leaning forward, interest piqued.

"Here, let me show you," Gemma said, as she pulled her smartphone out of her jeans pocket and tapped the screen to life. She cued up the video from the night before and turned the screen so Barry could see. The footage played, revealing shadowy figures among the rose bushes, their movements hurried and destructive.

"Is that who I think it is?" Barry asked in disbelief as the recognition dawned on him.

"Unfortunately, yes," Mavis said, confirming with a nod.

"Mrs Colchester's grandkids ..." Barry said, setting his tea cup on the table. His shock was mirrored in the tightening of his jaw. The three sat briefly in silence. Barry's disbelief hung in the air. "I can't believe it," he finally said, shaking his head. "Fancy sending your grandkids to damage gardens in the competition. What was she thinking? Shameful."

"Well, we are assuming Mrs Colchester is aware of what her grandkids are doing," said Gemma. "She may not know. We need to give her the benefit of the doubt."

Mavis nodded in agreement and then looked towards Barry. "What do you think we should do, Barry?"

"Confront Mrs Colchester, for starters. But Gemma is right; we won't go off half-cocked. Let's get her side of the story," Barry said decisively. "And we'll have to report this to the competition organisers. We can't let this stand. Too many people have put a lot of time and effort into their gardens."

"I agree. We need to nip this in the bud," Gemma added, her voice carrying a firm resolve. "Let's pay Mrs Colchester a visit when we close the shop."

"Good idea," said Barry, nodding.

"Right, I'll come back here to meet you both, then. You close at five pm, don't you?" asked Barry.

"Yes, meet us here at five," Gemma said, as Barry stood from the table.

He gave them a grateful nod. "Thanks for bringing this to my attention." With that, he strode out of the shop.

Later that afternoon, not too far from closing time, James and his girlfriend, Rhianna, walked into the shop. Gemma looked up from arranging a display of romantic holiday reads. "James. Rhianna, lovely to see you both," she said. "Were you looking for something particular today?"

"Just thought we would pop in on the way to the train station," James said, with a slight hint of concern in his voice. "I wanted to check if you were okay. Things seemed tense when I saw you and Cynthia at the corner shop yesterday."

"James is an empath. He really picks up on these things," said Rhianna.

"I do, I'm afraid. I'm very sensitive to other people's emotions," said James. "I think I get it from my mother." He smiled.

"Everything's fine, thank you," Gemma assured him. "I appreciate your concern. Cynthia? Oh, it was nothing. I was just checking that she was okay, as she was very much in shock when she found that poor George's body. She seemed ... unexpectedly flustered."

Rhianna's eyes sparkled with interest as she leaned in closer. "Flustered that you asked?" she asked. "That seems rather peculiar. You'd think she'd be grateful you were checking in on her. Like a good friend does."

Gemma laughed. "I know. It's all rather silly, isn't it? I think I just caught her at a bad time. We all have bad days."

James turned to Mavis. "Oh, Dad said he bumped into you at the Strutt Centre, Mavis. Quite the social butterfly, aren't you?" He smiled again.

Mavis straightened up. "Oh, yes, Norman and I had

a delightful chat," she replied. "I was there for a baking class in a different room, you see. I saw him in a room with the model railway folk, so I popped in for a good chin-wag."

"It's a brilliant place. They run some excellent classes there," James said. "With Gemma visiting Cynthia and you with Norman on the same day, it's almost like you two are on the case again; like with the business of that poor writer fellow, Dominic Westley."

Gemma smiled. "Oh, James, you have such an imagination! We only investigated Dominic's murder because authors dropping dead in your shop isn't great for business," she quipped. Her eyes darted to Mavis's amused expression. "I pop into Cynthia's shop all the time. For biscuits, usually. When it comes to custard creams, I am weak."

"Chocolate bourbons for me. Can't beat them," Mavis said with a chuckle. "Just popped my heard around the door to say hello, that's all."

Rhianna leaned in. "Gemma," she whispered, as if sharing a secret, "have you heard anything more about the man they've arrested? I know your David's on the case."

Gemma paused. "Not much to tell, to be honest," she said with shrug. "Just that a homeless man was taken into custody. Sounds like a clear-cut case. Such a sad story."

"Goodness. I hope he gets what he deserves for what

he did to poor George," Rhianna replied, her face etched with concern.

"I can't remember if you said before. Did you know George, at all? He must have been in your year at school," Gemma said.

Rhianna shook her head. "Not really. We were at school together, but he ... well, he ran with a different crowd. Quite a rough crowd, really." Her voice trailed off.

The bell above the door jogged them from their conversation as a customer exited the store. James glanced at his watch. "We should get going, Rhianna. We have a train to catch. We have plans in Derby. A film and then dinner."

"Sounds like a lovely evening," Gemma said.

"We're trying out that new Italian place in the shopping centre," James added.

Mavis smiled. "Ah, young love."

"Very romantic," Gemma mused, her thoughts wandering to her own relationship with David. "Let me know if it's any good. Maybe I'll persuade David to take me there."

"Of course," James said with a warm smile. "I just wanted to stop by on our way to make sure you were okay."

"You're too kind, but I'm fine. I think Cynthia was just having a bad day. We all have them," Gemma said to reassure him. "She's still quite shaken about discovering the body, I think. My asking about it must have stirred up some raw memories. Can't say I blame her. I was shocked to the core also."

James nodded. "Well, I'm glad you're okay," he said before turning towards the door, Rhianna at his side.

"Take care," Gemma called out after them, watching as the couple stepped out into the quaint bustle of the marketplace. She turned back to the counter and blew out a large puff of air. She allowed herself a moment's relief, her shoulders easing from their tension before she turned to Mavis.

"Such a pleasant young man," Mavis said. "They make a lovely couple."

Gemma nodded in agreement. "Perhaps we've been a bit too conspicuous in our sleuthing, though," Gemma whispered, leaning closer to Mavis so that only she could hear.

"Indeed. Seeing Norman and Cynthia on the same day might have stirred the pot more than we intended," Mavis said.

"I didn't feel comfortable fibbing to James and Rhianna. It goes against the grain, but we can't very well announce we're investigating, can we," said Gemma.

"Absolutely not," Mavis said. "Discretion is key. We'll be more careful in the future."

"Yes, discretion and perhaps a dash of subtlety next

time." Gemma smiled. "Right then," Gemma added, turning her attention back to the customers browsing the shelves. "Back to books it is."

## Chapter Twenty-One

As the working day drew to a close, Gemma turned the key in the Bookworm's lock. No time for relaxing, though. It was time to confront Mrs Colchester and put an end to the garden wars that had been raging. Barry walked across the marketplace towards them, right on time.

"Evening, ladies," he called out, tipping an imaginary hat. "All set for the showdown?"

Gemma chuckled. "Ready as we'll ever be, I suppose. I've sent you those video files if you need any evidence."

"Much appreciated, Gemma. I'll have a word with the competition chairperson tomorrow," he said.

Mavis clutched her purse a little tighter, her usually bright eyes clouded with unease. "I must admit, I'm all of a dither about facing her. Mrs Colchester is an amiable lady but stern as an old schoolmistress and has opinions firmer than my coffee and walnut cake."

"Never met her myself," Gemma mused, her mind already painting a picture of her from Mavis's words. "What I would like to know is why has this competition got her knickers in such a twist? Is it a large cash prize?"

"Good heavens, no," Mavis scoffed. "It's the prestige, I suppose. But to think she'd do something so underhanded for a bit of glory ..."

"All that effort in sabotaging gardens for prestige? Seems heavy-handed. If her garden is good, why not just compete like everyone else?" Gemma asked.

"Indeed," Mavis said. "That's the thing. Her garden is fabulous. I don't know what she's playing at. Prize-wise, there's a voucher for the Green-fingers Garden Centre, but it's about the participation, the community spirit. The mayor presents a trophy, and there's the honour of having your victory immortalised in the local *Gazette*."

They walked through the marketplace to the carpark. "Mavis," Gemma said, as they approached her car, "I've only ever heard Mrs Colchester referred to as Mrs Colchester. Does she have a first name?"

"Indeed she does," Mavis said, rounding the car to the passenger's side. "It's Dorris. Dorris Colchester."

Gemma wasn't one for confrontation, but in this case, it was necessary. They owed it to all the competition's entrants.

Gemma's car rolled to a gentle stop outside the Colchester residence. She peered through the windscreen at the mock-tudor house. "Lovely house," Gemma said.

"Isn't it just?" Mavis said from beside her.

Exiting the vehicle, they walked down the path to the front door. Gemma pressed the doorbell. Mrs Colchester answered, her expression one of mild surprise. She appeared to be a similar age to Mavis and was impeccably presented. She didn't have the look of a cheater; if cheaters have a look, that is.

"Good evening, Mavis, Barry," Dorris said in greeting with a polite smile. Mavis and Barry nodded at Mrs Colchester. Gemma noticed that both looked nervous.

"Nice to meet you. I'm Gemma Curtis, the proprietor of The Bookworm Bookshop," Gemma said, extending a hand that Dorris accepted with a firm shake.

"May we come in?" Mavis asked, her tone serious. "We need to discuss something serious."

"Serious? Why, yes, of course. Come in," Dorris said, with a graceful sweep of her arm. "Please, make yourselves comfortable in the lounge." The lounge balanced comfort with elegance. Burgundy and yellow wallpaper covered the walls while comfortable, plush sofas sat around the room and tasteful art adorned the walls. Dorris took her place in a high-backed armchair.

"Would anyone care for some tea?" Dorris enquired, her hospitality automatic.

"No, thank you," Mavis said, declining almost too quickly and folding her hands in her lap as she perched on the edge of the sofa. Gemma observed a subtle shift in Dorris's posture, a slight tensing of her shoulders and a fleeting dart of her eyes. "Dorris," Mavis began, her voice level, "have you heard about the unfortunate incidents with some gardens entering into the competition?"

"Only whispers," Dorris responded, her fingers intertwining anxiously.

"Has your garden been targeted at all?" Barry chimed in, leaning forward. "Any strange happenings?"

A pause — a breath caught and held — before Dorris shook her head. "No, nothing of the sort."

Barry nodded. "It seems all the top contenders in the competition have been targeted," said Barry. "My garden was hit, and so was Mavis's."

"Well, that's just awful," said Dorris.

"I wonder why nobody targeted you," said Barry.

"I honestly couldn't tell you. Perhaps my garden isn't seen as a good enough target."

"A previous competition winner? I find that rather strange," said Barry.

"Well, what can I tell you," said Dorris.

Gemma reached into her trouser pocket and pulled out her phone. She unlocked the screen and turned it towards Dorris, pressing play on the evidence that would shatter the tranquillity of the moment. "Nobody has tried anything with your garden," Gemma stated, her voice a mixture of accusation and sorrow. "And we know why."

The video showed a couple of youthful figures, unmistakable in their mischief. Dorris's face contorted into an expression of recognition and regret.

"They're your grandkids, aren't they?" Mavis's question hung heavy in the room, disappointment laced her tone.

Dorris's head descended, and she stared at the floor. Barry leaned forward, his voice soft yet carrying a piercing clarity. "Why, Dorris? Why do this? Over a simple competition?" The words seemed to crush the remaining fight from Dorris. Her shoulders slumped; her facade crumbled. Tears gathered in the corners of her eyes, spilling over like rain breaching the banks of a swollen river.

"I just wanted to win again," she sobbed, the sound heart-wrenching in its rawness. "For the third time ... It sounds so foolish when I say it aloud, but there's little joy left for me. Winning ... it made me feel alive, like I mattered." Her plea was a whisper. "Winning gave me attention, something to be proud of," Dorris continued, her voice cracking under the strain of her emotions. "I know it's no excuse, but those moments on the podium were ... They were the best moments of my life."

Nobody seemed to know what to say. The room went silent, hanging like thick fog. Mavis's voice cut through it, gentle yet incredulous, as she turned her bespectacled gaze upon the woman they once admired. "Why would you get your own grandkids to doing something like that?"

Dorris, her eyes rimmed with red, avoided their stares as she fumbled with the hem of her cardigan. "I had mentioned to them how important winning the competition was, and then they suggested the idea," she whispered, her voice carrying both defiance and sorrow. "They said they'd make sure the other gardens wouldn't win, for a price, of course. They wanted some spending money for their holiday. Offered to do it. I don't know why. It seems silly now. I'm so sorry, Mavis ... Barry ... Please accept my apologies."

Barry sat with his arms folded across his chest and shook his head in quiet disbelief. "Shameful," he muttered under his breath.

Gemma felt a tightening in her chest. She knew what came next; justice, however gentle its touch needed to be, must prevail. "How do their parent's feel about this?" asked Gemma. "They can't be happy about their children trespassing into other people's gardens and vandalising their property?"

"They don't know. They are at work all the time. I spend a lot of time looking after my grandkids," said Dorris.

Gemma sighed and wasn't sure if it was worth pushing further now that the cat was out of the bag. At the back of her mind, she thought that Dorris was the real-life Gangster Granny, and she wondered if David Walliams secretly knew Mrs Colchester. The thought nearly made her smile, but she suppressed it as she recomposed herself. "This will have to be reported to the competition," Gemma said, her tone firm but not without sympathy. "It's not fair to the other entrants."

Dorris nodded but couldn't make eye contact with Gemma. "I understand," she said, her voice brittle like thin ice.

"Many have spent their hard-earned money, pensions even, on making their gardens nice for the competition. You have also let down Belper," Gemma continued, her eyes finally locking with Dorris's.

A nod, more vigorously this time, came from Dorris. "I'll repay everyone for their damages," she said. "Every penny, I promise."

"Yes, that's the least you can do. Everyone will need a full apology too," said Mavis, as she rose from the sofa. Barry followed suit, his posture stooping momentarily before regaining its usual straightness.

"I'm sorry." Dorris's voice was but a whisper.

Mavis paused at the door, her hand on the polished brass doorknob. She turned. "I know," she said. "I can't tell you how disappointed I am, Dorris. I would have expected much better from you." The words seemed to hang there, suspended in the room's silence, before Mavis gave a small nod and stepped through the door, signalling an end to the confrontation.

Gemma followed, feeling the tension dissipate as they left the confines of the Colchester house behind. They walked in silence down the front garden path to the car. "Come on," Gemma said, her tone brighter now, trying to lift the spirits of her friends. "I'll drive you both home."

"Thank you," said Mavis, as she got into the passenger seat. Barry climbed into the back.

"Well, that was certainly awkward," he said.

"You're not wrong, Barry. But it had to be done," said Mavis.

Barry nodded. "Yes, it did," he said. "I'll speak to the competition organisers tomorrow and present them with the video evidence."

"Thank you. If you want me to pop along with you, let me know," said Mavis. Barry nodded, as if contemplating the idea. Mavis turned to Gemma, who was now in the driver's seat and about to start the car. "Are you doing anything nice this evening?" she asked, trying to change the subject.

"I'm seeing David. We're going for a few drinks," said Gemma, as she drove down the road.

"Ooh, lovely," said Mavis. "Say hello from me."

"I will," Gemma said.

## Chapter Twenty-Two

The blast of an alarm yanked Gemma from her sleep. In the darkness, she scrambled for her glasses. After her fingers closed on the frames, she put them on and blinked her surroundings into focus.

"Wha ... what's that noise?" she mumbled to herself, regretting the double rum and coke she had the night before after a few Aperol spritz's with David. He always made them so strong.

The bed's sidelight flickered on, bathing the room in a soft golden glow. Gemma jolted awake as she saw the glaring red notification on her phone screen. "Oh my god!" The words escaped her lips before she grasped their weight.

Beside her, David stirred, groggy but alert from a deep sleep. He shifted towards her as concern etched his features. "Gemma? What is it?" He looked at his watch to check the time. "It's 2:30 in the morning."

"The Bookworm," she gasped, her voice laced with panic. "The alarm's going off. I think there's been a break-in."

David propped himself up on one elbow. He watched as Gemma's fingers danced across her phone screen, summoning the security app.

"Can you see anyone?" asked David, his detective instincts kicking in.

She squinted at the grainy footage, her breath catching. "No, I don't think so. But the front window, it looks like it's shattered," Gemma said, her voice sounding stressed as she flicked through the security camera images. "Who would do that?"

"Get dressed. We'll go check it out," David said, his tone steady and measured as he sat up in bed.

Gemma nodded, attempting to still the flutter of nerves in her stomach. Deep down, she was glad her boyfriend was a trained detective who knew what to do. David got out of bed and pulled on last night's trousers and shirt with quick, methodical movements. Gemma threw on a T-shirt and jeans.

"Come on," David said. "I'll drive."

Gemma nodded, her heart thumped against her ribcage as she shoved her feet into her trainers without tying the laces. They made their way out of the house at speed, heading for David's car.

"Wait! The door!" he called out.

"Oh!" She spun around, her hands trembling as she shut the front door.

David unlocked his car, and they clambered in.

As they pulled up to the shop in the marketplace, the wail of the alarm assaulted their ears. Gemma leapt from the parked car and headed to the shop's door.

"Wait, Gemma. Let me check it first," David said, his voice calm as he looked towards the broken window at the front. He retrieved a heavy-duty torch from the boot of his car and turned to her with an expectant look. "The keys?"

She fumbled in her pocket and fished out the keys. Handing them over, she watched as David approached the storefront. His torch cut through the darkness, sweeping across the shelves laden with books. Gemma's heart ached at the sight.

"Shouldn't we call the police?" Gemma asked. David stopped, turned towards Gemma, and smiled.

"I am the police," he said with a chuckle.

"I mean police with a van and maybe a dog?"

"It's a broken window, not a bank job," he said as he rolled his eyes. "We'll be fine. Stay behind me." David stepped closer to the window and shined the light through again. Satisfied that the coast was clear, he unlocked the door and stepped inside to disable the intruder alarm with Gemma's key fob. The sudden silence was almost as jarring as the noise had been. "Stay by the door," David instructed. He scanned the shadows beyond the main area.

Gemma nodded and watched as he disappeared into the back room and then into the café. Her attention was drawn to the floor, where amidst the glittering shards of broken glass lay a solitary brick. A piece of paper, secured by a rubber band, clung to its rough surface.

Gemma glanced towards the café, ensuring David was still out of sight. Her heart thudded, she knelt beside the brick and peeled the note free. Unfolding it, the words leapt up at her: "YOU HAVE BEEN WARNED!" The letters were nondescript. Her mind raced with questions. Who would do this? And why? David returned from the back of the shop. Gemma's heart still raced, and her mouth felt dry. She held the note up so David could see.

"Note on a brick. Very original," he said with a faint smile, as if trying to lift the mood of the situation. "Could it be those kids you told me about? The kids who damaged the gardens? Seems like the sort of petty thing they might do."

"Could be, yeah. Revenge for them getting in trouble," Gemma said.

"Want to file a report? I'll get some uniformed officer's sent around."

"Not yet. Let me think," Gemma said.

David nodded. "Okay, but if you need to claim for the damage, you'll need a crime reference number."

Gemma folded the note into a square and slipped it into her back pocket.

"I'll see if I can get the CCTV footage from around the marketplace. See if we can see who it was," said David.

"Thank you," said Gemma.

"Got any sturdy cardboard boxes?" David asked. "Something to patch this up till morning."

"Boxes ..." Gemma repeated, her mind lurching back to the present. "Erm ... Yes, in the office. From yesterday's book delivery." David strode towards the office. Gemma watched him go, the tension in her shoulders easing now that she had a moment alone to think. She stood by the broken window with glass crunching beneath her shoes and looked out towards Cynthia's shop at the corner of the marketplace.

There was a light glowing from the flat above the shop where Cynthia lived. "Cynthia must have been woken by the alarm," she whispered to herself. "I should go and apologise for the noise later on."

David walked behind her, his arms laden with large cardboard boxes that seemed almost comically oversized in his grasp. He unfolded them, laid them flat and began sealing the jagged absence left by the shattered window. "This should hold until you can get someone out to replace the window," he said, securing the last strip of parcel tape with a firm pat.

"I'll call my builder. Hopefully, he can get the glass

replaced," she said. Gemma grabbed a broom from the office and set about sweeping up the broken glass. When she was done, she reset the alarm and locked the door.

"Alright, let's get you home. Try and get a few hours' sleep. You'll be knackered later on," David said. Gemma nodded and followed him to the car. As David started the engine and pulled away from the shop, Gemma gazed up again towards Cynthia's window. The light inside still cast a pale glow against the drawn curtains. A shadow moved inside.

"Are you okay?" David asked, his voice breaking through her fixation. His brow furrowed with concern.

"Yeah, I'm fine," she said, pointing up at Cynthia's window. "I think the noise of the alarm must have woken Cynthia. I'll pop around later and speak to her."

"Might be worth asking if she saw anything," said David.

"I'll make sure to ask," Gemma said, as David drove them back to her house to attempt to get some more sleep. It was nearly 3:30 in the morning, and she wasn't looking forward to a full day in the shop after a night of broken sleep.

# Chapter Twenty-Three

Gemma arrived early at the bookshop after trying, but failing, to get some extra sleep. As she turned the key in the lock, her hand trembled. With a steadying breath, Gemma pushed the door open and stepped inside. Her senses were on high alert. She reached for the alarm panel, swiping the fob to silence the shrill warning beeps.

Gemma pulled her phone from her pocket and tapped the number for Geoff Dunsworth, her builder. The call connected, and she switched to speakerphone as she began assessing the window damage more closely.

"Geoff? It's Gemma from the Bookworm."

"Morning, Gemma! What can I do for you?" Geoff asked.

"Could you possibly replace a glass window pane?

Someone decided to redecorate ours with a brick," Gemma said, trying to bring humour to the situation.

"Sorry to hear that. I can pop over this morning and take a look. Is it double-glazed?"

"No. Just single-glazed window panes," Gemma replied.

"Much easier to sort out then. I'll be over shortly to measure up."

"Thanks, Geoff," said Gemma. "See you soon." When the call disconnected, Gemma pocketed her phone, leaned against the counter and sighed.

It wasn't long until Ellie and Mavis arrived; their expressions of shock mirrored each other as they took in the sight of the makeshift cardboard panel where there was once a window.

"Good heavens! What happened here?" Mavis asked with concern, darting her gaze from the damaged window to Gemma.

"Someone didn't seem to like our window, so they smashed it with a brick," Gemma responded with a shrug. She watched Ellie's hand flutter to her rounded belly, her face etched with worry.

"Why would anyone do that? To a bookshop of all places?" Ellie asked, her eyes wide as saucers.

"The burglar alarm went off last night. It pulled David and me out of bed at an ungodly hour."

"URGH, not what you want," Ellie said. "I best get

the café setup. We are still opening, aren't we? Do you think it will put customer's off?"

"Yes, business as usual. Geoff is coming over to get the glass replaced," said Gemma. "If any customers ask, just say the window is being replaced. No need to mention the brick being thrown through it."

Ellie nodded and stepped past the shelves towards the back of the shop. Mavis shuffled closer to Gemma, her curiosity piqued. "In the movies, a brick through the window is usually accompanied by a note," Mavis prodded gently.

"Ah, yes. Now you mention it." Gemma reached into her back pocket and pulled out the crumpled note, unfolding it with care. She passed it to Mavis, who brought it close to her glasses for inspection.

"You have been warned!" Mavis read aloud in disbelief. "This is rather sinister."

Gemma nodded in agreement. "I'm wondering if it's Mrs Colchester's grandkids again. Maybe getting a little revenge?"

"That seems a little drastic for kids," Mavis said.

"It is, especially in the early hours of the morning," said Gemma, as she slipped the note into her back pocket. "It certainly won't dampen our spirits, though." Gemma hovered by the boarded-up window, her gaze drifting out to the marketplace. She turned back to Mavis. "Last night, when David and I were securing the shop, I noticed a light on in the flat above Cynthia's shop. Someone was standing near the window behind the curtain as we drove past. Presumably, it was Cynthia. I might pop over and apologise for waking her with the alarm and see if she saw anything."

"Yes, a good idea. We don't want to upset the neighbours. I'll come with you," said Mavis, just as the bell above the door jingled and Geoff Dunsworth walked in.

"Morning, ladies," said Geoff, as he looked at the cardboard barrier stuck where the window used to live. "Bleeding vandals. They're a menace."

"You're not wrong, Geoff," Gemma said, as she held up the brick. "Or maybe they were providing a brick for the new extension," said Gemma with a smile.

"Very generous of them," Geoff said, chuckling. "Let's have a look then." He fished a tape measure and notepad from his leather shoulder bag and stood by the window. The metal tape snaked across the window frame as he jotted some measurements.

"Will it take long to get some new glass?" Gemma asked, watching him work.

"Shouldn't take long," Geoff said, his eyes focused on the task. "I'll nip over to the suppliers and get some cut to size. I'll have you sorted out as soon as I can." Geoff could sense that Gemma was stressed. He smiled. "It will be done by the end of the day. In the meantime, leave this temporary cardboard in place. If I can't get the glass today, then I can cut some Perspex to size, which will be more robust overnight."

"Thank you, Geoff. That would be wonderful," Gemma said, with genuine relief. Geoff nodded, stuffed his tools back into his bag, and headed out, leaving Gemma and Mavis alone once more to focus on the business of selling books.

Later in the morning, Gemma glanced at the wall clock; the hands barely seemed to have moved since the last time she looked. It was a quiet morning, so she turned to Ellie, who was wiping down tables.

"Ellie, would you mind holding the fort? I'm going to pop over to the corner shop to apologise to Cynthia. Mavis is coming for moral support," Gemma asked.

"Of course, Gemma," Ellie replied. "It's all under control here. Don't you worry."

"Thanks, Ellie. We won't be long." Gemma smiled. With Mavis in tow, Gemma exited the bookshop, and they walked across the marketplace. They stopped in front of Cynthia's shop, which stood silent and still. Gemma reached for the door handle, only to find it unmoving beneath her fingers. "That's odd," she said, peering through the glass. "Cynthia's shop is never closed at this hour."

Mavis leaned forward, squinting until she saw upon the note stuck to the inside of the window. "Look at this, Gemma." Her voice held an edge of concern as she read aloud, "Due to unforeseen circumstances, the shop will be closed for the foreseeable future."

"Well, that's unexpected," Gemma said, her curiosity piqued. First, Cynthia gave her a good telling off when she accused her of interfering, and now she was conspicuously absent. They walked around the side of the shop, where a narrow alleyway led to the private entrance of Cynthia's flat. Gemma pressed the doorbell and waited, her ears straining for any sound of movement from within. There was nothing but silence.

"What now?" Mavis asked.

"I'm not sure," Gemma said. "I'll pop around again later. Perhaps Cynthia will be in then." Defeated, they headed back to the bookshop. As they approached the door, the postman, who was just leaving, waved at Gemma.

"Thanks for holding the fort," said Gemma, as she stepped through the door.

"No problem. The postman's just been," Ellie said, as she held out a stack of envelopes.

"Thank you," Gemma replied, accepting the bundle with a smile as Ellie retreated to the café. Gemma perched on the edge of the counter and rifled through the letters, her fingers dancing over bills and flyers until they paused at an envelope that stood out from the rest. Gemma tilted her head as she scanned the handwriting and postmark stretched across the front of the envelope. Gemma opened the envelope. "Well, that's odd. It's from Cynthia." Gemma's voice held a tinge of disbelief as she scanned the letter.

"What does it say?" Mavis asked. Her eyes were wide with curiosity.

Gemma read the first line to Mavis. "Gemma, I have a confession to make."

## Chapter Twenty-Four

Mavis, sat on a stool behind the counter, watched her with expectant eyes. "Cynthia posting a letter? She's only across the marketplace," Mavis said.

"I know, right? Very unusual," Gemma said, as she continued scanning the first page. "Listen to this, Mavis. Cynthia's stating that George was intimidating her for cigarettes and alcohol. But there's more."

Mavis leaned forward. "Go on."

"George used to conduct his ... dealings in her shop; drugs," Gemma continued, her brow furrowed. "He made her disable the cameras, and at times, when a dodgy customer arrived, they would close the store temporarily. Then he'd make drug deals right there among the magazines and greeting cards. Out of view of prying eyes."

"Good heavens," Mavis exclaimed. "That's brazen."

"Indeed." Gemma scanned the rest of the letter, her lips moving silently as she absorbed Cynthia's confessions. "She's been living in fear, Mavis. And ..." Gemma paused and went wide-eyed. "Gosh, she says she's not sad he's gone, but she didn't kill him."

"As shocking as that sounds, can you blame her for thinking that? Especially if he put her through all that torment?" said Mavis.

"Yes, I guess so. The letter continues to say there are people here in Belper who controlled George. That he wasn't working alone."

"Whoever they are, they're still out there," Mavis mused, her well-spoken words evoking with concern.

"It would seem so." Gemma let out a sigh. "She doesn't say who they are. But if George was taking orders ..."

"Then someone in this town means business," Mavis finished, her tone grave.

Gemma's mind raced, thoughts darting like swallows at dusk. She turned the page and traced It with her finger. "Even with George gone," Gemma read, "I still feel like they're watching me." Gemma looked up at Mavis, her mind churning with possibilities. Cynthia, the beleaguered shop owner, living in fear. "Cynthia knew what we'd been thinking," Gemma said aloud, more to herself than to Mavis.

"She thinks you suspected her of George's murder,

even if only a very tenuous suspicion?" Mavis said, leaning closer to be discreet.

"Yes," Gemma said, nodding, her pulse quickening as she delved deeper into the letter. "But she states she didn't do it."

"Of course she does," Mavis replied, though her scepticism was tempered by a softening in her eyes. "Even if someone was guilty, they would proclaim their innocence until the bitter end."

With a deep breath, Gemma read on, scanning through the text and summarising. "Cynthia's leaving Belper. Says she needs to escape, to find respite from all this. She feels shame for being George's accomplice." Her hand paused over the last sentence. "She's sorry for her part in all this; says she had no choice but to comply. She didn't mean to snap at me when I visited the other day."

"Escape?" Mavis's lips pursed in thought, her empathy clear. "Nobody should have to live like that, coerced into silence."

"I know. This is horrible," Gemma said. "But running away doesn't do much to make her look innocent, and with us having this confession letter about George's drug dealings in her shop, that puts us in a predicament."

"If whoever is watching her knows we have this information ... Well, that could be dangerous," Mavis said.

Gemma looked Mavis in the eye. "That brick that was thrown through the window. Do you think it could be a warning from George's handler? Instead of being related to Mrs Colchester's grandkids?" Gemma asked.

"Perhaps. It's hard to say," said Mavis.

Gemma refolded Cynthia's letter and slid it back into the envelope. For a moment, silence hung between the two women. The simple letter she held in her hands was very dangerous if anyone knew she was in possession of these facts. Gemma was no longer convinced the warning on the brick was related to the garden vandals, and now thought that it was about her and Mavis looking into the murder. The thought made Gemma feel sick to her stomach.

Mavis broke the silence with a sigh. "If all that's true," she said, "then poor Cynthia ... She must have been living in fear for ages. Possibly even years." She shook her head. "I can't even imagine how awful that must be."

Gemma nodded solemnly. Her throat felt tight. "Being extorted for cigarettes and alcohol is bad enough," Gemma said, her voice barely above a whisper, "let alone being forced to turn your shop into some sort of ... illicit drug den."

"Right on our doorstep too," Mavis murmured, her eyes narrowed in thought. After a moment, curiosity edged into Mavis's voice. "Do you think when you saw

Cynthia in her window last night that she was about to leave Belper?"

Gemma cast her mind back to the shadowy figure behind the curtains. "She must have been," Gemma conceded, the pieces of the puzzle aligned with a reluctant click. "Preparing to flee."

"The sound of our shop alarm going off may have frightened her even more," Mavis concluded.

"Something that is strange," said Gemma, "is why would Cynthia confess this to us? That's a massive risk to take."

"I think it's obvious," Mavis said. Gemma looked at her and smiled. "Cynthia knows you solved the Dominic Westley murder ..."

"Well, we both did, Mavis. Don't underestimate your part," Gemma said.

"Yes, quite," Mavis said. "But Cynthia also suspected that you might be investigating George's murder."

"A correct assumption."

"Therefore, this letter is a call for help. She is trusting you to solve this puzzle. She may see this as her only way out," Mavis said, and she was right. This was a call for help. If Cynthia was being watched, then sending this letter and going into hiding must have felt like her only choice to end this awful situation.

"You are absolutely right, Mavis. I didn't spot that."

"That's why we're a team, my dear," said Mavis.

"Something else that is strange," said Gemma, "is if all this was a secret, how come a parent at our reading event knew about Cynthia being intimidated?"

"That is a good point," said Mavis. "When I discussed it with Norman, he said that after Cynthia mentioned the intimidation, she suddenly went silent. Perhaps she sought solace and help, but then the intimidation escalated into being forced to assist with George's drug dealing? Threatened to be silent; hence, why she stopped talking about it all of a sudden."

Gemma nodded. "That would make sense. She may have confided in some people at first and then tried to suppress it and brush it off."

"Yes, that feels like the logical reason," Mavis said.

Gemma let out a long breath. "So that leaves the golden question. Who could be in charge of George?" Gemma asked. "The identity of this person or persons is our key. What if George had been rebelling against other gang members, and they murdered him? That's not too wild a leap, is it?"

"That's what I was thinking. This person sounds more like a gangster off a TV drama," Mavis uttered. "We have to tread carefully. Having this letter could be very dangerous."

Gemma smiled nervously. "You're not wrong, Mavis," Gemma said, feeling the weight of the situation press down upon her. The door jingled and someone walked in, but Gemma and Mavis were so preoccupied they didn't notice that it was David. He approached the counter, his eyes catching the cream envelope in Gemma's hand.

"Morning," he said cheerily. In a split second, Gemma panicked and pulled the letter below the counter. Not her best idea.

"What's that?" he asked.

Gemma's heart skipped as she fumbled for words, the letter felt like contraband under David's gaze. Deep down, she knew this was the time to come clean with David, especially now that the situation seemed to have escalated. "It's from Cynthia," she managed, her voice sounding distant to her own ears. "She's leaving Belper ... And, well, it seems that her shop served more than just newspapers."

David's expression morphed from worried to alarmed as he scanned the letter's contents. A silence stretched, fraught with unsaid fears, until he looked up, meeting their gazes with an intensity that made Gemma's stomach flip. "Please tell me you're not investigating George's murder," he said, a plea wrapped in the veneer of a question.

Gemma exchanged a glance with Mavis. She turned back to David.

"David, we need to talk."

# Chapter Twenty-Five

Gemma glanced quickly between Mavis and David. Ellie was nearby cleaning tables, and Gemma waved to catch her attention. "Ellie, could you ...?" she trailed off, motioning towards the bookshop counter.

"Of course," Ellie replied. "I've got this covered."

"Thank you. We won't be long." Gemma beckoned for Mavis and David to follow her into the back office, a small room lined with shelves of administrative binders alongside books waiting to find their way onto the shop's shelves. As the door clicked shut behind them, a bubble of nerves swelled in Gemma's stomach.

David's voice cut into the silence. "So, who's going to tell me what's going on?"

Gemma sucked in a breath. "David, it's just ..." she began, lifting her gaze to meet his. "Mavis and I, we can't accept that John — poor, helpless John — could do something so ... so dreadful."

Before David could respond, Mavis spoke, her voice firm. "He's always been such a mild-mannered and lovely man," she said. "He's always been very polite. Never asking for anything more than a bit of conversation."

David listened, the lines of his face softening in the dim light of the office. He sat on the cluttered desk, his arms crossed over his chest. He looked at Gemma and took a deep breath. "I get it," he said finally. "But the evidence we've got; it's not just compelling; it's overwhelming. John's prints are everywhere. On the vodka bottle that ... well, you know. And inside those gloves; his DNA is all over them. There are bloodstains on his clothes too." He paused. "The toxicology analysis of his blood also confirmed he was loaded on alcohol and ketamine, a combination that can drastically alter your personality."

The room seemed to close in around Gemma. "But has John said that he did it? Has he confessed?" asked Gemma. Her voice was hopeful yet held an edge of desperation.

David shook his head. "He says he can't remember anything about the evening in question. Complete blackout, which isn't unheard of when under the influence. Also, it's quite common for someone arrested for murder to maintain their innocence and deny the charges." He paused, his eyes softening. "Look, I know you two care about him, but this isn't your fight. The police have this covered."

Gemma nodded and bit her lip, glancing towards Mavis. "Then there's this letter." Gemma hesitated before continuing. "It's quite unnerving, David. I'm not sure we should discuss that here at the shop," Gemma said, a look of worry flashing across her face.

"Why not discuss it at my place this evening?" Mavis interjected, her voice carrying a note of authority.

David sighed, rubbing the back of his neck. "Alright. That sounds like a good idea."

"Seven o'clock?" Gemma proposed. "Then at least we are away from prying ears."

"Seven works for me. I'll come straight from the police station," David said. "Can I take that letter?"

Gemma's fingers hovered over the letter, the weight of Cynthia's despondent words pressing against her conscience. She looked into David's earnest eyes and surrendered the letter to his outstretched hand. He pulled the letter from the envelope and scanned its contents again.

"My God, this isn't good," he said. "Keep this to yourselves. Don't discuss it at all until we meet." David folded the letter and put it back into the envelope before he slid it into his coat pocket. "I'll see you at Mavis's house." David turned, leaving the confines of the office.

Gemma tracked his departure until the sound of the

front bell signalled his exit from the bookshop. She turned to face Mavis and slumped into the chair behind her, causing it to creak.

Mavis looked at Gemma. "I was expecting a good telling off for playing detective again," Mavis said.

Gemma chuckled. "He knows us too well by now. Besides, we've only been chatting with folks around town. I wouldn't say it's a full investigation, in the strictest of terms," she said.

"Well, we best get back to the shop floor. Those books won't sell themselves," said Mavis, hoping for a small glimpse of normality.

Gemma let out a laugh. "Lead the way, Miss Marple," Gemma said, rising to follow her friend. "Let me drive you home after we close up?" she offered as they stepped towards the door. "We can get ready for our meeting with David."

"Oh, that would be lovely. I've already baked some shortbreads this morning. I'll put those out."

"Perfect," Gemma said with a chuckle, imagining David's eyes lighting up at the mention of biscuits. "He can never resist biscuits."

They stepped out of the office into the main shop area of the Bookworm. Ellie was handing some change to a customer who had just purchased a Brandon Sanderson fantasy epic. "Thanks for covering, Ellie," Gemma said.

"No problem at all," Ellie replied, turning towards

them, her maternal glow apparent. She looked up at Gemma. "Is everything okay? You look a bit ... off."

"No, I'm fine. Just shop things. Nothing to worry about," Gemma deflected, brushing away the concern. "Has it been busy?"

"Quiet as a library," Ellie said, with a gentle laugh. "Though there was one odd chap. Quite tall, stick thin and bald. Looked quite scruffy. Not your typical book enthusiast, if there is such a thing. He looked around but didn't touch a thing. I asked if he needed help, and he just grunted and walked out without a word."

The description sent a chill down Gemma's spine, as she was hit with a wave of paranoia. She exchanged a quick, uneasy glance with Mavis, whose eyes echoed her concern. A sudden thump of her heart made Gemma feel queasy, but she masked it with a smile. "Thank you, Ellie," Gemma managed. "You're a star." As Ellie waved off the compliment and returned to her tasks, Gemma looked at Mavis. The tension hung between them. Gemma thought she was probably being paranoid after the letter, but part of her wondered if this strange man had any relation to what Cynthia mentioned about being watched.

## Chapter Twenty-Six

Gemma sat in the dining room of Mavis's well-kept home, fiddling with her necklace. The makeshift murder board dominated one wall, laying their investigation bare, although Gemma wasn't sure what David would make of it. This made the extent of their investigation very evident.

"Are you okay?" Mavis asked.

Gemma let go of her necklace. "I'm fine. Just a little on edge. That letter from Cynthia has left me a little rattled."

"Me too. It was when Ellie mentioned about that strange man coming into the store. Felt a little suspicious," said Mavis.

"Yeah, that worried me too," said Gemma. "Perhaps we are just being paranoid. David will know what to do."

Mavis's doorbell echoed through the house.

"Ah, that'll be him now." Mavis bustled out of the dining room to let him in.

Gemma sat upright and composed herself, but when David followed Mavis back into the room, his demeanour wasn't stern or serious. He looked relaxed as he glanced around the room.

"Mavis, your house is very nice," he said, his voice radiating warmth.

"Thank you. Very kind," Mavis replied. She gestured to the plate of biscuits. "Shortbread, David?"

His eyes lit up as he reached for a biscuit. "Don't mind if I do. Thanks."

"Coffee?" Mavis asked, already knowing the answer as she picked up the coffee pot.

"Yes, please. Thank you," David responded, accepting a mug from Mavis. He ambled over to the condiments and dropped five sugar cubes in his cup before stirring his coffee with a spoon.

Gemma opened her mouth, a tentative "sorry" escaping, only to be cut off by David's raised hand and reassuring smile.

"I'm not here to have a go at you about investigating the murder," he said, his voice light.

Relief washed over Gemma, and her words came out in a rush. "I thought you were going to give us a good ticking off after we received that letter."

David chuckled. "I don't tell you what to do, Gemma. I never have."

"True," she said with a nod.

He stood, surveying the murder board taped to the wall with genuine interest. "This is just like on the tele," he said, pointing at the web of clues sprawled in a big spider diagram.

Mavis beamed at the comparison. "Yes, just so. Don't you have similar boards at the police station?" she asked.

"Nah, we record it all on the computer these days. Then everyone involved can access it."

"Ah, yes, much more convenient. I like the old-fashioned ways myself," said Mavis.

David smiled as he settled into his chair and retrieved a well-worn notepad from his coat pocket. "I still like a good notebook, though."

Mavis cocked her head, a playful twinkle in her eye. "Are we being interviewed, Detective?"

"Nothing so formal," he said with a laugh, flipping open the cover. "Just a habit, to organise my thoughts. Let's start from the top then," he said, pen poised. "You've already told me you don't believe John could be guilty, even though the weight of forensic evidence against him is very strong."

Mavis leaned forward. "Well, as I said at the shop earlier, it's just so out of character for him. He's a lovely, mild-mannered man."

"We know John had a history with the victim, George," Gemma added, her voice steady but thoughtful.

David hummed as he contemplated this. "And how did you come by this information about John's history with the victim?"

"My good friend Barry, from the food hub at the Baptist church," Mavis said. "John confided in him about George's intimidation."

"Even the mildest-mannered people can be pushed too far," David said, scribbling notes that danced across the page. "Everyone has a snapping point."

Gemma fiddled with her necklace again. "Yes, that's true," she said. She let go of the necklace and looked up at David. "You mentioned before about the alcohol and ketamine mix in John's blood …"

"That's right," David said.

"I was talking to my friend Jen. She's a pharmacist at the supermarket, and I had coffee with her recently; just a casual chat, you understand." Gemma paused, and David nodded. "We discussed the effects of mixing ketamine with alcohol."

David chuckled. "That's quite a specific topic for a light-hearted coffee catch-up, isn't it?"

"Well, you know me. Details are my cup of tea, or coffee, in this case." Gemma smiled. "Mixing alcohol and ketamine is risky. To affect John but not render him unconscious or worse ... it takes a certain finesse in dosing."

"True," David agreed, tapping his pen against the notepad. "You'd need more than just basic knowledge to pull that off."

Gemma nodded and leaned forward, hands resting on the polished wood of the table. "Also, about the church; I checked on the reverend after the incident. He talked about the CCTV system and how it had been tampered with a few weeks prior, creating a blind spot by the back door and a nearby gap in the fence."

"Convenient, but we have taken this into account after speaking with the reverend," David said.

"Too convenient," Gemma asserted. "Planning such a precise act with camera tampering and blind spots is one thing, but for John to then take a drug that could have floored him? It doesn't add up."

David nodded, processing her words. "The forensic evidence isn't in John's favour, though. He hasn't even claimed innocence. Says he doesn't remember if he did it or not."

Mavis picked up the plate of shortbread and offered them to Gemma and David.

"Another biscuit?"

"No, thank you," said Gemma.

"Thanks," David said, as he held up the biscuit like a prize trophy. "Right then." David shifted his attention back to the matter at hand. "What else have you been investigating? How does Cynthia play into this for you?"

Gemma leaned back in her chair. "Well," she began, "our initial suspicions about Cynthia stemmed from her reaction to finding the body; overdone, like something out of an amateur dramatic rehearsal." Gemma paused, remembering how the scene had unfolded. "We didn't think much of it at the time, apart from Cynthia being flamboyant." Gemma hesitated, recalling the disarray at the scene. "Then there was her lipstick; the bright pink one she's known for. It was lying there on the floor near George's body." Gemma's gaze drifted to the murder board, her brow creasing. "But that day, Cynthia was wearing a different shade."

David took a bite of the shortbread, nodding as he chewed thoughtfully. "Yes, we have that lipstick bagged up as evidence, but it isn't that suspicious, given her volunteer work at the church and frequent access to that particular room. When we spoke to her, we learned that she was in the bell chamber the previous day for a rehearsal as well as sweeping the floor, so she probably dropped it then."

Gemma watched David's expression and noted the flicker of doubt that crossed his features before masking it with another smile. Mavis's hand shot up, then settled back down as a chuckle escaped her lips. "I don't know why I raised my hand," she confessed. David's shoulders shook with mirth, and Gemma grinned.

"It's your home, Mavis. No need to ask for permission. This isn't an official police interview," said David.

"Anyway," Mavis continued, "when I bumped into Norman at the Strutt Centre, he mentioned Cynthia had taken quite a fancy to him."

David tilted his head, a puzzled expression crossing his face. "Norman, he's the church warden, isn't he?"

"That's the one," Mavis said. "Well, Cynthia tried to kiss him recently at the church."

David looked up in surprise. "And how did Norman react to that?" David enquired, his pen poised above his notepad.

"He reacted like any happily married man would. He felt horrified!" Mavis declared. "I'm not sure it applies to your investigation, but it seemed worth mentioning." Before they could further dissect Norman's unexpected encounter, Mavis leaned forward, her gaze sharp. "Gemma, tell David about what you heard at the children's reading."

Gemma sat upright and raised a finger, as if having a eureka moment. "Well reminded, Mavis," Gemma said. "One mum told me that George had been intimidating Cynthia for cigarettes and alcohol from her shop."

"Yes, her letter mentioned that too." David's scribbling paused as he looked up, intrigued. "She never mentioned that to the officers when they spoke to her, though." David tapped the pen against his chin. "That's a very relevant detail, if true. That gives her a firm motive."

Gemma nodded. "That's what we thought. I casually brought it up with Cynthia at the shop, trying not to sound too investigative." She sighed. "But Cynthia snapped at me. Accused me of being nosy."

David's snigger broke the brief silence. "Well, she wasn't wrong about that, was she?"

"No," Gemma admitted, smiling guiltily at David. "She wasn't. I could have approached that one a bit more carefully. But it was such an odd reaction for her. I must have touched a nerve."

"Understandable," David muttered, scribbling notes. "If you are concealing something and somebody probes, it will put you into a panic state. A typical fight-or-flight response. We catch people out in interviews with that all the time."

Gemma picked up a biscuit, while David caught up with his notes. He dotted an exaggerated full stop and then looked up at Gemma.

Mavis's eyes lit up as if a lightbulb had gone off. "Cynthia told Norman about the intimidation at first, but then she clammed up, wouldn't speak another word about it." She tapped her finger against her chin thoughtfully. "Right around the time those drug exchanges in the shop started, I'm willing to guess."

"Could be significant," David murmured. He laid

Cynthia's letter on the table. His fingers brushed over the words as he scanned the letter.

"The main thing that concerns me," David began, "is the idea of the corner shop being used for coordinated drug exchanges." He shook his head, a frown creasing his forehead. "Going to those lengths to intimidate a local business into turning off their CCTV ... it's something a well-organised gang would do. A shop owner doesn't just relent. There would have been months, or even years, of intimidation leading up to this."

Gemma exchanged a worried glance with Mavis. "You mentioned nothing about drug gangs when we were engaged before," she said, a mild tremor lacing her voice.

David looked at her. "These types of gangs tend to be very violent, Gemma. I've seen some very gruesome scenes." His eyes momentarily lost focus, as if haunted by memories best left unspoken.

Mavis's hand fluttered to her chest. "Goodness. That sounds shocking."

"It is," David said. "The dealers on the street are one thing. They are opportunists who are down on their luck and want to earn some quick cash. It's easy to catch them; they're not the brightest. The handlers further up the chain are organised crime gangs who are very good at covering their tracks and evading capture. The dealers will take the heat, and if they talk and try to give up any of their handlers ... Well, let's just say it's not in their best interest to speak to the police."

"They would rather go to prison than talk?" asked Gemma, surprised.

"In some cases, yes. It's the lesser of two evils," said David.

"Dare I ask what the alternative is?" asked Mavis.

"You don't want to know. They are connected in prison and can exact revenge on them inside. They can also go after family members. Some cases I have dealt with are so bad, I couldn't even bring case files home in case you saw the pictures, Gemma."

Gemma drew a hand up to her face. "Gosh, you mentioned none of this," she said.

"Some things are best left unsaid," David replied. "This is why I'm concerned." He steepled his fingers as he considered Gemma and Mavis with a grave expression. "You see, the thing is," he said slowly, "I'm not aware of any new drug gangs operating in the area, which is what's making me nervous." He paused, glancing at the makeshift murder board that dominated the wall. "At the moment, I can't be certain George's murder isn't connected in some way to gang activity, even if indirectly. We arrested John for the murder, but clearly George was working for a gang, and that worries me."

"Do you think they are connected?" Gemma asked.

"At this stage, I don't know," David replied. Gemma

nodded. Her brow furrowed as she took in David's words. "The note on the brick," David continued, tapping a finger against the tabletop, "it says you have been warned, but it doesn't specify about what. Could be the murder, could be Cynthia and the whole drug situation."

"Or both," Mavis interjected.

"Yes, or both," David agreed. "There's the link with George bullying John, but all this is circumstantial at the moment. We need concrete and physical evidence to link the two."

"Which means more digging," Gemma murmured. Her mind raced with possibilities, despite the danger they suggested.

"Actually," David said, smoothing the wrinkles in his shirt, "I'm going to have uniformed patrols stepped up in the area as a precaution. And I need you both to promise me you won't investigate further."

"Of course, David," Gemma replied, though a small part of her rebelled at the thought of stepping back. "Although you know you can count on us for anything that might help."

"Anything at all," Mavis said. She placed a hand on David's arm in a comforting gesture.

"Good." David gave them a grateful smile. "Make sure to let me know if you hear anything you believe to be relevant."

"We will," Gemma assured him. She paused as a

thought entered her head. "David, are the police going to search for Cynthia now she's gone missing?" Her voice wavered with concern.

He shook his head, his expression solemn. "Technically, she isn't missing. If Cynthia wants to go away for a while, then that's her decision. We can't step in unless we believe she's in immediate danger or if she's reported as missing by a family member." The room fell silent. Gemma knew David was right, but she didn't like the answer. Nobody spoke, and David took another biscuit. Gemma thought about Cynthia, wondering what she was doing at that moment and hoping she was okay.

Mavis, ever the one to break tension, clapped her hands together. "Well, onto other matters," she said. "The judging for the gardens is tomorrow. Though I must admit, I'm still quite shaken from Mrs Colchester's tomfoolery."

"Ah, yes, the annual Belper Blooms competition," David said with a smile. "I'm sure you'll do well, Mavis."

"Thank you," Mavis replied with a gentle smile.

"Mrs Colchester's got nothing on your green fingers," Gemma chimed in, grateful for the shift in conversation.

"Let's hope so," Mavis said with a sigh. "Let's hope so."

"Anyway," David said standing and stretching his back, "I should be off. I'm on a late shift tonight." He offered them both a reassuring nod. "Remember what we said about staying out of trouble?"

"Of course," Gemma replied, though the idea of sitting by wasn't in her nature. "We'll keep our ears to the ground and out of trouble."

"Good. And Gemma," he added, pausing at the doorway, "try not to worry too much. We'll sort this out."

"Thanks, David," Gemma said, as he left the house through the front door.

## Chapter Twenty-Seven

The next day, Gemma sat behind the counter and flipped through a novel. It had been a quiet day, with only a trickle of customers. The previous evening's discussion played on her mind as she reread the same paragraph several times. Despite David's well-meaning caution, she couldn't help but feel the itch of curiosity under her skin. She was compelled to delve deeper into George's murder.

Gemma glanced at the clock above the counter. The morning had dragged. She attempted to immerse herself in her book to distract her wandering mind. After a short while Mavis entered. She was in a chipper mood that radiated through the shop like a breath of fresh air, and she made a beeline for Gemma.

"How did the judging go, Mavis?" Gemma asked, relieved that her friend had arrived to distract her.

"It went splendidly!" Mavis said, as she sat herself on the stool next to Gemma. Her glasses perched on her nose gave her the look of an excited owl reporting good news.

"Did the judges say anything about the whole Mrs Colchester business?" Gemma asked, leaning forward, eager for any scrap of information to take her mind off last night.

"Nothing specific. They just lamented how foul play is a terrible business and not keeping with the idea of community spirit," Mavis said, waving a dismissive hand. "They confirmed she's been disqualified from the competition."

"That's good news, at least," Gemma said. "There's no place for cheaters around here." Mavis's tale of horticultural triumph was cut short as the bell above the door announced a new arrival. At last, a customer, Gemma thought, as she glanced up, her professional smile at the ready. The customer, a man in his thirties, was wearing a black buttoned shirt and dark blue designer jeans.

"Good morning," he began, approaching the counter, "I'm looking for a science fiction series that's ... well, imaginative, I suppose, focusing on positive themes? Something action packed, but not too violent?" He paused. "I read a lot of military science fiction, but I'd like something a little less intense for a change."

"Ah," Gemma said. "I have just the thing." She

beckoned him to follow her and stopped next to the science fiction shelves. "Here we are," she said, as her hand swept over a colourful array of spines before extracting three volumes. "The Diary of a Martian series. It's penned for the younger crowd but has a loyal following among adults as well."

"How young?" the man asked.

"Not too young. A middle-grade reading level. Think Artemis Fowl, Percy Jackson or the first three Harry Potter books. That sort of thing," Gemma said.

"Sounds perfect." The man tilted his head, curiosity piqued as he scanned the covers depicting Martian landscapes and childlike wonder.

"It's a trilogy. Well, a trilogy of novels and a sidequest novella," Gemma continued, her voice enthusiastic. "It's written from the perspective of a human child growing up in a Martian colony. The future it paints is one of hope, and there's a brilliant redemption arc that resonates well with readers. It's one of my favourites."

"Great. I'll take the first one and check it out. If I like it, I'll come back for the rest," he said. His eyes lit up at the prospect of some adventures on Mars.

"Great choice. I think you'll love it," Gemma said, leading him back towards the counter. Mavis loved nothing more than seeing a customer's excitement as they embarked on a new literary voyage. As the computerised point-of-sale system beeped, the customer scanned his bank card, sealing the deal. Gemma placed the book in a Bookworm branded paper bag and handed it to the customer.

"Thank you for the recommendation," he said, wearing a massive smile. "I'm going to go home and start book one straight away."

"Enjoy," said Gemma, as the man turned and exited the shop with what Gemma thought looked like a spring in his step.

Gemma's phone buzzed with a text message from Jack. "There's a new update for the point-of-sale computer. Can I pop in sometime and install it for you?"

She tapped a quick reply into her phone. "There's the murder mystery readers' club in tonight. How about then?" Jack's response popped up almost immediately: a thumbs-up emoji.

"Jack's coming by later to do something to the computer," Gemma said to Mavis.

"Such a lovely boy, always so helpful," Mavis said, with a fond chuckle.

"Absolutely," Gemma agreed.

Business in the afternoon picked up from the quiet morning, and a steady stream of customers kept Gemma and Mavis busy. A box of Richard Osman's recent novel arrived and promptly left the shelves as quickly as Gemma could put them on display. She ordered two more boxes. As the final customers left the store, the members of the murder mystery readers' club trickled in, their animated voices filling the shop with a buzz of anticipation. Out of all the clubs and societies that used the shop as a venue, this was one of Gemma's favourites.

Judith, the club's president, made her way to Gemma. "Evening, Gemma! I'm rather excited about our debate tonight," she said, beaming and tucking a stray lock of hair behind her ear.

"Oh?" Gemma leaned forward, her curiosity piqued. "What's the topic?"

"We've been reading a modern cosy mystery this week," Judith explained. "So we're debating the merits of cosies versus traditional murder mysteries and police procedurals."

"Sounds like a fun discussion," Gemma replied, imagining the lively exchanges of opinions that were about to unfold. "I might just listen in." The club members settled in after buying drinks from the café and seated themselves in their favourite chairs.

"Welcome, everyone." Judith's voice rose above the gentle murmurs and chit chat. Her voice commanded the attention of the room, and her posture radiated enthusiasm. "I hope this week's mystery has given you all much to ponder."

A ripple of assenting nods travelled through the group, though Gemma noted the varying degrees of energy in their expressions; some faces were alight with excitement, while others held more reserved gazes. Gemma noticed that the latter were more critical of the week's club read.

"Let's dive right into our topic," Judith continued. "Tonight, we are discussing the relative merits of cosy mysteries versus traditional crime novels. Thoughts?"

A gentleman in a tweed jacket cleared his throat and adjusted his spectacles before speaking up. "In my view," he began, his voice measured, "cosies can be rather superficial. I argue they lack the psychological depth and complex storylines in which traditional murder mysteries excel."

A few heads nodded thoughtfully, considering the critique. Gemma tilted her head, pondering the idea, but she disagreed. She was about to contribute her thoughts when another person joined in.

"Ah, but there's something to be said for the emphasis on character and community," countered a woman with a warm smile. "Cosy mysteries delve into the fabric of tight-knit societies, offering us characters that grow and evolve. They might not explore the darkest corners of the mind, but they celebrate human connection and give us a complexity rooted in relationships and communal ties."

Gemma nodded. The woman was right. Cosy mysteries were as much about the characters and where they lived as they were about the murders themselves.

Judith scanned the group. She lifted her head, inviting another voice to join the debate. "Anyone else?" she asked. She had a twinkle in her eye and clearly relished the idea of a good literary debate.

A man wearing a smart green jumper over a shirt cleared his throat before he spoke up. "The settings," he began, his voice confident yet touched with a hint of criticism, "are often too idyllic, too perfect to be on the stage for murder. It strains credibility, doesn't it? The tranquillity of these small towns, the charm of their teashops and bookstores; it hardly seems the place for crime."

Across the room, a tutting sound cut through the murmurs of agreement. A woman shook her head. "On the contrary," she countered, "the serenity is precisely the point. It's escapism; intentional and crafted. These settings amplify the shock of the crime. A compelling contrast. It's not just about solving a mystery; it's about finding peace amidst the chaos, knowing that justice will restore the community's gentle rhythm."

Mavis, who sat beside Gemma, nodded vigorously. "Exactly!" she exclaimed. "They're like comfort food. Cosy mysteries wrap you up and reassure you that all will be right in the end." Gemma nodded.

The gentleman who raised the original argument nodded as he considered the different viewpoint. "I never considered that," he said. "I guess I'm just so used to gritty, hard-edged stories. I never stopped to consider that sometimes people would want something more calming."

"Any other thoughts?" Judith asked.

A new objection arose from a stern-looking woman at the back. Her frown was etched with the weariness of one who had faced this debate many times before. "They can be predictable, formulaic even. We've all seen the patterns: the unlikely detective, the convenient resolution. Where's the originality?"

The room fell into a restless hush, heads nodding in silent agreement.

But then, as if on cue, a spirited retort rose from a young woman with an eager expression. "Genres thrive on conventions," she said. "Cosy mysteries offer us familiarity, yes, but within their framework lies infinite variety. Authors play with these tropes, bend them, give us fresh perspectives. The joy is in the details, the subtle twists."

Gemma found herself buoyed by the well-articulated defence of a genre she was passionate about. She couldn't help but call out, "Hear, hear!" Her cheeks flushed red as everyone turned to look at her. Gemma sank into her chair. The lady who offered the original counterargument smiled at her.

The vibrant discussion ebbed and flowed, and Gemma felt a sense of pride that the Bookworm was alive with good-natured discussion around the written word.

Judith's voice rose above the din. "Let us remember," she began, her tone both gentle and firm, "that cosy mysteries hold a dear place in our hearts for a reason." The room fell into a respectful silence, every eye fixed on her. "They weave together the threads of mystery with an embracing warmth, a comfort that shelters us from the harsh realities of the real world." Gemma leaned forward, hanging on Judith's every word. She certainly had a way of commanding the room. "These stories are more than just pages bound by spine and glue; they are worlds where community prevails and relationships matter. Where the sharp edges of the world are softened, and moral resolutions remind us of the good in humanity." Gemma felt a swell of pride for the genre she so adored as she nodded in agreement. "Cosy mysteries," Judith concluded, her eyes sweeping across the group, "are not merely tales to pass the time but lifelines to those seeking solace in a story well told." Nods rippled through the crowd like waves, even from those who had voiced their scepticism moments before.

As the group murmured among themselves, the bell above the door jingled. Gemma's attention shifted as Jack stepped inside. She greeted him with an enthusiastic wave, her smile brightening the already light-filled shop.

"Jack, how lovely to see you!" Mavis said as she bustled to the counter alongside Gemma.

"Always happy to lend a hand," Jack replied with a

grin as he settled into the chair behind the counter next to Gemma. He exuded a quiet confidence, the kind that came from knowing one's way around computers.

"Can I get you anything?" Mavis offered.

"A coffee would be lovely, thank you," Jack said. Mavis nodded and turned towards the café.

# Chapter Twenty-Eight

Mavis bustled back to the counter and placed a steaming mug of black coffee brimming with sugar, just how he liked it, in front of Jack. He nodded his thanks as his fingers glided across the computer keyboard to start the software update on the point-of-sale system.

"What does this update give us?" asked Gemma.

"Bug fixes and security patches mostly," he said without looking up, the screen reflecting in his eyes. "Can't be too careful nowadays, what with everything connected to the internet."

"Very wise," Gemma said with a thoughtful nod.

Mavis sat beside her. "Jack, I must thank you again for allowing me the use of your cameras. They were like guardian angels looking over my garden."

"No problem at all, Mavis," Jack said with a genuine

smile, his attention momentarily diverted from the screen. "How do you think it went with the judges?"

"Oh," Mavis said, her expression folding into a mock pout, "those judges could outplay professionals at a poker table. Nothing but 'umms' and 'ahhs,' not a hint of favour or disdain." She chuckled. "Still, one can hope."

"Your garden is excellent, Mavis. If there's any justice, yours will come out on top," Jack said.

A modest blush coloured Mavis's cheeks, and she clasped her hands together. "Well, I have my fingers crossed, but you haven't seen the others. Some of them are very good indeed."

Gemma leaned closer to the computer screen, inspecting the monotonous progress bar of the software update. Jack tapped his fingers rhythmically on the counter, but then sat up straight and turned to Gemma.

"Oh, you'll never guess who I saw today," said Jack.

"Who's that?"

"George's girlfriend, or ex-girlfriend now, I guess. She was walking through town earlier," Jack said.

Gemma looked up in surprise. "Oh, I hadn't realised he had a girlfriend. Tell me about her. What's she like?" Gemma asked as she tilted her head towards Mavis, then back at Jack. In a voice barely above a whisper, she confided, "Although we're not supposed to be discussing George's case," she said, as she smiled at Jack. "It's ... complicated."

"Ah, okay. Forget I mentioned it. Sorry," he said, returning his attention to the point-of-sale system.

"Although ..." Gemma interjected, the irresistible pull of intrigue drawing her back in, "no harm in hearing about George's girlfriend, right?" It was a balancing act, tiptoeing around the edges of propriety and curiosity.

Jack smiled at Gemma. "Of course," he said, a willing accomplice in their not-quite investigation. "No harm at all."

"Her name is Lily Thomas," Jack said. "She was in my year at school."

"Did you know her well?" Gemma asked, leaning against the counter, her curiosity piqued.

Jack chuckled, glancing up. "Not really. She ran with the popular crowd, and I ... Well, let's just say I wasn't exactly on their radar. Would be surprised if she even knew my name, even when I sat behind her in German and geography."

"Oh, don't sell yourself short, Jack," Gemma said. "Everyone brings something special to the table."

"Nah, it's fine." Jack shrugged off the compliment with ease.

"So, what's the story between Lily and George?" Gemma asked, pressing on. "Were they still together when George ... you know?"

Jack hesitated. "I'm not sure about the details. I

heard their relationship was quite fraught, but that's all hearsay. Can't say for certain."

"Fraught? Interesting," Gemma murmured, more to herself than anyone else. It was the first whisper she'd heard of George being romantically entangled.

"Does Lily work around here?" Mavis interjected.

"Yep, at that fancy hair salon on King Street. The new one in the old bank building," Jack replied.

"King Street, hmm," Gemma mused aloud. The gears of her mind were already turning. Gemma's lips twisted as she made a humming noise.

"That sounds like a plan forming," Mavis said, her eyes crinkling with a knowing smile. "You're plotting something, I can tell."

A mischievous grin played on Gemma's lips. "I think a trip to that hair salon on King Street might be in order," she said, tilting her head to one side as she picked up the end of her ponytail and inspected the ends. "It has been a while since I went to the hairdressers. Could do with getting these split ends sorted, and David's taking me out at the weekend ..." Gemma paused and smiled. "Time I treat myself to a cut and blow dry."

Jack chuckled while finishing the update installation. "I thought you might find that information interesting," he said, arching an eyebrow.

"I'm not investigating, of course," Gemma clarified with a wink. "Just getting my hair done. Want to look my best when I go out with David."

"Certainly doesn't sound like investigating to me. If Lily is there and the one cutting your hair ... Well ... What a coincidence," Mavis said, amusement twinkling in her eyes.

"Precisely," Gemma said with a nod.

Jack stood, stretching his back after the time spent hunched over the computer. "All set now," he announced, giving the screen a satisfying pat.

"Thank you, Jack," Gemma said, her appreciation genuine for more than just his technical skills.

"Good luck with the investigation ..." He paused, then smiled. "I mean, haircut."

"Yes, it's just a haircut," Gemma said, her chuckle softening the words.

"Of course," Jack said as he grinned. "I'll see you both soon." He walked to the other side of the counter and headed towards the door.

"Bye, Jack," said Gemma.

"Toodle-oo," said Mavis.

As the last members of the murder mystery club gathered their belongings and left the store, Gemma turned off the lights for another day. She and Mavis locked the door and headed home.

## Chapter Twenty-Nine

The next day, bright and early, Gemma approached the Bookworm with a bounce in her step. The rattling of metal against the marketplace drew her attention to where Geoff Dunsworth, the affable builder, had unhitched a compact digger from behind his flat-bed truck.

"Morning, Gemma!" Geoff called out, wiping his brow with the back of his hand. "Big day today."

"Indeed, it is," Gemma replied, her eyes bright with anticipation. "I can't wait to see the new café extension take shape."

"First things first. We've got to get these foundations dug," Geoff said, patting the side of the digger. "The window you had from us is holding up well too, I hope?"

"Perfect," Gemma said.

With a hearty laugh, Geoff signalled for his crew, who had just arrived, to manoeuvre the digger towards the back of the building.

Gemma unlocked the front door of the Bookworm and was greeted by the familiar sight of endless spines of books lining the shelves.

"Good morning," Ellie called out as she followed Gemma into the shop.

Gemma turned to face her. The swell of her belly announced the imminent arrival of new life, a fact that Ellie carried with grace. "Ellie, you're here early! Are you feeling alright?" Gemma asked with concern in her voice.

"Never better," Ellie replied. "This little one has been playing football all night," she said, patting her stomach. "Thought I'd get the day started and get here early."

"Make sure Sienna handles more table service today so you can take it easy," Gemma instructed. "And head off early this afternoon."

"Will do." Ellie chuckled, resting a hand on her pronounced curve. "At least I can still see my toes; I consider that a win."

Gemma laughed as Ellie headed towards the café. Gemma walked into her private office and pulled her phone from her back pocket to check the time. It had just gone nine in the morning. She sat down behind her desk and dialled the number for the hair salon.

"Hello, I'd like to book an appointment for a cut and blow dry," she said into the receiver. A brief silence filled the air before she continued. "Could I have Lily, please?" Gemma listened attentively, nodding to the affirmation at the other end of the line. "Yes, 11am works. Thank you." Gemma hung up the phone after giving her name and number just as the bell above the door jangled.

"Yoo-hoo," Mavis called out.

Gemma left the office to meet her. "Morning, Mavis. How are you?"

"Morning, Gemma," Mavis said as she hung her coat on the stand.

"I just booked myself that haircut over at the salon," Gemma said with a smile.

"Definitely not investigating," Mavis whispered as she smiled at Gemma.

Gemma smiled. "Just getting a haircut ... Just happens to be with the murder victim's ex-girlfriend. Total coincidence."

"Perfectly normal," said Mavis.

With their laughter fading, they busied themselves among the shelves, straightening books and making sure the shop was presentable. The rest of the morning ambled along to a steady stream of customers buying books and then being convinced to get a coffee and slice of cake using their generous customer discount.

Gemma glanced at the wall clock behind the

counter, its ticking hands nudging her towards the time of her appointment. With a gentle pat on Mavis's arm and the affectionate assurance that all would be well in her absence, Gemma stepped out from the shop and into the marketplace. It was a beautiful, sunny day with only a few clouds in sight.

Gemma walked past Cynthia's store, which was still closed. She stopped by a bench and looked up at the window above the shop where Cynthia lived, wondering what she was doing at the moment. A sharp sense of pity, tinged with a hint of suspicion, hit Gemma.

Gemma had been thinking about this while lying in bed the previous night. Cynthia's letter told a grim story of intimidation, abuse and fear, yet Gemma couldn't help wondering if Cynthia's letter was a clever ruse; a distraction. These thoughts didn't sit well with Gemma, as she did feel sorry for her, but she didn't have any proof that Cynthia was telling the truth. All she had was a letter and a brick through her window. She pushed these thoughts to the back of her mind and continued to the salon.

Upon entering, the warm hum of hairdryers and the soft murmur of conversation greeted her. The lady at the appointment desk offered Gemma a smile.

"Morning, I've an 11am appointment with Lily," said Gemma.

"Good morning. Is it Gemma?" the receptionist asked, her fingers dancing over the keyboard.

"That's right," Gemma said. The receptionist ushered Gemma over to a chair at the back wall of the salon.

"Please, take a seat. Could I get you anything to drink? Tea? Coffee?"

"A cup of tea would be lovely. With a dash of milk and no sugar, thank you." Gemma replied, easing herself onto the plush seat, her gaze wandering through the array of vibrant hair product bottles lining the shelves.

Moments later, a young woman emerged from the back of the salon. She wore smart jeans and a black blouse embroidered with the salon's logo. Gemma felt a burst of butterflies in her tummy.

"Hi, I'm Lily," she introduced herself. "What are we doing for you today?"

"Hello, Lily. I'd like a few inches off and the layers neatened?" Gemma asked, her voice friendly and encouraging.

"Of course. Let's start with washing your hair," Lily said, gesturing Gemma over to a sink. Gemma sat and leaned back, and Lily began wetting her hair after checking that the water temperature wasn't too hot. As she massaged in the shampoo, Lily sparked up a tentative conversation, as hair stylists do. "You run the bookshop, don't you? I've passed by it so many times."

"Yes, that's me," Gemma said. "There's nothing quite like being surrounded by books all day. It has its own set of challenges, but I wouldn't trade it for the world."

They fell into a comfortable chat about the quirks of small business ownership and the usual conversations about holidays. Gemma listened with genuine interest as Lily described the satisfaction of a well-executed hairstyle. Even amidst the idle chit-chat, Gemma could sense something off about Lily. The conversation was flowing but mechanical. Lily finished washing and conditioning Gemma's hair, wrapping her head in a towel before ushering her to another chair in front of a mirror.

Lily removed the towel and brushed Gemma's hair before she picked up some scissors and began cutting with the ease of a seasoned artist. The scent of hair products, a mix of sweet coconut and ammonia chemicals, drifted through the air, creating a comforting atmosphere much like at the bookworm with its aroma of coffee and cake. The conversation gradually steered towards more local matters in the town, beginning with the local food fair that coming weekend.

This was it. Gemma was going to probe. Her mouth felt dry, as she didn't want to go too fast like she did with Cynthia. "Speaking of local happenings," Gemma ventured, watching Lily's reflection for any sign of discomfort, "it's been such a shock with what happened at St Peter's."

Lily paused mid-cut, her eyes meeting Gemma's in the mirror before resuming her task with a forced steadiness. "Yes, it was a terrible ordeal," she acknowledged, her voice a notch quieter than before. "I don't know if you know, but the man who died, George, he was my ex-boyfriend. We split up about a week before he died."

Gemma feigned surprise, her brows lifting in a well-practiced innocence. "Oh ... I'm sorry for your loss. I didn't know you and him dated," she said. "That ordeal must have been so difficult for you."

There was a palpable pause as Lily set the scissors aside, her gaze locking with Gemma's in the reflection. "This is going to sound awful," Lily began, her tone edged with a complex mix of relief and resignation, "but I'm not sad that George is gone."

# Chapter Thirty

Gemma's reflection in the mirror faltered for a moment. She opened her mouth, but nothing came out. Before she could find the words, Lily continued.

"I sound like an awful person."

"No, you don't. There are always two sides to every story," Gemma replied carefully, her thoughtful gaze met Lily's in the mirror. "What is your story if you don't mind me asking?"

With a sigh, Lily began unravelling the tale of her life with George. "He was rough ... very rough with me. If he was frustrated or stressed, then it made him lash out," she confessed, her hands never ceasing their work, even as her voice wavered.

Gemma's heart clenched in sympathy. "I'm so sorry, Lily." Her response was genuine. As Gemma refocused on Lily's reflection, her eyes homed in on something she hadn't noticed before; makeup meant to conceal a bruise near her eye.

"Is that bruise his handy work?" Gemma asked, her voice low as she tried to be discreet.

Lily paused, meeting Gemma's gaze again in the mirror. "Yes," she admitted. "It's healing, but it was hard to conceal at first."

Gemma watched as Lily resumed trimming her hair. Gemma admired her resilience, as she couldn't imagine what it would be like to be in a relationship where you're treated that badly. When Gemma and David were first together, she never felt unsafe or threatened in any way. The problems she thought her relationship endured at the time paled in comparison.

"Why not leave if it was that bad?" asked Gemma.

Lily set the scissors down with a clatter and sighed, her fingers brushed loose locks of hair from Gemma's neck. "I tried once before. I got as far as packing a bag, but George found out," she confessed. "He made it clear," she said and paused. "He said I'd never leave him. He threatened to hurt me worse than before ... and then my family."

"You just said you had split up with him the week before his death, though. What changed?" asked Gemma.

"I found out he tried to give some drugs to my sister.

She never took them, she's not like that, but she said he'd try to give them to her for free."

"Oh my god! Why would he do that? That's awful," said Gemma.

"Yes, it is. He did it to get to me. I challenged him over it, and we had a blazing row. That was when he hit me again. At that point, I just wanted to get out, so I packed a bag and left that evening when he was out of the house."

"What on earth possesses people to do this to other people?" asked Gemma.

"That's only part of it," said Lily.

"How do you mean?"

"I'm pretty sure there was someone else," Lily said.

"Someone else? Another woman?" Lily nodded. "Oh, Lily. That's awful," Gemma said.

Lily laughed, picking up the scissors once more but not cutting. "He'd come home late, smelling of a citrus perfume. Not something a man would wear, and certainly not like any of mine."

"Citrus?" Gemma asked.

"Yeah, not lemon ... More orange, I guess, but sweeter."

"Oh, like orange blossom?" asked Gemma.

"Yeah, actually, that's exactly what it was," said Lily.

Gemma had a sudden realisation. She'd smelt orange blossom perfume only recently. Could it be a coincidence? She wouldn't say anything now, though. This was a conversation to have with Mavis.

"I never caught him at it. He was far too good at covering his tracks." Lily shook her head, her hands resuming their work with newfound precision. "But every time he came back reeking of that perfume, I knew it wasn't just business keeping him out late. He didn't even try to hide it. I don't think he cared."

Gemma felt the full weight of Lily's story, and it was quite distressing. Being entangled with a man like George must have been tough, and though she despised the thought of murder, she couldn't help but feel relief on Lily's behalf.

"George's line of work," Gemma ventured, "what did he do?"

Lily glanced at her through the mirror. "Drugs," she said matter-of-factly, as if revealing a preference for tea over coffee. "As I said, he tried to give some to my sister to get her hooked."

"Give some for free so you pay for more?" asked Gemma.

"Yes. Very callous. He never kept them in the house, though, so it was always difficult to prove."

Gemma feigned shock and concern. "Did you know who he worked with?" she asked.

"No. George was secretive about everything, and I learned early on to stay out of it." Her voice was flat, resigned. "Sometimes, I hoped he'd get caught. Maybe then I'd be free."

The admission hung in the air, dense and potent. Gemma remained silent, allowing Lily the space to breathe. Again, Gemma found herself empathetic to Lily's plight. It's a sorry situation when you hope your boyfriend gets arrested for dealing drugs because it would make your life safer. As Lily was being quite open, Gemma thought she would probe further.

"If you had already split up with him, I guess you don't know what happened the night he died?" Gemma asked.

"No, I hadn't spoken to him since we broke up. I was fearful that he might try to get some kind of revenge on me for leaving, but nothing happened. I told my sister to stay away from him too," said Lily.

"Did the police ask if you saw him that night?" Gemma enquired, her tone soft but insistent.

Lily nodded. "Yes, they did, and I told them I hadn't seen him. I told them about the abuse he had put me through, and they asked where I was that night."

"What did you tell them?"

"I've been crashing at a friend's house since we broke up. I needed some space. My friend was away for a few days for work, so I had some alone time to think." Lily let out a laugh. "I didn't see anyone that evening. I know how this all looks ..."

"How does it look?" Gemma leaned forward, encouraging Lily to continue.

"Like I had every reason to want him dead after ..." She hesitated. "Well, you know what he did to me and then my sister," Lily admitted, her fingers pausing for a fraction of a second before resuming their task. "If they hadn't arrested that homeless man, I'd probably be their number one suspect. I wouldn't blame the police for thinking that."

Gemma absorbed this with a quiet "hmm" and thought to herself that there was an orderly queue of people wishing the same fate for George. "You must have been quite surprised when they arrested that man. John, I think his name is," she said, trying to downplay how much she knew.

"Surprised, yes. I mean, why would he want to murder George?" Lily's question lingered in the air.

"I heard a rumour that George had been bullying him," Gemma said.

"Wouldn't surprise me." Lily's lips tightened into a thin line. "George treated everyone like they were beneath him. Always calculating what he could get out of people. A defenceless man would be just another target for him."

The salon's atmosphere remained lively around them, filled with the drone of hairdryers and idle chit-chat, yet the space between Gemma and Lily felt isolated.

Gemma shifted her gaze away from the reflection, settling on a stack of magazines by her side. The glossy covers boasted bold headlines and promised escapism, but the true stories, she knew, were unfolding right here amid the hum of everyday life.

Gemma felt the tension that had wound tightly around the room as Lily's hands moved through her hair, working in layers with the scissors. They sat in silence for a while as Lily worked.

"What will you do now?" Gemma finally asked.

"Actually," Lily began, her voice lighter, "I've been thinking about entering this hairdressing competition. It's quite prestigious." A hint of excitement crept into her tone. The first genuine spark Gemma had seen in the young stylist since their conversation began.

"Really? That sounds wonderful, Lily." Gemma offered a supportive smile. "You're talented. I'm sure you will do well."

Lily's eyes met hers in the reflection, a glimmer of hope shining in them. "Thanks, Gemma. It feels good to focus on myself for a change."

"If you ever need someone to talk to or just want to escape, the Bookworm is always open." Gemma's invitation was sincere. "A good chat over a cuppa can do wonders, and I'll throw in some cakes." Gemma took one of her Bookworm business cards from her pocket and handed it to Lily. "Also, my phone number is on here if you just want to phone for a chat."

"Thanks. I might just take you up on that," Lily said, her gratitude clear.

With her haircut now complete and her hair dried, Lily held up a mirror so Gemma could admire her handiwork from the back. "It's lovely, thank you," she said, catching Lily's eye one last time in the mirror before rising from the chair. She was led to the front desk of the salon so she could pay, and then she headed towards the door.

"Bye, Lily. Take care of yourself," Gemma said.

"It was lovely to meet you, Gemma. Thank you so much for listening."

Gemma stepped out into the street. Mavis would be eager to hear about everything Gemma knew. The walk was short, yet it gave her enough time to order her thoughts. The revelations of George's actions, including his cheating, the admission of Lily's abuse and the plight of an accused homeless man swirled within her. There was a lot to process, and she wanted to get Mavis's thoughts.

Gemma heard a voice in her head. It was David telling her not to get involved. She scrunched her face at the thought. She knew she should just leave it and not say anything, but she just couldn't help herself. All she was going to do was chat with Mavis. What harm could that cause?

## Chapter Thirty-One

Later that evening, Gemma stepped into Mavis's dining room, eager to share the day's information. A sense of comfort settled over her as she watched Mavis bustle about with mugs of coffee and heard the rustle of a biscuit packet as chocolate hobnobs appeared on a floral plate. Mavis sat next to Gemma, her pen poised, ready to leap up and make notes on the large sheets of paper taped on her dining room wall.

"Go on, then," Mavis urged. "What did Lily say? You were all hush-hush at the shop."

Gemma took a sip of her coffee. "Well, it was quite revealing," Gemma said. "George was ... he was terrible to her, Mavis." Gemma's voice was lower than usual, as if whispering a dark secret. "He was quite abusive, both verbally and physically. She even had a bruise still healing near her eye, concealed with makeup."

Mavis's eyes widened in horror as she reached for a hobnob, her hand trembling ever so slightly. "That's awful, Gemma," she whispered, biting into the biscuit with less than her usual gusto.

"More than that," Gemma continued. "She tried to leave him once, but he threatened her. Said he'd hurt her and her family if she did."

"Good heavens!" Mavis set her biscuit back on the plate. She reached across the table to squeeze Gemma's hand. "No one should live in fear like that. It's atrocious." Mavis grabbed her pen and started scribbling on the murder board.

"Yes, it's a terrible way to live," Gemma agreed, reaching for a biscuit herself. "She was trapped in that relationship with nowhere to go. But Lily did say that she had finally left him a week before he died."

Mavis turned to face Gemma. "Oh, interesting. Why did she finally decide to leave if he'd threatened her?"

"Lily found out George had offered drugs to her younger sister to presumably get her hooked." Mavis gasped in shock. "He probably did that deliberately to get at Lily via her sister. A way of exerting control."

"Despicable," said Mavis.

"Lily had enough at that point and packed a bag to leave. That was after he hit her, leaving the bruise. She had been staying at a friend's house since." Gemma swirled the coffee in her mug, watching the steam rise like whispers. "George wasn't just an abusive bully,

Mavis," Gemma began. Her voice was steady despite the turmoil that churned inside her. "He was probably unfaithful to Lily too. She hinted at her suspicion of another woman being involved."

Mavis sat forward. "Another woman? And he had the audacity to cage Lily in such a toxic bond?" Her tone was laced with indignation.

"Yes, although she'd never caught him," said Gemma. "Lily described how he'd return home sometimes smelling of women's perfume, orange blossom, to be precise."

"Orange blossom, you say ..." Mavis echoed, her eyebrows raised. Gemma watched as realisation dawned in Mavis's sharp eyes. "Rhianna? Surely not. She's devoted to that lovely James."

"Yes. Remember at the summer fair?" Gemma said as she leaned forward. "I mentioned I liked her perfume. It was orange blossom too."

"Yes, I remember!" Mavis's voice spiked with surprise before softening again. "Could it be a coincidence?"

"Or, could it just be a popular perfume. Hard to say," Gemma said as she picked up another chocolate hobnob. "But it's a lead worth exploring. I need to drop it into casual conversation somehow."

"Careful," Mavis said. "We must tread lightly. We don't want to stir a hornet's nest or wrongfully accuse her, or even make poor James think his girlfriend is up to no good, when most likely she will be innocent. She doesn't seem the type."

"Of course," Gemma assured her, though her mind raced with possibilities. "It's all speculative until we know more."

"Speculative indeed." Mavis reached for her pen and scribbled more notes across the murder board. "But you have an eye for detail, Gemma. And a nose for the truth, it seems."

"Let's hope so." Gemma smiled, reaching for her mug to get a sip before setting it back down with a delicate clink. "There's more," Gemma said. "I asked Lily about George's line of work."

"Line of work?" Mavis echoed, her eyebrow arching in amusement. "That's an interesting way of describing his 'dealings'."

Gemma chuckled. "Not sure what I was thinking. It just kind of ... came out," she said, shaking her head at the understatement. "Lily confirmed he was a drug dealer, but it was always kept away from the house. Of course, I feigned ignorance to all of it."

"Smart," Mavis said, nodding. "And what Lily said lends credence to Cynthia's story about George dealing in her shop."

"Yes, it does," Gemma said. "What's more, Lily said she often hoped he would be arrested for it, not that she would ever grass him up."

"Oh my," said Mavis.

"Having him arrested would certainly give her the opportunity to get away from him."

"You can't fault her logic," Mavis said. There was a pause before Mavis asked, "Did Lily say anything else?"

"Yes," said Gemma. "I saved the best, or worst, depending on how you look at it, to the end."

"Goodness," said Mavis.

"The biggest shock came when Lily admitted she was glad that he was dead."

Mavis gasped, her hand raised to cover her mouth. "That is quite the admission."

"It is," Gemma agreed. "It took me quite by surprise. She didn't even try to hide it. Said his death finally gave her an escape from his abuse and any further torment. Even more so than hoping he would be arrested for dealing drugs."

"Escaping a prison without bars," Mavis murmured to herself as her pen hovered above the paper on the wall, reluctant to commit such a private confession to their chronicle of events.

"That's one way to put it," Gemma said, folding her hands on the table. "With the mental and physical torment Lily endured, while murder is undeniably wrong, I can't blame her for feeling that way. Stress, anxiety and fear can play terrible tricks on the mind. Even though she'd left him, she was still living in fear."

"Nobody could blame her thoughts in this situation, even if they were twisted," Mavis conceded, her voice hollow with sadness.

Gemma glanced out the window into Mavis's picture-perfect garden, deep in thought as she wrestled with the idea that anyone could be glad another human was dead to resolve a dire personal circumstance. Gemma couldn't imagine ever being in such a situation.

Mavis leaned forward, her eyes alight with curiosity. "Gemma," she began in a hushed tone, "it feels wrong to even say this, but do you think Lily could have been involved in his murder? Like a crime of passion?"

Gemma pursed her lips as she considered the question. "My gut says no," she replied. "Lily's openness about not mourning George ... I can't see it as a front. If she were involved, wouldn't she play the part of the bereaved girlfriend to avoid suspicion?"

"Perhaps," Mavis pondered, tapping her pen against her chin, "Lily feels safe to express such sentiments now that John's been arrested."

"That's true," Gemma conceded, though she shook her head slightly, as if to dispel the thought. "But even then, if she had a hand in his death, surely silence would serve her better." She sighed. "I can't completely rule her out, but I'm not convinced Lily could do it." Gemma paused. "Or maybe I just don't want to believe she could kill."

"Does she have an alibi?" Mavis said.

"I asked that, and she doesn't," Gemma confirmed.

"She said she was alone, staying at a friend's house, but her friend was away on a business trip; no one saw her after she finished work that day. Lily told me she had discussed this with the police already. She knows that if John hadn't been arrested, then she may have been considered a suspect."

"If we look at this logically, Lily had the motive to murder George. She was mentally and physically abused," said Mavis.

"Yes, we could argue she had the motive. A potential crime of passion. A young woman pushed to the limits whose alibi we can't verify. We can't say for sure she stayed in that evening," said Gemma.

"And as for opportunity," said Mavis, "could she gain access to the church and commit a murder without leaving DNA evidence, get John intoxicated on vodka and ketamine and then get him to carry out the crime to the point the police say the evidence is compelling against him?"

Gemma chuckled. "Well, when you say it like that, it seems very unlikely," Gemma said. "Unless ..."

"Unless she was in cahoots with John and they planned it together?" Mavis suggested.

"It's a possibility, I guess, but Lily seemed unaware that George had been bullying John. She could be deceiving us, though," said Gemma. "One to ponder on."

Mavis nodded, her gaze thoughtful as she scribbled

additional notes. "Your appointment with Lily at the hairdresser's has certainly provided us with much to think about," said Mavis.

"And I came away with a nice hairdo, too," Gemma said with a smile to lighten the tone of the night's revelations.

"Very nice it is too," Mavis agreed.

Gemma stood and stretched her arms. "For us, though, the next step is confirming whether Rhianna is George's mystery woman," she said. "I'm about eighty percent sure it's her, based on the scent of the perfume. I know it's gut instinct, but I've always followed my gut."

"Discretion will be key," Mavis said as she stood. "We must tread carefully."

"Of course," Gemma agreed, her mind already turning over their next steps. "I haven't quite figured out my approach yet."

"Time enough for that another day," Mavis said. "It's getting late. You should head on home."

"Yes, I still need to give Baxter his dinner and let him out in the garden," said Gemma. With that, Gemma headed towards the front door.

## Chapter Thirty-Two

On Sunday, Gemma surveyed the bustling high street, transformed into a vibrant sea of stalls and strings of bunting for the summer food festival. The smell of sizzling burgers mingled with the aroma of fresh pastries created an atmosphere that was both homey and exciting. She stood behind the Bookworm's stall, displaying an array of popular books on a table next to an espresso machine.

"Sienna, remind me to sample those fancy doughnuts from that new local company. I spotted them further up King Street," Gemma said. "If they're as delicious as they look, we might stock them at the café."

Sienna flashed a grin. "Sure thing, Gemma. I've had them a few times, and they're amazing. Especially the salted caramel one."

The war memorial gardens at the top of the high

street thrummed with the sound of live music from a group of local musicians, lending a cultural heartbeat to the day. Gemma sat back in a camping chair and took in the sights and smells of the food festival as she drank a coffee that Sienna had made her.

Unexpectedly, Mavis appeared, weaving through the crowd with her silver hair reflecting sunlight and her signature handbag looped over her arm. Mavis was supposed to be off this weekend, but there she was, dressed as smartly as always.

"You're supposed to be putting your feet up," said Gemma.

"I know, but I thought I'd pop into town and look around," she said.

"Well, stay for a cup of tea," Gemma said, as Sienna prepared her a cup of Earl Grey from the insulated urn of hot water.

"Lovely," said Mavis as she accepted the tea from Sienna and settled into a spare camping chair next to Gemma behind the table.

The stall enjoyed a steady stream of customers; they came for the coffee and cake, and many left with a book tucked under their arms. It was during a lull in activity that a man in his late forties approached, eyeing the literary spread with interest.

"Ah, Lee Child," he said, picking up a copy of *The Killing Floor*. "Jack Reacher's quite the character, isn't he?"

"Absolutely," Gemma replied, her eyes lighting up at the thought of discussing a well-known thriller. "There's something satisfying about seeing the little guy take on the big imperfect world, isn't there?"

"Vigilante justice," the man mused, flipping the book over in his hands. "Not that I'm endorsing it in real life, but in fiction, it can be quite the thrill."

"Definitely," Gemma agreed, her laughter mingling with his. "A bit of escapism never hurt anyone. Makes us root for the underdog."

"I'll take it," said the man. "Not read the first Jack Reacher book for a very long time."

"Enjoy your read," Gemma said, as the man handed over the payment. He gave a nod of thanks and wandered off, disappearing into the sea of festival-goers.

"I do like seeing a happy reader," Gemma said to Mavis, who nodded.

The scent of freshly baked bread and simmering curries wafted down the street as the food fair was in full swing. Norman, James and Rhianna meandered down King Street towards Gemma. The Bookworm's cosy stall brimmed with eager customers, but Gemma's keen eye caught the trio's approach before they reached her.

"Morning, Gemma! Mavis!" Norman called out, his voice carrying over the clamour of the festival.

"Hello," Mavis said, smiling at them.

"Good morning," Gemma echoed, her gaze lingering on Rhianna for a moment longer than the others. The distinct fragrance of orange blossom tickled her nose, triggering a silent alarm in her head. Without a word, she shot Mavis a glance that spoke volumes. Mavis returned the look with a slight nod, a silent conversation passing between them.

"Isn't it just a lovely day for the fair?" Mavis continued.

"Absolutely. We were going to head into the memorial gardens and see what entertainment is on this afternoon," Rhianna said, unaware of the looks exchanged between Gemma and Mavis. Her smile was as bright as the summer sun shining down on them.

As they chatted about the festivities, a tall, bald man crept closer to the stall. Gemma's intuition prickled, and the hairs on her arms seemed to stand to attention; something about the way he slinked forward set off alarm bells in her mind. She recalled Ellie's description of a suspicious character last week and wondered if this could be the same person.

"Can I help you with anything?" Gemma asked, trying to sound casual as she addressed the stranger.

He didn't reply, his hand already darting into his bag. In one swift motion, he withdrew a tin of paint and flung its contents across the carefully arranged books. A collective gasp rippled through the crowd as the man turned and ran away from the stall.

"Hey!" James shouted, springing into action. He dashed after the vandal, disappearing into the crowd.

"James, be careful!" Rhianna's voice rang with panic, but her plea was lost in the commotion.

With wide eyes, Mavis gasped in shock, and Gemma put her hand on Mavis's arm. "Catch your breath," Gemma said, her concern clear as she watched Mavis take slow, deliberate breaths.

"Who would do such a thing?" Mavis murmured.

Gemma offered a comforting pat on Mavis's arm. Gemma felt like bursting into tears but tried hard to suppress her feelings to help calm Mavis and Sienna.

Norman glanced down the high street with a look of concern on his face. "I'm going to find James," he announced, leaving Rhianna at the stall with Gemma.

"Be careful!" Gemma called after him. She turned her attention back to the splattered paperbacks, her fingers lifting each casualty from the table. Quite a few books had borne the brunt of the paint attack.

"What drives some people to do this?" she muttered, straightening up to find Rhianna's gaze on her.

"I don't know. Some people are just wired wrong," Rhianna replied.

Offering a smile, Gemma sought to lighten the mood. "Is that the orange blossom perfume you are wearing again? You must tell me where you got it from. It's lovely."

"Thank you," Rhianna responded, a hint of warmth in her polite tone. "It's Jo Malone. You can layer them in different fragrances, but this is just orange blossom on its own."

"I might have to treat myself," Gemma said. "I was getting my hair done the other day," she said, pointing her finger down King Street to the hair salon. "Lily, George's ex; she was my hairdresser." Gemma watched Rhianna closely, noting the almost imperceptible tightening around her eyes. "We got talking, and Lily mentioned orange blossom perfume too. I knew it reminded me of someone." Gemma paused while looking at Rhianna.

Rhianna stiffened, but then smiled. "Well, it is a popular fragrance."

"Yes, I know. It just reminded me, that's all," Gemma said. She thought it best not to push any further. Before they could say anything else, James reappeared, his chest heaving from running, his forehead dotted with sweat. "He was too fast," he panted, disappointment evident.

Norman followed shortly, his disapproval clear. "You shouldn't have chased him, James. He could've been dangerous."

"Sorry, Dad. It was just instinct," James said in defence, his shoulders slumped slightly under Norman's stern gaze.

"Did anyone recognise him?" Gemma interjected, hoping to grasp some clue from the chaos. "We think he came into our bookshop earlier in the week."

Heads shook in unison. "No idea," James said.

Rhianna looped her arm through James's, her earlier poise restored but laced with urgency. "Let's go home. That is quite enough excitement for one day," she said.

"No, let's get food first," James said, still catching his breath. "I could do with a burger after all that running." Rhianna nodded.

"Take care," Gemma said. The trio bid their farewells and departed. Gemma turned to Mavis. "What did you think of that when I brought up Lily?" she whispered, her voice barely rising above the hum of the surrounding festival.

Mavis nodded. "She looked unsettled, but she covered it well." she said with a knowing tilt of her head.

"Do you think she was with George?" Gemma asked.

"Hmm," Mavis said with pursed lips. "I'm not sure."

"Me neither, Mavis. I wonder if James has ever suspected anything? Poor thing," said Gemma.

## Chapter Thirty-Three

It was Monday morning, the day after the food fair, and Gemma was back in the Bookworm. She was trying not to think about the paint attack, as it increased her heart rate with anxiety, and failing miserably; the thought kept entering her mind. The bell above the door jingled as a customer entered the shop, and she couldn't help but flinch. Her heart skipped as she peered around the corner of the local authors' display.

Gemma turned to Mavis. "I'm a little on edge today," she said.

"I doubt he'd have the gumption to show his face here after yesterday's spectacle," Mavis said, her voice carrying from where she was tidying the biographies section.

Gemma pursed her lips, trying to shake off the anxiety. "I can't help it, Mavis. Every time that bell rings, I see that tall, skinny menace with his pot of paint."

Ellie walked over from the café at the back of the store. "Morning, you two. Sienna told me about the food fair fiasco."

"It was awful, Ellie. Thankfully, only a few books were damaged, but the fact that someone would want to do that is pretty scary. Do you remember the man you said came in last week? The one who seemed all shifty?" Gemma asked.

"Vaguely, yeah. He'll be on the CCTV, won't he?" Ellie suggested, with an optimistic tilt to her voice.

"Of course! I didn't think to look," Gemma exclaimed, feeling foolish for not thinking about it sooner. She fetched her phone from the back pocket of her jeans and quickly navigated to the security camera app. With a swipe here and a press there, she found the timestamp from that day.

"Here he is," Gemma said as she expanded the image of the bald man entering the shop. A chill ran down her spine. "It's him. The same person."

Ellie squinted at the frozen frame. "That's creepy. Makes me feel all jittery inside. First, a brick through the shop window, and then knowing he went from lurking around inside the shop, to ... that." She gestured towards the market square and high street outside. "Do you think it was him who threw the brick?"

Gemma was about to say she didn't think so, but

she paused to think about it. "You know, it would make sense. Unfortunately, it wasn't caught on camera. I'd bet a pack of custard creams it was, though."

The door's bell sounded again, and Gemma looked up. She smiled as David entered. She was sure glad to see him. "Morning," Gemma said as he stepped over and planted a kiss on her cheek.

"Morning, ladies," David said, nodding towards Mavis, then Ellie. Gemma retrieved her phone, and her fingers unlocked it to reveal the paused image of the man from the food fair. She tilted the screen towards David. "This is the man who threw paint at us."

"Mmm, I don't recognise him. Could you send me that photo?" David asked as he observed the image with keen interest.

"Of course. I'll do it right now," she said, tapping on her phone to share the image.

"Would you mind if we talked in the back office for a moment? You as well, Mavis." David's request caught Gemma off guard, but she nodded, leading the way. They settled into chairs around her desk cluttered with book orders and invoices.

"Is everything alright?" Gemma asked, her eyebrows raised in concern.

He hesitated, choosing his words carefully. "We've located Cynthia," he began as he watched their expressions shift from anticipation to apprehension.

Gemma's heart began beating like a kettle drum at an orchestra. "I thought she wasn't considered missing?"

"She wasn't," David said. "But she's been involved in a hit-and-run accident near Leeds."

"Goodness gracious!" Mavis said, her hand fluttering to her chest. "Is she alright?"

David's face softened. "She's got a broken leg and some cuts and bruises, but she'll live. One of my officers is already speaking with her at the hospital, along with the local police."

Gemma leaned back in her chair. Cynthia's situation was dire, yet knowing she was alive brought a sense of relief. The room fell into a contemplative silence. "Do you have any idea who was driving? Who hit Cynthia?" asked Gemma.

David shook his head. His gaze was steady but troubled. "Cynthia mentioned to my officer that she felt as if someone had been watching her for a while before the accident. We've scoured the CCTV footage from Leeds, but whoever it was knew what they were doing. We found the car abandoned and torched."

"Torched?" Mavis's voice trembled. "As in set on fire? How dreadful."

"The driver never appeared on camera," David continued. "They abandoned the car in a blind spot, out of sight of any CCTV. And the car was reported stolen just the day before."

"Sounds professional," said Mavis.

"Yes, that's what we think too," said David.

Gemma's stomach knotted. She looked down at the grainy wood of the table, tracing a knot with her fingertip. "So Cynthia was right. She sensed danger and tried to escape it."

David nodded, his expression sombre. "It seems so."

Pushing his chair back, he stood, the legs scraping against the floor. "I should get back to the station. There's a lot to do, but I wanted you both to know what was happening."

"Thank you, David," Mavis said, her voice carrying warmth. With a grateful smile, David nodded and turned to leave.

## Chapter Thirty-Four

Gemma returned to the counter after David's unsettling visit. Cynthia Norton had been the target of a hit-and-run attack, and it was almost too much for Gemma to fathom. This was all getting very serious, as if a murder on its own wasn't serious enough, but also, drug dealing, a hit and run, vandalism ... What next?

"Tea?" Mavis offered. Gemma forced a smile as she nodded in gratitude, and Mavis bustled towards the café.

Gemma turned her attention to a recent delivery of books that needed logging on the computer and displaying on the shelves. As she scanned books, a customer approached the counter. "Afternoon, Gemma," she said.

"Hello, June. Lovely to see you," Gemma said. June

was a regular customer of the Bookworm and would buy a new book there nearly every week. "What can I help you with today?"

"I'm after that new one by Richard Osman; *We Solve Murders*. Heard anything about it?" June asked, her eagerness palpable.

"Ah, it's fantastic! We just had a new box of them arrive the other day." Gemma's spirits lifted as she spoke of one of her contemporary favourites. "A globe-trotting murder mystery filled with wit. It'll have you chuckling and guessing all the way through."

"Perfect! I loved *Thursday Murder Club*; I couldn't put it down." June's eyes sparkled, reflecting the joy only a fellow book lover could understand.

"Then you're in for a treat," Gemma assured her, handing over the hardback with a flourish. After the customer paid and left, Gemma's phone vibrated against the wooden surface of the counter. With a cautious swipe, she unlocked the screen to reveal a text message from an unrecognisable number. She read the message to herself: "If you want to know what's really happening. Farm track, parking spot, just after Ashop Road off Over Lane. 2am." The words seemed to hover before her eyes, each one laden with ominous potential. Mavis walked over carrying two cups of tea and placed them on the counter. Gemma handed her the phone. "Who do you think this is from?" Gemma asked, her voice barely above a whisper.

Mavis peered over her glasses, her lips pursed in concern. "I don't have the foggiest, but it sounds dangerous," she said.

Gemma bit her lower lip. "I wonder if it's Lily. She might know more about George's 'dealings' than she let on."

"That's a possibility," said Mavis. "She has already confided quite a lot."

"It could be her way of trying to expose what George was up to without implicating herself," said Gemma.

"Is it her phone number?"

"I don't know. I never got her number, but I think I need to find it out now. I did give her my business card which had my number on it. Yes, it must be Lily," said Gemma.

"Unless it's one of those disposable phones. What are they called … I've seen them on the TV … Burner phones. That's it," said Mavis.

"It's a line of enquiry, for sure," Gemma said, but then paused. "We need to see what's going to happen at that location at 2am, but I'm not going to skulk around a dark farm track at night like some sort of detective in a thriller. Nothing good ever happens down farm tracks in the dead of night. It could be anyone. Could be someone trying to help, or worse, someone trying to lure us into a trap."

"Good heavens, no. That would be far too dangerous," Mavis said with a shudder. But the cogs were already turning in Gemma's head, sparking an idea. She composed a new text to Jack, whose knack for gadgets had helped more than once. "Do you still have those cameras you lent Mavis for her garden?"

A reply came almost instantly, as if Jack sensed the urgency behind her text. "Yes. I got them back from Mavis once the judges had finished with her garden."

"Could you bring them? Need your help after work," Gemma replied, her plan crystallising with each sent message.

"I'm home from 4pm. Pick me up?" Jack's text read.

"Will do. Thank you," Gemma replied with a sense of determination.

She turned to Mavis with a reassuring smile, though her stomach was a tangle of nerves. "We're going to get to the bottom of this, Mavis. Without risking our necks."

Mavis watched her. "Just remember, we're booksellers, not secret agents. Be careful."

Gemma nodded, feeling the weight of responsibility settle on her shoulders. "I'll be extra cautious, Mavis," she said in assurance, her voice steady despite the flutter of apprehension in her chest. "We'll just set up those cameras and leave straight away. If anyone's about, we won't risk it." Mavis nodded, and they went about the rest of their day doing what they did best; selling books.

As the clock hands swept towards four, Gemma approached Mavis and Ellie. "You two going to be alright holding down the fort?" she asked, slipping her phone into the back pocket of her jeans.

"Go on. We've got this, don't we, Ellie?" Mavis said, casting a supportive glance towards the younger woman, who nodded.

"Absolutely," Ellie said, her voice bright.

"If there're any issues with shady characters coming in, call Geoff. He's out at the back of the café with his crew, laying the new foundations for the extension." Ellie and Mavis nodded. "His number is behind the counter next to the phone," Gemma said.

"Off you go. We'll be fine."

Gemma's car rolled to a stop in front of Jack's house, the engine idling as she waited. A moment later, Jack appeared with a backpack slung over one shoulder. He opened the door and slid into the passenger seat.

"Thanks for coming at such short notice," Gemma said, her voice filled with gratitude.

"Anytime," Jack replied, fastening his seatbelt. "So, what's the plan?"

Gemma pulled out her phone and handed it to him, displaying the cryptic message. "We received this message. We're not totally sure what it's concerning. Could be about the brick through the window, the paint attack at the food fair or even something to do with George. We're not sure," she explained, watching his reaction.

Jack's raised his brows as he read the message, and he let out a low whistle. "Wow, this is some serious stuff," he said, handing back the phone. His eyes sparkled with a mix of concern and excitement. "I feel like Q from James Bond. I only have cameras though, no bulletproof Aston Martin DB5s."

"You mean you can't reprogram a satellite to look directly at this location?" Gemma teased with a smile.

Jack laughed. "I think we'll have to stick to motion-controlled trap cameras for now," he said.

"I want to see if we can hide the camera and record whatever happens at that meeting and retrieve them tomorrow," Gemma said.

"Well, the cameras are already prepped. The batteries are charged, and I'll turn the motion alarms off so they don't make any noise when activated. We're good to go," Jack said, confirming with a nod.

Gemma smiled and started the car before driving through Belper's winding streets. It didn't take long to get there. Belper was a small town. "Here we are," Gemma announced as they arrived at the farm track.

Hedges loomed around the area, creating a natural barrier. She drove up to what looked like a small parking area at the side of the road and killed the engine. She scanned the area through the windows, searching for any signs of movement.

"Coast looks clear," Jack whispered. He grabbed his backpack and stepped out. Gemma followed suit, remaining vigilant of her surroundings. Jack moved stealthily, placing three cameras among the foliage, ensuring a panoramic view of the upcoming clandestine rendezvous. "Done," Jack said, ducking back into the car.

"Brilliant," Gemma said. She breathed a sigh of relief, feeling a rush of adrenaline as they departed from the scene and drove back to Jack's home. "Are you free tomorrow to collect the cameras?"

"Shift at the sorting office isn't until the afternoon; I can help you in the morning," Jack responded, his tone reassuring.

"Thank you, Jack. You're a lifesaver," Gemma said, allowing herself a small smile. She pulled up to the curb outside Jack's house.

"Here we are," Gemma said, the engine idling as Jack unbuckled his seatbelt. "Thanks again, Jack. I appreciate your help."

"No problem. Always happy to help. I hope you find what you're looking for on the cameras."

"Me too," Gemma said. She just wanted all this talk

of murder and drug dealing to be finished with. "I'll swing by at 9am tomorrow?"

"Perfect. See you then." With a nod, Jack stepped out onto the pavement and back towards his house.

## Chapter Thirty-Five

The next day Gemma and Jack entered the shop after retrieving the cameras from their hiding place. Mavis looked up from behind the counter. She smiled as she saw Gemma and Jack. "Did you get what you needed?"

"I hope so. The cameras were still there, so that's a good thing," Gemma replied.

"Good thing they were camouflaged, and it would have been dark," Jack added, patting his backpack where the cameras now lay hidden.

"Let's go into the office and take a look," Gemma said. She glanced towards Sienna, who was wiping down tables in the café. "Sienna, could you watch the front for us?"

"Of course," Sienna said.

With a nod of gratitude, Gemma led the way to the

back office. Mavis shuffled along beside her, and Jack followed. As the door shut, sealing them away from the rest of the world, Gemma felt a surge of determination.

Jack unzipped his backpack and retrieved his laptop. The soft whirr of the machine coming to life broke the silence of the back office. With swift clicks, he extracted the SD card from each camera, slotted them into the side of his computer and, one by one, copied the video files from the memory cards. Jack dragged the files into his video editing software and lined up the timestamps like a conductor arranging his orchestra.

"It all looks a bit fuzzy to me," Mavis asked, peering at the computer screen.

"Patience, Mavis," Gemma said, a half-smile playing on her lips despite the tension knotting in her stomach. Gemma leaned forward as she watched the grainy night vision footage play.

"Here we go," Jack said. The first car materialised on the screen, its headlights piercing the darkness. A door opened, and a figure clutching a briefcase stepped into the camera's unflinching gaze.

Gemma's breath hitched. "Oh my god. It's him. The vandal that threw paint at our stall," she said, recognition washing over her in an icy wave. The tall, bald man was illuminated by the ghostly green of the night vision.

As the video continued, another vehicle rolled into view, parking alongside the first. A man emerged, his features obscured by shadow, carrying a holdall bag large enough to stow away countless secrets. He met the bald man halfway between the cars, and the exchange was silent but charged with meaning.

Jack leaned closer, squinting at the screen. "It looks like they are doing a drug trade," he said, sounding like an expert who had binged far too many TV shows on Netflix.

Gemma nodded. "I think you're right," she said.

Gemma leaned in. Her breath caught in anticipation as she watched the figures on the screen. The second man's words were a distorted murmur muffled by the limitations of the night vision camera.

"Can't make out what they're saying," Mavis grumbled, frustration masking her usually cheery demeanour.

"Let me try something." Jack's fingers tapped on his laptop keyboard. "I'll enhance and boost the audio."

"Do you want me to repeat the word 'enhance' like they do on CSI?" Gemma asked, smiling.

"Ha, yes. That adds to the magic," Jack said as he enhanced the sound.

After a moment that seemed to stretch far too long, Jack hit play on the video. This time, the voices emerged clearer and menacing. The unknown man's voice cut through the static. "Have you sorted out the people investigating the boy's death?"

The bald man replied, his tone nonchalant despite the gravity of his words. "We're working on it. Intimidation has silenced the people involved."

"Intimidated ..." Gemma echoed under her breath, the word leaving a sour taste.

The other man's response sent a chill down her spine. "If you don't get it sorted, we'll do it for you. We can't be dealing with groups that are carrying so much risk. I don't like loose ends. They're bad for business."

Gemma exchanged a grave look with Mavis. The implications were stark and terrifying.

"Is he implying he'll come and ... sort *us* out?" asked Mavis, whose voice trembled.

Gemma looked up at Mavis. "It won't come to that. I promise," Gemma said, although she wasn't sure she believed it herself. Before they could fully process the threat, a third figure stepped from the car. Gemma's eyes widened, a gasp escaping before she could clamp down on her shock. Recognition dawned upon her, cold and undeniable. "Is that who I think it is?" Gemma's voice trembled with disbelief.

Mavis squinted, her sharp gaze locking onto the screen. "Gosh, I think it is." Their shared realisation hung heavy in the air. The mystery person's assurance was chillingly professional. "I can assure you everything regarding George's death will be dealt with," they said and paused before adding, "and nothing will be related back to you. You have my word."

The man with the holdall's reply was a blunt, stark warning. "It better be, or there'll be consequences."

Gemma could feel the tension in the room. Hearing

these people make a direct threat like this was very unnerving and frightening. But Gemma knew she had what she needed to end this nightmare. She continued watching the video as the exchange of the briefcase and holdall played out before them, captured in the ghostly green hues of the night vision camera.

As the vehicles dispersed into the night on the video, Gemma felt a resolve form within her. She knew what had to be done next. "I need to speak to David," she said, her voice steady with newfound determination. "We have found George's killer."

## Chapter Thirty-Six

Gemma pushed open the heavy wooden door to St Peter's, and Mavis shuffled in beside her. The familiar scent of polished wood greeted them. Baxter, Gemma's trusty labrador, trotted ahead, nose to the ground, tail wagging at the prospect of new company.

"Ah, Gemma, Mavis, you're here," Reverend Simon said, his voice echoing off the high vaulted ceiling. He had arranged chairs into neat rows near the altar.

"Good evening, Reverend. This is my good friend Jack," Gemma said, gesturing towards Jack, who nodded.

"Good evening, Reverend. Do you have anywhere I can plug in my laptop?" asked Jack. "I'll want to show a video."

"Yes, of course. By the altar, you will find power and a cable for the projector," said the reverend.

"Thank you for allowing us to meet here, Reverend," Gemma said with a nervous smile. "We have some matters to discuss regarding the demise of young George Peters."

"Yes, of course. Anything I can do to help." The reverend bent down and gave Baxter a hearty pat on the head. "Good boy," he said, as Baxter responded with an appreciative nuzzle against the reverend's hand.

Mavis turned to Gemma. "Shouldn't we wait for David to get here?" she asked. Gemma shook her head.

"No, he said to gather all involved here and keep them talking. He'll be here soon."

"Could that be dangerous?"

"I don't think so, not with this many people," said Gemma as she bit her bottom lip. She knew full well the plan was risky, but David explained that keeping the guilty occupied in a large group would mean they wouldn't be able to warn any of the other gang members that the police were on to them.

As the sound of jovial conversation drifted in from outside, Gemma turned to see Norman, James and Rhianna entering the nave. James and Rhianna laughed together, their faces glowing with a shared secret joy.

"Look at you two," Mavis said, her spectacles reflecting the light as she peered at them. "You seem happy!"

Rhianna extended a hand, showing the diamond ring that adorned her finger. "We just got engaged," she said, her eyes sparkling almost as much as the gemstone itself.

"Congratulations!" Mavis said, and Gemma echoed the sentiment.

"Come, come, let's sit," said Reverend Simon as he gestured towards the arranged seating. "Would you care for some tea or coffee?" he offered, showing the small table near the altar adorned with an eclectic collection of mismatched mugs and a large hot water urn. James guided Rhianna to a chair before accepting the offer of refreshments.

The heavy wooden door of the church creaked open, interrupting the hum of idle chatter. A figure, unsteady on crutches, made her way into the nave. The echo of her uneven gait reverberated off the ancient stone walls. It was Cynthia, her leg encased in white plaster.

"Ah, Cynthia! You made it," Gemma called out, rising from her seat. Her voice was laced with concern as she hurried over. "Thank you for coming." She reached Cynthia just as Reverend Simon provided a steadying arm to help her navigate the chairs.

"Of course," Cynthia replied, albeit with a shaky voice. "But why call me here?"

"It's an important parish meeting," the Reverend interjected before guiding Cynthia to one chair and then going to the tea and coffee table to get her a drink.

"Here, have some tea," he said, returning and handing her a steaming cup. "Just how you like it."

Before they could settle, another figure appeared at the entrance, silhouetted by the fading light of day. It was Lily, wearing a rock band T-shirt and ripped blue jeans. Her eyes were apprehensive, and she hesitated at the door.

As she stepped forward, Gemma caught a fleeting expression of shock on Rhianna's face. She quickly smoothed it over with a smile. Gemma looked at James, who didn't seem to have noticed. Beside her, Mavis leaned in, her sharp gaze missing nothing, and they exchanged a knowing look. They had both sensed the undercurrents swirling beneath the surface.

"Hello, Lily. How are you?" Gemma asked in greeting, closing the distance between them. The younger woman accepted Gemma's embrace, her hug tight but brief.

"Fine, I guess," Lily said, her voice quick. "Just a bit ... confused about all this. I've never been a part of the church before."

"Understandable," Gemma assured her, holding her gaze. "All will be revealed soon, I promise."

They parted, and Lily found a seat, folding her hands in her lap as if to anchor herself. Gemma returned to Mavis, her mind working through the puzzle pieces, each person's arrival adding weight to the gravity of the evening's purpose.

Gemma rose from her seat, commanding the attention of the church's nave. Gemma looked at her watch. *Come on David, where are you?* she thought to herself before addressing the assembled group with a warm smile.

"Thank you all for being here," she began, her voice resonated through the nave. "I appreciate your willingness to gather at short notice. I want to talk about the murder of George Peters."

Cynthia shifted in her seat and almost dropped one of her crutches. "Why? The police have already made the arrest," she said.

"Yes, they have," Gemma said, nodding. "But there are some points I'd like us to consider together." She took a breath before recounting the day of the craft fair. "We start on the day of the craft fair here at St Peter's, where Norman and Cynthia were heading to the belfry to prepare for the demonstration," Gemma explained, her tone turning sombre. "And then ... we heard Cynthia's scream fill the church."

"It was terrible. An awful scene, like out of a horror movie," said Cynthia.

"Horror doesn't cover it," Gemma said. Her gaze drifted, as if she could still see his lifeless eyes staring into nothingness. "It was a violent and brutal attack." She remembered how she had sprinted towards the chaos that day, her mind racing but focused. "I knew we had to preserve the integrity of where George lay. Thankfully, David — Detective Inspector Haynes — was already there at the fair, helping with our book stall. He came to the scene and then called his team from the police station. Norman helped Cynthia down from the chamber while I waited for David." Gemma's recall was clinical and detached.

The group listened, hanging on every word. "Before we found George," she continued, "John, a local homeless man, was staggering around at the craft fair." She paused, letting the image settle. "He reeked of vodka, completely unaware of his surroundings. We escorted him outside, gave him some tea and something to eat, but it was clear he wasn't ... present." Pity softened her features. "Later that day," she continued, "he was arrested for George's murder. The evidence against him seemed overwhelming."

"Seemed?" Cynthia's voice quivered, echoing off the walls.

"Yes, seemed," Gemma said, locking eyes with Cynthia. "Compelling, even. But let's consider the facts post-arrest." She paused before continuing. "Toxicology found alcohol in John's blood, which was no surprise considering his state, but that wasn't all. Ketamine was also found in his system; a dangerous sedative." Murmurs of concern spread, like ripples across a pond. "Alone, each is harmful in different quantities. Together

..." she said, her voice dropping to highlight the severity, "well, let's just say, it's a concoction that requires careful mixing, knowledge of its potent effects. Too much can be fatal."

"Why would someone do such a thing?" the reverend asked, his hands clasped in front of him.

"A very good question, Reverend. Did John obtain and mix this dangerous cocktail himself, or did someone give it to him?" Gemma paused to let the question be absorbed. "And then there's the matter of the church's back door. Unlocked by John, supposedly, while he was under the influence of this potent cocktail. The same door where the CCTV had a convenient blind spot after it was vandalised."

"Convenient indeed," mumbled the Reverend, stroking Baxter's ears as the dog sat at his feet.

"Moreover," Gemma said, pacing a step forward, the crowd's collective gaze following her movement. "John would have had to lure George up to the belfry to commit the crime." She let the words hang in the air, laden with doubt.

"Under the influence of alcohol and ketamine?" Jack questioned as scepticism furrowed his brow.

"Exactly," Gemma said, her lips pursed. "All while under the influence. It doesn't quite add up, does it? Technically possible? Yes. Realistically possible? I don't think so." The room fell silent. "Let's keep our minds open," Gemma concluded. "There's more here than meets the eye."

"He could have committed the murder and then taken those drugs to drown out what he'd done," said James.

"That's a possibility, apart from the fact that the bottle of vodka that also contained ketamine was the murder weapon. Don't forget, the death was caused by blunt force trauma to the head, followed by a stab wound in the abdomen with the broken bottle."

Norman leaned in his seat and raised an eyebrow. "Wasn't there forensic evidence all over the bell chamber? Fingerprints and such?" Norman asked.

Gemma nodded. "Yes, some. John's fingerprints were found on the vodka bottle," she said. "Also, his boot prints were all over the bell chamber."

Cynthia perched uneasily on her chair with her leg outstretched in its plaster cast. "Well, it doesn't look good for John. This is quite compelling evidence. Fingerprints and footprints everywhere," Cynthia said.

"It is," Gemma conceded. "But don't you think it's a little convenient? The CCTV system taken out of action at just the right place? Entry to the church wasn't recorded. That must have required a lot of planning."

Reverend Simon added, "Or a coincidence. John was a regular around here. He could have seen the camera was broken and taken advantage."

"True," Gemma said, but her eyes told a different story.

Shifting the conversation, Gemma's tone softened. "I've also learnt from a friend who volunteers at the food hub that John often spoke of being bullied by the victim, George. Repeatedly intimidated."

Lily spoke up, her voice tinged with bitter experience. "I'm not surprised. George was horrible to most people, especially those who were weaker than him. A true bully."

James nodded. "Then John had a motive. Pushed to breaking point, maybe?"

"Perhaps," Gemma said. "It certainly seems that way." Gemma clasped her hands together. "Despite everything, Mavis and I can't quite accept that John is capable of such violence." She glanced over at Mavis.

Mavis nodded. "I've had many a chat with John over the years," she said, her voice rich with empathy. "He's always been a mild-mannered kind soul."

James, his expression earnest, leaned forward from where he sat beside Rhianna. "Surely, though," James said in a measured tone, "being pushed to breaking point can make even the gentlest person do the unthinkable."

Gemma nodded, acknowledging the point. "The thing is," she said slowly, pacing in front of the group, "this murder was too calculated, too precise and brutal.

It just all seems a bit much for someone who might suddenly snap. This wasn't just someone lashing out on the spur of the moment. This murder took planning."

## Chapter Thirty-Seven

As Gemma addressed the group, the once calm weather outside turned to intense rain that pummelled the church roof with a ferocity that mirrored the intensity gathering in Gemma's eyes. She looked up at the roof, startled by the sudden change in the weather and looked nervously again at her watch. She would have expected David to be here by now, along with more police officers. She was feeling nervous that she may have to reveal the killer without having someone here to arrest them. *What if something has happened to David?* she thought as her mouth went suddenly dry. Gemma turned to face the small assembly at the front of the church.

"I want to continue by discussing you, Cynthia," Gemma said, her voice cutting through the drumming rain.

At the mention of her name, Cynthia's eyes widened, and a look of shock flitted across her features. Gemma addressed the rest of the group. "As I have already mentioned, it was Cynthia, along with Norman, who unlocked the bell tower that fateful day," she said, pausing just long enough to ensure the gravity of her words settled over the gathered group. "And when they discovered George's body," she said, her tone softening a fraction while recalling the scene, "Cynthia let out a scream so blood curdling it alerted everyone in the church to the horror within."

The silence that followed was broken only by the relentless rain pattering against the stained glass windows of the church.

"Mind you," Gemma continued, as she locked eyes with Cynthia, "I thought your reaction, while understandably upset, seemed ..." She searched for the word, not wanting to offend but feeling duty-bound to honesty, "a tad theatrical."

"Of course I was upset!" Cynthia shouted. "I take a little offence at being called theatrical, Gemma."

Gemma raised her hands. "Please, Cynthia," she implored, "just let me finish." Gemma paused at the front of the congregation before her. "Another thing," Gemma said, drawing the room's focus, "a minor detail, but you were wearing red lipstick that day. Unusual for you, since you favour pink."

"That's correct," said Cynthia.

"And we found your pink lipstick on the floor of the belfry, near poor George's body," said Gemma.

From her seat, Cynthia looked up, her expression a mixture of surprise and defensiveness. "I might've dropped my pink one the day before," she said. "Norman and I ... we clean up there regularly. Part of our duties. I couldn't find it in the morning of the fair, so I just wore red instead."

"Of course," Gemma acknowledged with an empathetic nod. "But as it was part of the crime scene, I had to mention it."

Norman added, "It gets terribly dusty up there when the bells are rung."

Just then, a flash of lightning illuminated the church's interior, followed by a thunderous clap that made Mavis and Cynthia jump.

"Despite all this," Gemma continued, "I thought little of it regarding Cynthia. She seemed to be just a hapless person who discovered the body." She paused. "But we had a children's story time event at the bookstore, and I overheard a conversation between some parents who suggested that George ... well, he apparently intimidated you, Cynthia. For cigarettes and alcohol from your shop."

"Typical," Cynthia snapped, bitterness lacing her retort as she dismissed the gossip with a wave of her hand. "Tongues wagging in this town over something that's nobody's business but my own."

The words hung heavy in the air before Gemma continued. "Do you remember the other week when I came to visit you in your shop?" asked Gemma.

"I do," said Cynthia.

"I wanted to check in with you to see how you were doing, as finding a body like that must have been a shock."

"Yes, it was a shock. Horrible," she said, her eyes dull as frosted glass.

"Can't begin to imagine," Gemma said. "But then I asked about the lipstick I found near the body."

"Which, as I said, I could've dropped anytime," Cynthia said, her shoulders rising defensively.

"Of course," Gemma agreed, her voice still gentle but persistent. "But it made you a little irate at the time. Then I asked you how well you knew George," Gemma said, watching as Cynthia's facade cracked with the question.

"Many people knew of him. He had a reputation," Cynthia replied, mild irritation lacing her voice.

"True, but with him intimidating you, that must have been quite frightening. Or did it make you angry?" Gemma asked.

At the mention of the intimidation rumours, fire flashed in her eyes. "Well, wouldn't you be angry?"

"Yes," Gemma conceded. "How was he intimidating you?"

Cynthia sighed. "At first, he would come into my

store and start knocking products off the shelves, just being a nuisance. Then he would get more verbally abusive. He was gradually cranking up the intensity over a month or so," she said.

"And then?" said Gemma.

"Then he would come up to the counter, get in my face and explain that Belper was a dangerous place, that I needed him. I assumed he was after money, but he would help himself to cigarettes and booze from my shelves."

"Worth a lot of money, I take it?" said Gemma.

"Yes, two to three hundred pounds at a time. He said provided I kept him supplied, he would ensure that I was kept safe and well looked after."

"So a protection racket?" asked Gemma. "There's more to the story, isn't there?" Before Cynthia could retort, Gemma recalled another piece of the tangled puzzle. "Mavis ran into Norman at the Strutt Centre," she said. "He confirmed the intimidation story we overheard at the children's story time reading."

"What of it?" Cynthia muttered under her breath.

"He said you had confided in him about the intimidation, but then you suddenly stopped mentioning it. Just went silent on the subject."

"And?"

"Well, why was that? From Norman's perspective, either the situation resolved itself, or it was because you had a bit of a thing for Norman. But after his rejection, you stopped talking to him about your problems. Either way, if something as serious as intimidation was playing on your mind, why would you suddenly stop mentioning it?"

Norman coughed. "Is all this strictly necessary? I mentioned this to Mavis in confidence," Norman said, a hint of stress and annoyance in his voice. He glanced at Mavis. "I trusted you with that information."

Mavis looked at Norman. "I apologise, Norman, but we were trying to piece together Cynthia's involvement in this story."

"Indeed," said Gemma. "It seemed off that you would mention several times something that was concerning you, intimidation in this case, and then suddenly stop talking about it."

Cynthia shrugged. "First, I stopped talking about it because George threatened me and said I had to keep quiet, or I would be hurt. He must have found out that I discussed it with people. And as for me having a bit of a soft spot for Norman, well, quite frankly, that is no ones' business," said Cynthia.

"Okay," said Gemma who was feeling uncomfortable probing Cynthia like this. "As I was telling you all this when I was in your shop, your demeanour changed to one of aggression, where you asked me to leave. You were getting quite irate."

"Can you blame me? Coming into my shop and speaking to me like that? You would react the same if I came into your bookshop and did that," Cynthia snapped.

Gemma nodded. She couldn't deny that would be the case. "You were probably relieved when James interrupted our discussion by coming into your shop to buy a magazine."

Cynthia shook her head. "I'm not being funny, Gemma, but where is all this going?"

"All in good time. Please bear with me," Gemma said. Cynthia shrugged her shoulders and shook her head. "So, moving on. We had an incident at the Bookworm, where someone threw a brick through our window in the early hours of the morning," Gemma said as she looked around the room. "There was a crude message tied to the brick. It said 'You have been warned!'" Mavis, sitting beside her, nodded.

Cynthia, clearly looking a little irritated, said, "You're not accusing me of that, are you?"

"Please, let me finish going through the details," Gemma said, raising her hands to calm Cynthia.

"Terrible business that was with the brick. Not what you'd expect around here," Mavis said.

"Yes, quite," Gemma said. "After David temporarily boarded the window, I'd spotted a light on in your flat, Cynthia. It was late, or rather early, depending on one's perspective, and I had assumed the noise from our alarm had woken you."

"It was loud enough to wake the dead," said Cynthia.

"The next day, still feeling guilty for the disturbance, myself and Mavis walked over to your shop to offer our apologies for the disruption. Yet when we arrived, the door was locked, and the closed sign hung in the door."

"Am I not allowed to close my store?" asked Cynthia.

"Yes, but it never closes," Gemma said. "We then went to your flat and knocked on your door, but we were met with silence."

Cynthia looked away from Gemma, her gaze fixed on the ground, as if she knew what was coming next.

Gemma addressed the group as a judge talking to the jury. "Upon arriving back at the Bookworm, the postman had already made his morning delivery. A letter. Upon opening the envelope, we found a rather revealing message; a plea from Cynthia scrawled in hurried print. It told of a darker tale where George had used Cynthia's shop as a front for his illicit drug dealing. The letter explained how he would demand you turn off the CCTV and close the shop to accommodate his dealings."

"That must have been quite frightening," Mavis said to Cynthia. "Being manipulated like that."

Cynthia nodded. "You can only imagine," she said. "Everything we discussed about his intimidation was leading up to this. They were gradually wearing me down, and said that if I did this for them, once, maybe twice a week, where I disable the camera and close, they would stop taking my cigarette and alcohol stock. I couldn't afford to keep taking those losses, so I had no choice."

"Your letter continued, saying that you had someone else watching over you. Making sure you stayed in line. Making you feel as though George wasn't alone in his dealings. He was working for someone else."

Cynthia nodded. "Yes, I felt as though I was constantly being watched. It was hard to prove, but the feeling was unsettling."

"But then you said you had to leave. Go into hiding," said Gemma.

"Yes, after you began asking questions, I could sense more scrutiny on me. Strange looks from people, rough-looking people coming into the shop. I felt very unsafe. I didn't know whether they were involved, or I was just being paranoid."

"Even though, by leaving suddenly like that, it didn't help profess your innocence," said Gemma.

Cynthia's reaction was immediate and visceral. "I didn't kill him. Are you crazy?" Her words cut through the patter of rain, sharp and desperate.

"But you must see how it looks, and with everything George was putting you through, it would be a powerful motive," said Gemma. "It looks suspicious." Cynthia shrugged. "Not only is it a motive," continued Gemma, "but you would have had the means to commit the murder with your access to the church."

"At that moment, I was more concerned about my safety. Not that it did me any good," she said, tapping the plaster cast on her leg.

"Yes, we heard about the car accident," Gemma said softly, turning towards the woman, who seemed to shrink under the collective gaze. "That must have been terrifying."

The word was barely out before Cynthia's dam broke, her tears mingling with the sound of rain. As if on cue, Mavis moved and rested her hand on Cynthia's shoulder.

"Never been so scared in my life," Cynthia sobbed, her shoulders heaving as Mavis wrapped an arm around her.

## Chapter Thirty-Eight

Gemma paced the front of the nave. She could feel the eyes of the group on her as she moved. The storm outside raged on, adding an ominous atmosphere to the evening. Gemma's heart thumped in her chest as she tried not to think about why David hadn't turned up yet. She was getting very close to the point of revealing the killer and she didn't have any support. She swallowed hard and tried to ignore the thought that something might have happened to David. *You're just being paranoid*, she thought.

"Jack, here," Gemma gestured towards where Jack sat, trying to appear inconspicuous, "saw George's girlfriend, or ex-girlfriend at the time he died, I should add, walking through town the other day."

At this, Jack offered an awkward wave before

retracting his hand, as if he wished he could disappear into the woodwork.

"And she's here with us today; Lily," said Gemma. The group turned as one to look at Lily, who sat somewhat defiantly, arms crossed. With a sheepish smile, Gemma admitted, "I must confess. I didn't even know George had a girlfriend." A few murmurs whispered through some members of the group, echoing Gemma's surprise. "Lily works at the new hair salon on King Street. So, I booked myself in for a cut and blow dry; overdue, anyway." Her attempt at humour fell flat as Lily stared at Gemma.

Lily's voice cut through the murmurings, sharp and laden with accusation. "So you came to the salon just to question me?"

"Yes. I did. Sorry," Gemma said with genuine remorse. "But it was to get to the bottom of this murder." Another crash of thunder punctuated her words, as if the heavens themselves were demanding justice. "I must say I was impressed with your candour, Lily. When you said you weren't sad that George was dead ..." She let the sentence hang between them, recalling the initial shock that had gripped her.

"George didn't start out violent," Lily interjected, her voice animated yet filled with deep-seated pain. "He changed; he just got worse." Her eyes flickered with memories, haunted by the shadows of her past.

Gemma nodded, her heart aching for the young

woman's plight. "When you explained the years of emotional and physical abuse ... well, I couldn't blame you for feeling relieved."

"I tried to leave him once before," Lily said. "But George ... he threatened my family. I had no choice. I told you this." She swallowed hard, her eyes darting towards the stained glass windows as if seeking an escape from the memory. "I was trapped," she said, pausing before looking back at Gemma. "Everything changed when he offered drugs to my little sister. He tried to get her hooked just to spite me," Lily continued, her voice now barely above a whisper. "That was the final straw. I left, despite everything and no matter the risk to me. I'd had enough."

Mavis's sharp intake of breath echoed around the stone walls, while the reverend's expression morphed into one of shock. He traced the sign of the cross with a hand through the air.

"Then you left and moved in with a friend," Gemma said, guiding the narrative back to safer ground.

"Yes," Lily said, nodding and grateful for the change of subject. "She took me in without question."

"It's always good to know you have friends who have your back," said Gemma. "I want to talk about something else that might be uncomfortable, so please bear with me." Lily nodded. "What I want to do is bring to light that George was also having an affair while he was with you," Gemma said.

"Yes, that's right. It wasn't just a one-off. It was constant, but I never caught him in the act," said Lily.

Gemma stepped closer to Lily, her gaze kind yet probing. "I'm sorry to hear that. It must have been very difficult to deal with. You mentioned he'd come home covered in the scent of perfume?"

"Yes, he would come home smelling of citrus, orange blossom," Lily clarified, a note of disgust coloured her voice. "He didn't hide it. He didn't wash it off. It was as if he wanted me to know. Like he was taunting me with it. Just another part of him trying to exert control over me."

As if on cue from Lily's admission, a peal of thunder rattled the intricately coloured windows, and the flicker of lightning cast an eerie glow over the congregation huddled within the church. Baxter let out a small yelp at the sound of thunder. Reverend Simon stroked the dog's back to calm him. Gemma was glad she hadn't left Baxter home that evening.

Gemma's pulse raced, knowing she was getting to the main point of the evening. She took a deep breath to calm her nerves and paced before the group, her keen eyes scanning the worried faces. She paused, turning to face Rhianna, who was no longer smiling.

"Rhianna," Gemma began, her voice steady despite the storm's rising crescendo outside, "I mentioned the scent of orange blossom to you before. It's a scent I've noticed you often wear. In fact, I commented on how much I liked it at the craft fair the day George's body was discovered."

"Yes ... But ...," was all Rhianna could muster as she tried to avoid eye contact. Gemma stood before her, looking at her, waiting for more of a response.

The silence in the church was palpable. Rhianna's eyes widened, darting from Gemma to James, who sat by her side. The air bristled with tension as everyone waited.

"Okay," Rhianna conceded, her cheeks flushed a delicate pink. "It ... wasn't an affair, just a fling, and it was over. I'd moved past it." Her words tumbled out, a mixture of confession and defiance.

"What was it then? Just sex? With my boyfriend?" Shouted Lily, who was fidgeting in her seat, her face flushing red. It must have taken monumental restraint not to launch herself at Rhianna. Gemma was impressed, although she wasn't going to say anything aloud. Now wasn't the time for that.

James, usually composed and calm, shifted uncomfortably in this seat, his agitation visible. "I know about this," he said, his voice a notch higher than usual. "As Rhianna says, we've moved past it. Rhianna made a mistake. Flings aren't illegal, but thanks for bringing it out in the open. It's just what I wanted to think about after we got engaged," James said through gritted teeth.

Gemma nodded, acknowledging the admission.

"True, they're not illegal, but this love triangle presents a powerful motive," she said, her eyes narrowing thoughtfully. She turned to Lily, who looked like a cornered animal, fierce yet frightened. "Your history with George and his physical and emotional abuse, along with him seeing another woman, gives you a very strong motive, Lily," Gemma said, watching the woman. "But without the means or opportunity, it seems unlikely; unless you conspired with someone."

"Like who?" asked Lilly. "Who do you think I could conspire with?"

"It could easily be possible that you knew of George's treatment of poor old John. Between the two of you, you could easily pull off a crime like this."

Staring at Gemma, Lily's eyes widened and her cheeks as flushed red as fire. "Of course I didn't," Lily protested. "I'm innocent! I mean, okay, I hated George, and yes, I was relieved when I heard he was dead, but that was just anger over how he treated me and what he tried to do with my sister." Lily was trying to spit her words so fast that she stumbled over them.

"The other option is that you joined up with Cynthia here," said Gemma.

"I beg your pardon!" Cynthia shouted.

Gemma raised a hand, urging Cynthia not to interrupt. "If you think about it logically, you both had very strong and undeniable motives, the means, with

Cynthia's access to the church, and the opportunity, as neither of you have verifiable alibi's. Do you see how this looks?"

"This is ridiculous," said Lily. "I've never even met Cynthia before today."

"You were at your friend's house the evening of the murder. You already told me you were alone while your friend was away on a business trip. Even by your own admission, if John hadn't been arrested for the murder, you would be considered the prime suspect, so you knew how it would look."

Lily's gaze faltered; vulnerability flashed across her features. "I know I said that, but do you really think I did it?" she asked.

"I will admit, I thought it was a distinct possibility," Gemma said. "And no one here would blame you after hearing your story. The years of mental and physical abuse; everyone has a breaking point, and I think you either reached it or were dangerously close," Gemma said, pausing to take a breath. "The constant infidelity. The callous act of offering drugs to your younger sister as a kind of punishment for you. It would take a strong will not to snap with all of that."

Everyone in the room held their breath, the collective anticipation nearly as charged as the atmosphere outside. Gemma stepped closer to Lily, and placed her hand on her shoulder.

"Even with all of these competing motives, I don't

believe you did it, Lily. If you have shown me anything, it is just how brave and resilient you are after all that torment. But I do believe I've pieced together the truth," Gemma declared. "Do you want to know who did it?" Gemma asked, clasping her hands together.

## Chapter Thirty-Nine

"The revelation about the killer came quite by surprise," she began. The assembled group's eyes were fixed on Gemma with a mix of anxiety and anticipation. The tension in the room was thick enough to cut with a knife.

She continued, "I received this cryptic SMS message." Her fingers fished out her phone, tapping the screen to life and illuminating the message. "Suggesting we check out the farmers' track parking spot at 2am. It was a real bolt from the blue, I can tell you," Gemma said. Her gaze flicked towards Lily. "My first thought was that it was from you, Lily. I had just given you my phone number, but I had not taken yours in return."

"Me, really?" Lily's voice quivered. "Everything was very secretive with George. I didn't know of his dealings, and I knew better than to pry for my safety."

"I agree. I don't think it was you. I don't think you would have been privy to any drug deals, especially after you split with him," Gemma said. "So if we rule out Lily for the moment, who else would want to send me this key piece of information?" Gemma paused for dramatic effect and to see if anyone owned up. They didn't. "First, we needed to find out what the message was referring to. What was going to happen at 2am on that farm track?"

Mavis nodded in agreement. "And that's where Jack comes into play." Jack looked up from where he sat with his laptop, and his cheeks flushed red at being called out.

Gemma glanced at Mavis and smiled. "Jack has some motion detection night vision cameras."

"Those cameras are very good," Mavis added. "They helped catch the vandals damaging gardens entered into the local gardening competition."

With a nod from Gemma, Jack knew it was his cue and began working on the laptop keyboard. With a click, the church's projector whirred to life, casting a glow on the white screen behind the altar. The video flickered, revealing the parking area on the farm track, where headlights pierced the dark. A thin, bald man emerged from a vehicle.

Gemma pointed towards the screen, but addressed the group. "That's him," she said, her voice steady yet charged with the anticipation of justice. "The same man who vandalised our food fair stall."

Cynthia gasped. "I recognise him. He's been in my shop before."

"For good reason," said Gemma. "He's probably the one who was keeping an eye on you."

Jack's hand hovered over the pause button, waiting for Gemma's nod before allowing the scene to play on. The tension in the air was palpable. Another figure appeared carrying a large holdall, and the group watched the drug exchange take place, along with the disturbing discussion about dealing with anyone looking into George's murder. Then, the third person in the video stepped out of the car for everyone to see.

"Pause it, please, Jack," Gemma said, her eyes never leaving the frozen image on the projector screen. She turned to face the group. Her heart thumped so hard she thought it might burst out of her chest. She thought she could hear blood pumping in her ears. *This is it*, she thought, *Now or never*.

"Do you want to explain, James?" she asked, her question hanging between them like a challenge.

Laughter, cold and unexpected, erupted from James. "Well, aren't you clever, Gemma." His voice held a mocking edge. "But please, you first."

"Very well," Gemma began, unflinching under his gaze. "In my mind, James, it's clear that you're the one pulling the strings; the dealer at the top of the chain who was controlling George, and therefore Cynthia."

Cynthia's gasp cut through the silence. "No, not you, James," she said, as if she didn't quite believe it.

"Very astute of you," James conceded, his words dripping with sarcasm.

Gemma pressed on. "With George involved with Rhianna, it stands to reason you wanted him out of the picture. Eliminated." James offered a slow, impressed nod, not unlike a teacher acknowledging a student's correct answer.

Gemma's looked over the small assembly, her eyes finally resting on Rhianna. "I believe it was you who sent me that message, Rhianna," she said softly, yet with gravity that made the others lean in. "Who else would know such detailed information about the drug deal locations?" Gemma looked at Rhianna and saw the colour drain from her face; a look of pure fear. James's eyes flashed towards Rhianna, who shivered, tears pooling like morning dew at the corners of her eyes. "Could it be," Gemma mused aloud, "that amidst this twisted love triangle ... you still harboured feelings for George? Is that why you sent the message? A pang of remorse, perhaps?" Rhianna's trembling intensified, though she kept her hands clasped in her lap. She nodded, refusing to make eye contact.

Gemma's mind flickered back to the start of the evening's meeting. The moment Cynthia stepped through the ancient wooden doors and the subtle shift in James's body language. His usual polished confidence had seemed to crumble slightly; his hands had begun a nervous dance upon his thighs, his legs canting towards the exit as if yearning for escape.

"Your body language spoke volumes, James, when Cynthia stepped into the church this evening," Gemma said, her tone matter-of-fact. "You were practically telegraphing your discomfort."

"Ah, so you're a body language expert now?" James retorted, a sarcastic smile playing on his lips despite the red flush that still clung to his cheeks.

"Well, I have read some books on it, so yes." Her voice rang with unwavering certainty. Gemma poised herself like a detective about to unveil the last piece of an intricate puzzle. "So, Rhianna," Gemma began, her voice carrying an assertive edge. "Why did you send me that message?"

Rhianna's shoulders slumped. A fragile sigh escaped her lips. Her eyes, rimmed red from tears, met Gemma's with a plea for understanding. "Like Lily, I've been trapped," she confessed, each word weighted with fear. "Being inside a gang like this ... it's terrifying." She paused and looked up at Gemma and then Mavis. "Having a fling with George was a mistake, but being made to be involved in his death as my punishment just showed how little I meant to James. I just can't live with what I've done." She wiped tears from her eyes and then looked directly at James. "I know I need to pay for what

I've done, and so do you James. That's why I sent the message."

From the corner of her eye, Gemma caught James shifting uncomfortably. His polished exterior was cracking, his usual polite facade giving way to a vulnerability he could no longer hide. "But we just got engaged!" he protested, his voice tinged with a mix of disbelief and desperation.

Rhianna's laughter held no humour. "And what would you have done if I said no?" she countered, her question hanging heavy in the air between them.

James's response was almost inaudible; a sheepish murmur barely heard over the storm outside. "Fair point."

"The game's up, James," Gemma declared, her tone firm. "Want to tell us how you did it? Killed George, that is? You may as well. Show us how clever you really are."

The rest of the group held its collective breath, waiting for the confession that would bring closure to the dark chapter that had clouded the town.

# Chapter Forty

Everyone's eyes were fixed on James, whose confession they awaited with bated breath. In the tense silence, a slow clap echoed. It was jarring and out of place. Norman stood tall with an air of smug satisfaction and applauded his son's downfall.

"I really must congratulate you, Gemma. Someone with your gumption would be an asset to my business," he said, addressing her directly. His voice was smooth as silk, yet it carried the chill of malice. "You have uncovered the monkey," Norman said as he gestured to his son, James, "but what you didn't expect was the organ grinder."

Gemma looked at Norman and couldn't conceal her look of shock. Neither could Mavis, from the gasp she let out, followed her by muttering, "Norman, how could you?"

Norman delved into his waxed canvas shoulder bag and pulled out a cold metal handgun and a mobile phone. A collective gasp shuddered through the room like an aftershock of thunder as everyone took a step back from Norman.

Norman's arm extended upward, the gun's barrel pointing at Rhianna. "You're a disgrace, Rhianna, and you will be dealt with like one," he said, his words slicing through the air. He gestured with the gun for her to move away from James and stand next to Gemma, Lily, Mavis, Jack, Cynthia and the Reverend. Baxter, ever loyal, growled, sensing danger.

"Norman, there is no need for this," Gemma implored, attempting to weave reason through the madness.

"If you had taken heed of our warnings, then there would have been no need. But you couldn't help yourself, could you?" Norman's response was a calm yet firm rebuke, silencing her with a chilling calmness. "James, bolt the door," Norman commanded. Obedience flitted across James's face as he moved to secure the church entrance.

"Why, Norman?" Mavis asked. Her voice trembled like the flickering candle flames. "Why are you doing this?" Despite the situation, Norman's expression softened, a momentary glimpse of regret brushing his features.

"I am sorry, Mavis, that you have become caught up

in this," he said almost gently. "But you should have kept out of it."

The church lit up again as another flash of lightning burst, and the rain continued to hammer down. Norman's stance left no doubt they were all pawns in a much larger game, one that he intended to win at any cost.

As the door's bolt clunked into place, sealing their fate, James turned and ambled back through the nave. Norman tapped away on his mobile phone.

Gemma's heart thrummed against her ribcage, almost as loud as the storm outside. How could she have not seen or guessed that Norman was at the top of the gang's tree? She wished David was there, as well as the rest of the Derbyshire constabulary.

"We will have some visitors meeting us here soon," Norman announced casually, pocketing his phone and fixing his gaze on the small crowd gathered like sheep for the shearing.

"Visitors?" Reverend Simon asked, his voice quivering. "What do you mean by that?"

"Do you really think we can let you walk away from this?" Norman's tone was chilling, devoid of any warmth. "There is too much at stake, and you all know too much. You have Gemma here to thank for sealing your fate." Norman looked at his watch, his gun still covering the group. "But don't worry. It'll all be made to look like an accident." He smiled. "James, take their phones."

James complied and passed among the group, confiscating their belongings, including Jack's laptop. As he placed them on the floor, he stood facing the hostages.

"James, you may as well tell everyone what they want to know about George. We have a brief wait for the others to arrive," said Norman, in a tone dripping with arrogance.

James cleared his throat. "George ... well, he had to go for several reasons." His cool gaze landed on Rhianna, who flinched under the weight of his scowl. "Having a fling with Rhianna was only part of it," he said, pausing to study Rhianna's reaction. "Only a small part, though," James continued. "He was also stealing from us; overcharging for drugs and skimming the money from the top."

"Couldn't you have just talked to him?" Mavis asked, her voice laced with the simplicity of a time when disputes were settled over cups of tea and slices of Victoria sponge.

Norman laughed out loud. "We're not an organisation with one-to-ones, appraisals and objectives," James said, as he smiled sarcastically. "You're too nice for this, Mavis. But that's not how our world operates." He turned cold eyes on Rhianna, who was sobbing. "Part of her punishment for infidelity was to be involved in his murder. To help tidy up the problem, if you will."

The cruelty of the confession hit Gemma hard. To be punished for a fling by being forced to kill the person involved was a new level of callousness that Gemma didn't expect to ever encounter.

"The homeless man, John, was nothing more than a patsy," James began, his voice eerily calm. "We left him a gift, one laced with ketamine. A bottle of vodka from dear Cynthia's store," he said, smiling at Cynthia. "So at least you benefited from the purchase of the murder weapon."

"You're all heart," Cynthia sneered.

Gemma looked at Cynthia, who appeared calm. Had she resigned to her fate? Or were her emotions thrashing inside like Gemma's?

"George had been tormenting John for months," James continued, his tone almost conversational. "It made perfect sense ... he'd be the ideal scapegoat."

Rhianna's whimpers grew louder, her shoulders shaking. Gemma's hand itched to comfort her, but she hesitated. No matter how much she empathised with her situation, she was still involved in a brutal murder.

"Then came the lure," James said. "A simple message from Rhianna, and George was putty in our hands. He never stood a chance."

"The church CCTV," Norman said. "I took care of that," he admitted nonchalantly. "As the church warden, who would suspect? And this lovely church has been a perfect venue for some of our trades.

Nobody would suspect comings and goings from here."

Reverend Simon's face crumpled. "How could you, Norman? This is a sacred place..."

"Drug deals under the cover of night," Norman interrupted, his voice smooth and unrepentant. "The church was merely a means to an end."

"George never suspected a thing," James continued, the veneer of his polite demeanour now stripped away to reveal the icy calculation beneath. "Rhianna led him inside for what he thought was just another secret rendezvous. Little did he know ..."

Gemma's breath caught as James detailed the treachery. She looked at Rhianna, whose tears glistened like crystals under the church lights. The image of John, the innocuous scapegoat oblivious to what was going to happen to him, haunted Gemma's thoughts. It was a level of callousness that would even shock her in a novel, let alone in real life.

"Once they were inside and John was out for the count on our special cocktail," James recounted, his voice carrying an eerie calm, "I put on John's boots and jacket. Surgical gloves shielded my skin from the evidence as I took the vodka bottle, covered in his fingerprints, and snuck into the church," he said, pausing to relish his moment in the spotlight, like any narcissistic psychopath would. "With George unaware, I snuck up on him and struck a blow over the head, then stabbed him with the broken bottle. It was over quickly. He wouldn't have suffered, which was a shame." He spared a glance at Rhianna. "She fled on my command, while I made sure John's prints told a story he could never speak."

"And Gemma," said Norman, addressing her directly, the smirk audible in his tone, "your fascination with that lipstick was no coincidence."

Gemma's eyes narrowed, her mind whirling. "Why?" she pressed, needing to understand the depth of his depravity.

"Simple annoyance," Norman replied with a dismissive shrug. Cynthia's infatuation had been inconvenient, so he had plucked her bright pink lipstick and planted it where it would sow further doubt.

"Destroying lives, intimidation, bullying … and then attempting to implicate poor Cynthia? You're a class act," Gemma said, her voice rising above the storm raging outside.

Norman's shoulders lifted in a nonchalant gesture, his response as chilling as the air that surrounded them. "Yes."

Mavis stepped next to Gemma. "When I spoke to you at the Strutt centre. You talked openly with me about George's intimidation of poor Cynthia. Why? Why tell me those things if you were their architect?" Mavis said.

"All part of the ruse, dear Mavis. It's nothing personal," Normal said. Mavis let out a loud tutting sound to mark her disappointment.

"The keys found on John, another little flourish?" asked Gemma.

"A nice touch, yes?" said Norman. Gemma shook her head.

"And that little display at the food fair? Chasing after the man who threw the paint over our table? A performance for our benefit, no doubt?" said Gemma. James smiled.

"A little performance to throw you off the scent. Putting that drama GCSE into practice. I thought it was a good piece of dramatisation."

There was a sudden bang on the church door that echoed throughout, causing Gemma to flinch in fear. Was this it? Was this how it would all end?

James gestured at Jack to step forward. "Open it," he commanded, a dangerous edge to his voice. Jack rose from his seat and stepped towards James, who grabbed him by the collar and pushed him towards the church door. James stayed close behind. "Try nothing stupid, or Dad may get a little trigger happy."

Jack's hands trembled as he reached for the bolt on the door, his eyes darting back to Gemma in silent apology. She watched, her own heart pounding against her ribcage.

With a creak, Jack slid the bolt and gradually cracked the door. Before he could comprehend the scene before him, he stumbled aside, tripping over his own feet and sending James sprawling to the stone floor. Like a flood breaching a dam, David and what looked like half of the Derbyshire constabulary burst into the church.

In the heat of the chaos, Gemma patted trusty Baxter on the head and then pointed at Norman. "Jump, Baxter!" she shouted. Baxter sprang into action with a growl and lurched forward. Norman, caught off guard, was knocked over by the canine's protective fury. The gun he had wielded so threateningly slid across the floor and stopped by Mavis's feet.

Mavis crouched down and picked up the weapon with two fingers by its trigger guard, her words a flutter of shock. "Oh my word. It's a gun! What do I do?"

"Pass it here, Mavis," came the calm, authoritative voice of Reverend Simon. "I used to be in the army." He took the firearm from Mavis's trembling fingers, handling it with the ease of someone who was well trained. He deftly de-cocked the gun, ejected the magazine and cleared the remaining bullet in the chamber with the ease of an experienced soldier. He then dismantled the gun's slide section and laid the disassembled pieces upon the lectern.

He smiled at Mavis. "As I said," he stated with a solemnity that drew a nod of respect from Mavis, "ex-military."

Meanwhile, the police wasted no time securing James and Norman. Their swift movements ensured that cuffs clicked shut around wrists. Gemma looked at Rhianna, whose tear-streaked face was a portrait of regret and fear. With a subtle nod from Gemma, David directed an officer to restrain her as well, her fate now entwined with those who had used her as a pawn.

As David approached, Gemma's pulse quickened, her eyes fixed on the unfolding scene. David, with a knowing smirk, addressed the defeated culprits. "I bet you weren't expecting us to arrive, were you?" He waved a mobile phone like a trophy before their bewildered faces. "We received your message, though. Just after arresting your bald headed accomplice."

Norman's shoulders slumped, the fight draining from him as he looked towards the stone floor.

"While Gemma was keeping you all busy here," David continued, his voice steady and assured, "my team and I were rounding up your little network." A faint smile played on his lips as he recounted the dealers' swift collapse under pressure. "You can rely on one thing with a lot of these lower-level drug dealers. They are not very intelligent, and when cornered and apprehended by a huge quantity of police officers, they will say anything to cut a deal."

The gravitas in David's voice filled the church as he read the criminals their rights and the police caution. Gemma watched as another officer bagged the gun and ammunition, preserving the evidence of Norman's treachery.

When the last of the police exited the church and the van doors closed, Gemma felt the tension release from her shoulders. She turned towards David and wrapped her arms around him. "You took your time getting here. I was expecting you sooner," she whispered, her voice thick with relief.

"I'm sorry. The arrests took longer than expected. I tried to get here as soon as I could, especially after receiving that text message." David hugged her tight, an embrace that signalled to Gemma that he regretted being so late. "In hindsight, I wish I hadn't agreed to let you gather the group here. What if you'd been hurt?" said David.

"It didn't go how I thought it would, but it all worked out for the best," said Gemma. She couldn't be angry. She was just relieved that it was over.

"Did you have any inkling that Norman was involved?" asked David.

"None, what-so-ever," said Gemma. "Norman was a man that everyone seemed to trust. He even had Mavis fooled all these years."

Mavis scrunched her face. "He did. I feel so silly now," she said.

"Unfortunately, that's how some of these professional criminals work. They get into positions of trust in their community so that nobody will suspect them," said David. "It's really quite devious when you think about it. They are at the top of the pyramid, giving orders, but not getting their hands dirty. Nobody would ever suspect them."

David embraced Gemma again; the warmth of his hold assuring her it was over. "They'll be going to prison for a very long time," he said against her hair.

Releasing Gemma, David enveloped Mavis in a hug. "Are you okay?" he asked.

Mavis nodded. "Yes, my dear. I'm just glad you're here." Her voice shook, but her spirit remained unshaken. "When will John be released?"

"First thing in the morning," David confirmed, his words lifting the weight of injustice from the air. "We'll inform him tonight, but I don't want to release him in the middle of the night if he doesn't have somewhere to go."

## Chapter Forty-One

The next morning, the sun had come out, making the previous night's storm a distant memory; well, the rain and thunder anyway. The storm that had raged inside the church would leave a lasting memory.

Gemma and Mavis were back in the Bookworm, where the welcoming aroma of freshly brewed coffee and cinnamon filled the air. After the previous evening, the shop never smelt so good. Gemma stood by the counter with Mavis, unpacking a box of books that needed shelving, gripping normality with both hands. Barry was also there to check on Mavis after he heard the news about the standoff and the arrest.

"I still can't quite believe it," Barry said, shaking his head in disbelief. "Mavis and Gemma, super sleuths!"

Mavis let out a chuckle. "I'm just relieved George's murderer has been found. I'm so disappointed about James, Rhianna and Norman, though. I thought they were good people."

"They had us all fooled, Mavis," said Gemma. "I am relieved it's over, though. Last night was quite scary."

"Just goes to show, never judge a book by its cover," said Mavis. As they pondered the deceptive nature of appearances, the bell above the door rang, and Jack sauntered in.

"Jack, how are you?" Gemma asked.

"I'm good, considering," Jack said.

"Well, we couldn't have done it without you," Gemma said. "Your help was invaluable."

"Ah, I didn't do much," Jack said, with his hands in his pockets. "Just helping a friend." A pause followed before he added, almost casually, "I've just come back from having coffee with Lily."

Gemma's eyebrow arched playfully. "Oh, really?"

"Yep," Jack said, chuckling. "After everything settled down with the police and the arrests, she approached me. Said she remembered me from school and thought I was brave for what I did." His cheeks flushed with a mix of pride and embarrassment. "She asked if I wanted to go for coffee."

"See, she did notice you back then," Gemma said, smiling.

Jack's response was a smile that carried a hint of disbelief. "Yeah, I suppose she did."

The bell above the door jingled again as David swept in with a slightly dishevelled figure in tow. "John, here you are, the people who believed in you to the end," David said with a smile. John, the once-accused, now exonerated man, extended a hand. He clasped David's, gratitude shining in his eyes.

"I ... I can't thank you enough for uncovering the truth. And for letting me get a shower and breakfast before I left," said John.

"Least I could do after what you've been through, but it's Gemma and Mavis who uncovered the truth," replied David, shaking John's hand firmly. He glanced at his watch, his face creasing with a sense of duty. "I have to head back, though. There's a mountain of paperwork and evidence waiting for my attention."

Gemma watched as David excused himself and departed. She turned her full attention to John. "John," she began, her voice soft, "I'm so glad you are free. This must have been such a terrible ordeal."

"Thank you. It has been quite frightening. But I was treated well while in my cell," John said.

"Detective Inspector Haynes said that you didn't profess your innocence," said Mavis.

John sighed. "The truth is, I couldn't remember anything from that night. There was a part of me that wasn't sure if I had done it or not." He looked down at his weather-beaten hands. "Deep down, I thought I wasn't capable of committing such a crime, but I couldn't be sure."

Mavis put her hand on his arm. "It's a terrible thing not to trust your own memory," she said.

John nodded, then added in a voice hardly more than a whisper, "But I wasn't eager to leave either. A roof over my head, three meals a day and safety. It was more than I've had in a long time. It was quite comfortable, really."

"John," Gemma said, her throat tightening at the admission. "That's just ... it's not right that you'd prefer a cell over freedom."

"Sometimes...," John's voice was resigned, "freedom comes with a cost too steep for those like me." The exchange lingered in the air, tasting of bitter truths about society that Gemma wished she could sweeten.

"John," she said, "what will you do now?"

A shadow of uncertainty crossed his worn face. Then he straightened his shoulders, as if reaching a decision. "I'm thinking of visiting my son," he said somewhat hesitantly. "He lives near Norwich, a place called Reedham."

"Yes, I've heard of it," Gemma said, her brow furrowing. "Does he know about ... your situation?"

"Ah," John said, his voice fading, "no, he doesn't. It's the shame. I didn't want him to know his old man ended up on the streets. He has his own life to lead ... A family. I didn't want to become a burden."

Gemma spoke softly, her heart going out to him. "What do you think will happen when you show up?"

"He's kindhearted," John replied, a glimmer of hope sparking in his eyes. "I just need to ask for help. But ..." He paused. "I think it's best I leave Belper after everything that's happened. I don't fancy being a local spectacle or target."

"Then it's settled," Gemma announced with more cheer than she felt. "I'll get you an open return ticket to Norfolk. If things don't work out, you come right back here, and we'll figure something out together."

Before John could express his gratitude, Barry, who had been listening in, interjected with an idea. "Hold on a tick," he said. "John, you and I are a similar build. I've got spare clothes at home. Let me pop over and fetch them for you."

"Barry, that's incredibly kind of you," Gemma said.

"Anything for a friend," Barry said with a wink before heading towards the door. "Back in a jiffy!"

As the door closed behind him, Gemma turned back to John with an encouraging nod. "We'll have you looking sharp for your son."

"Thank you, Gemma," John said, his voice rough with emotion. "Means more than you can know."

"Think nothing of it," Gemma replied. "It's the least

we can do. Let's get a coffee and some cake while we wait for Barry. It's on me."

John smiled. Gemma, Mavis, Jack and John headed to the café and took a seat. Sienna took their orders and promptly returned with their drinks and cakes before scurrying back to the counter to serve another customer.

"Thank you," John said. "This is lovely."

Mavis sipped her tea, which steamed her glasses a little, and then turned her keen gaze upon John. "You know," she began, setting her cup down with a gentle clink, "I've always known in my gut that you weren't the one behind such a cruel act."

"It's true," said Gemma. "Mavis said right from the start that there was no way you would have committed this crime."

John's eyes glistened with unshed tears. "That ... That means everything, Mavis."

"When we heard about the toxicology report, the pieces just didn't fit. I spoke to a medical expert, a friend, and they confirmed your state at the time made it nigh impossible for you to commit such a premeditated crime. We just couldn't ignore that, could we?"

"Impossible," Mavis agreed, patting John's hand.

"Thank you both for believing in me when I was doubting myself," John said. They sat and enjoyed their drinks and cake, and it wasn't long before Barry bustled back into the bookshop, a large holdall swinging from his grasp.

"Here we go!" Barry announced, placing the holdall at John's feet with a grand gesture. "I've packed some of my best shirts, trousers, even a blazer. There's also a wash kit — brand new, mind you — with all the essentials for a gentleman on the move."

John, taken aback by the generosity, could only stammer out a heartfelt, "I ... don't know what to say, Barry."

"Say, you'll look dashing when you reunite with your son," Barry replied as he took a seat around the table.

"Barry's right. We want you looking your best," Gemma replied. As John peered into the holdall, rifling through the neatly folded clothes and toiletries, a sense of hope seemed to lift the shadows from his face. "You can use the toilet at the back of the store if you want to get changed and ready," Gemma said, gesturing over to the back of the café.

"That would be lovely," John said, standing and retrieving the bag. "I won't be long."

"Take all the time you need," said Gemma. She fished her phone from her jeans pocket and navigated to the rail service website. "Reedham, Norwich," she muttered to herself, confirming an open return ticket that would grant John the freedom to navigate this new chapter of his life without the constraint of time. The printer behind the counter whirred to life, churning out the crisp paper ticket. Gemma went to retrieve the ticket and quickly came back. "Got it," she announced, brandishing the paper like a trophy as she placed it in an envelope.

It wasn't long before the toilet door creaked open and John emerged. The lines of worry that once etched his face seemed softened now, his jaw clean-shaven, and his hair slicked back into respectability. The clothes, courtesy of Barry's wardrobe, fit him well, adding a layer of dignity that homelessness had stripped away.

"Blimey, you look like a new man!" Barry exclaimed, standing from his seat with an approving nod. "Ready for that fresh start?"

John's smile was hesitant but genuine as he approached the group, the weight of gratitude heavy in his gaze. "I can't thank you all enough," he said, his voice thick with emotion. "You've all done so much for me."

Gemma handed him the envelope containing the ticket. "There are plenty of trains from Belper to Nottingham. You change there, and it's a direct train to Reedham." John nodded and smiled.

Barry clapped John on the shoulder. "Come on. I'll drive you to the station."

Gemma and Mavis both hugged John, and Jack offered a firm handshake. Barry led John out of the store to his car in the nearby Coppice carpark.

Gemma turned to Mavis and Jack, her eyes tracing the space John and Barry had just vacated. "I do hope he'll be alright," she said, smiling.

"He will be," Mavis said, assuring Gemma with the wisdom of her years. "I have a good feeling."

Jack nodded in agreement. "Yeah. Sometimes, all it takes is one good turn to change a person's life. You've given him more than one."

As they returned to the rhythm of bookshop, the air seemed lighter, the shelves brighter, and the world outside just a little kinder.

## Chapter Forty-Two

Later that afternoon, Gemma stood in the local river gardens, a pleasant park and picnic area, and looked out at the river Derwent flowing past the old red brick mill. It was a warm day with a cloudless blue sky, which was much better than the sudden storm the previous night. Mavis and Barry stood by Gemma's side, but Mavis seemed distracted. Gemma couldn't blame her. The winners of the gardening competition were about to be announced.

"Quite the turnout," Gemma said, trying to distract Mavis to help calm her nerves.

"Isn't it just," Mavis said. She glanced around, noting the absence of a particular individual. "No sight of Mrs Colchester, not that I'm surprised."

Barry, standing tall beside them, scanned the crowd once more before nodding. "She wouldn't want to show her face. She must be feeling quite ashamed of what she did," he said, echoing Mavis's sentiment.

"Did John get his train okay?" Gemma asked.

"He did, yes. He's looking forward to being reunited with his son," said Barry.

"It's a shame he didn't feel like he could go before he fell down on his luck," said Gemma.

"I know, but I can see where he is coming from if he didn't want to be a burden and felt shame for his situation. They are powerful feelings to overcome," said Barry.

"I guess so," said Gemma. "Well, I really hope it works out for him."

"I have a feeling he's going to be okay," said Barry.

The trio made their way towards the bandstand, where a gathering of townsfolk had already formed a semi-circle. Mavis smoothed her blouse, while Barry subconsciously brushed a hand against his ironed shirt. Gemma smiled. They were both trying very hard not to show how nervous they were, but Gemma could tell.

As Belper's mayor ascended the steps to the bandstand, there was a collective hush of anticipation within the crowd. He stood behind the microphone, his presence commanding. "Welcome, residents and visitors of Belper, to the annual garden competition award ceremony!" he said, his voice booming across the park.

Gemma clapped along with the others as the mayor announced the winners of the container garden category, her hands coming together in crisp, encouraging pats. Her smile widened as the names for the herb garden category were read out, each clap a celebration.

"Best vegetable patch now," Barry said, looking at the printed leaflet of the running order.

Mavis nodded in response as she stared with intent at the mayor standing on the bandstand. "Winning isn't everything. It's just a competition," Mavis whispered, more to herself than anyone else.

Gemma heard the words clearly and offered a reassuring nod as Mavis tried to downplay the importance of a win to herself. Gemma recognised this as a self-preservation technique; she read it in a psychology book. "Your garden's a stunner, Mavis," she said, before looking at Barry. "Both of yours are."

"Thank you, dear," Mavis replied.

Gemma looked at her own copy of the leaflet and then glanced at Mavis and Barry, their hands clasped behind their backs like schoolchildren awaiting their grades. "Here goes," Gemma whispered to them as the mayor approached the microphone with another envelope.

"And now I'd like to announce the winners of the prize marrow competition," he said, his voice echoing through the speakers.

Mavis leaned in to Barry, "You've got this. Your marrows are large and firm."

Gemma tried to suppress her inner child as she

nearly laughed at Mavis's comment, but she composed herself as the mayor spoke.

"In third place ..." the mayor said. "We have Humphrey Barton." The audience applauded. Gemma watched as Mavis's gaze flickered with fleeting disappointment when neither her nor Barry's name was called out. "And in second place, we have Colin Smith." More applause erupted from the crowd.

Mavis and Barry exchanged glances again. The mayor opened another envelope containing the name of the winner. For Gemma, time felt like it was running in slow motion, just like in the movies when something impressive was about to happen. "And the first place in the prize marrow competition goes to ..." Dramatic pause. "Barry Spencer!" The crowd responded to the mayor's declaration with a crescendo of applause. Gemma clapped until her palms stung.

"Congratulations, Barry. That's marvellous," Mavis said, turning to Barry with a proud nod. He seemed stunned before he grinned and made his way through the crowd to the steps of the bandstand.

"Your marrows are legendary now, Barry," Gemma called out after him, which made the crowd laugh. The mayor handed Barry an envelope containing his garden centre vouchers and then shook his hand while posing for a photograph with the local *Gazette*. He walked back to Gemma and Mavis with a massive grin on his face.

Mavis stared at the mayor on the bandstand. It was

time for the best garden category, which was always Mrs Colchester's territory — or had been. Gemma squeezed Mavis's hand, sensing her friend's apprehension.

"Second place," the mayor started once again, prolonging the suspense as he called neither Mavis's nor Barry's name. The second-place winner collected their prizes from the mayor. "And now, for the coveted prize, first place for the best garden goes to ..."

"Let it be Mavis. Let it be Mavis," Gemma implored to herself.

The dramatic pause stretched on, the silence teetering on the brink of impatience, before the mayor lifted the card from the envelope. "Mavis Rawlings!" said the mayor.

The crowd erupted, filling the park like the finale of a fireworks display. Mavis stood frozen, a statuesque figure in disbelief.

"Mavis, you've done it!" Barry's voice cut through the jubilation as he patted Mavis on the back. "Well deserved."

"Did I really win?" Mavis asked, stunned by the announcement.

"Absolutely," Gemma confirmed. With a gentle nudge, Gemma encouraged Mavis to step forward to the steps of the bandstand.

As Mavis ascended the steps, a wave of pride washed over Gemma, and the crowd's rapturous applause seemed to lift Mavis, carrying her towards her trophy.

"Bravo!" Gemma cheered, her voice mingling with the others.

The mayor handed Mavis her trophy and garden centre vouchers. He gave her a firm hug and then had a photo taken by the local *Gazette* photographer. Mavis held the trophy up for the crowd to see as they continued their applause before she descended the stairs and headed back towards Gemma and Barry.

Watching Mavis return to the fold, clutching her prizes, Gemma couldn't help but reflect on how the pieces of her own life were fitting together so neatly. With the murder case closed, Belper breathed easier, and justice served its course. John, a man wronged by fate, would once again embrace his son. And her relationship with David was growing stronger each day.

The thought of the Bookworm also buzzed in Gemma's mind, as she looked forward to completing the extended café and all the events she and Mavis would host there. The future looked bright.

"Here's to our future, Mavis," Gemma whispered, though her words were lost in the applause.

"I'll drink to that," Mavis replied with a smile.

"Let's celebrate properly," Barry suggested. "To the pub we go!"

"Lead the way, my dear," Mavis said, hooking her arm through Barry's and Gemma's as they made their way towards the exit of the River Gardens.

## The End

Thank you for reading ***The Bookshop Mysteries: A Murder at the Church***. We would be grateful if you could leave a review for this book at the store you purchased it. Reviews really help authors.

Gemma and Mavis return for more crime solving adventures in Book 3 - ***The Bookshop Mysteries: A Legacy of Lies***.

Thank you.

# Join the Reading Club

The Bookshop Mysteries is set in a real town, Belper (Derbyshire) in the United Kingdom, and is set in real locations. If you would like to see what these locations look like, then you can join our reading club to receive a free book: The Locations of the Bookshop Mysteries.

By joining the club we will let you know about new releases, special offers, and exclusive behind-the-scenes details about how we write the books.

https://www.sareevesfiction.com/join

*Also by S. A. Reeves*

***In the Bookshop Mysteries series:***

A Bitter Pill
A Murder at the Church
A Legacy of Lies
A Deadly Deceit

# The Bookshop Mysteries

Love the Bookworm Bookshop and Café? You can buy exclusive merchandise with the Bookworm's logo, from mugs, bags, t-shirts, hoodies and more.

Order from http://sareevesfiction.com
or scan the QR Code.